Captivate Me

HARMONY WEST

Copyright © 2023 by Harmony West

Cover Design © 2023 by Beholden Book Covers

Published by Westword Press

All rights reserved. No part of this book may be reproduced in any form or by any electronic or mechanical means, including information storage and retrieval systems, without written permission from the author.

This is a work of fiction. Names, characters, places, and incidents are the product of the author's imagination or are used fictitiously. Any resemblance to actual events, locales, or persons living or dead is purely coincidental and not intended by the author.

ISBN (paperback): 979-8-9881181-2-1

ALSO BY HARMONY WEST

Saint and Sinner Duet

Her Saint

His Sinner

Diamond Devils Series

If You Dare

Drown in You

Devil You Know

Die for You

Standalones

Always with You

Captivate Me

To the readers who want the prince and the beast.

CHAPTER ONE
CASSIE

*E*very day, I have to watch the man I love kiss my best friend.

Theo St. James. Whose face I see in the constellations. Who I've been in love with since eighth grade.

When he smiles and bends down to kiss Noelle lying in the grass, I turn away, hoping Addison and Piper don't notice how I can never seem to stomach watching the love birds.

Maybe they'll assume I'm jealous that Noelle and Theo are in love while I'm perpetually single. Maybe they'll miss that I'm only jealous because it's her he's in love with.

The sun beams down on us, an uncharacteristically warm day for March, hence the dozens of students stretched out like cats on the quad.

Theo plops down next to Noelle. "Hey, pretty girl." Ugh. Gag me.

Actually, I wouldn't mind Theo gagging me.

The light catches his profile, illuminating the sturdy edge of his jaw and the skin that's already tan from baseball practices. His sandy hair falls in adorable curls over his temples and down the nape of his neck. His bicep swells as he props himself up with one arm. My mouth goes dry, but I have to pretend like it doesn't. Four years later and I'm getting sick of pretending.

"Sorority girls only," Addison's nasally voice teases him. Her black dress clings to every curve—the one she's wearing for Kyle when she sees him in class later, the guy who's been leading her on since her freshman year. He takes her on a date, fucks her, then ghosts her for a week until she finds him in bed with another girl. She throws a tantrum, dresses hot to make him regret his decision, and the cycle begins anew.

"Leave him alone." Piper swats Addison's arm, batting her long, Disney-princess red hair over her shoulder. Then she coos at Noelle and Theo, "They're *in love*."

"We're not nearly as bad as you and Neal," Noelle objects, propping herself up on her elbows. A couple of guys passing by check her out. She gets so many looks that she doesn't even notice. Meanwhile, girls like me, who would give anything to be noticed, stay invisible.

My outfit is cuter than usual today. In high school, I lived in ripped, faded jeans and frayed sweatshirts. Now that we're in Chi Omega, I've upgraded my wardrobe, swiping my card knowing that the haul would cost me a whole paycheck. Today's Instagrammable outfit is a gray skirt and black scoop neck blouse. But no one notices. Not when Noelle van Buren is beside me.

She's in a white crop top and jeans. Though the outfit would look average on anyone else, she could pass for a glamorous French model. Her bleached blonde hair falls in perfect waves as always, and her makeup is just minimal enough to make you wonder if she's wearing any at all.

Piper pretends to pick at her nails, but a little smirk plays at her lips. "I have no clue what you're talking about."

"We can hear you two through our wall every night. Right, Cassie?" Noelle's piercing blue gaze lands on me.

"Totally." I do my best impression of Piper's high, whiny moan, and Theo flushes crimson.

I bite back the smile that threatens to curl at my lips. I want to see him blush when he makes me moan for real. But I shake the thought away. He's not mine.

When Noelle does an impression of Neal's brutish grunts to accompany my moans, our friends laugh. Moments like these, I almost think Noelle and I are a good match. That it makes sense we've been best friends this long.

Then I remember everything she's done.

Still, being close to Noelle means being close to Theo. I love everything about him. I love how easily he smiles. The happiness that always seems to glow from his perfect, bowtie lips to his sparkling green eyes.

I just wish he was smiling for me.

After high school, Theo and I were supposed to get into Westbrook University—one of the best STEM universities on the East Coast—and study for our respective STEM majors together. Noelle was supposed to attend Yale or some other Ivy League her parents bribed her way into. Noelle and Theo would realize long distance isn't for them and break up.

Leaving Theo St. James all mine.

Except Noelle's mom pushed her to come here. At least, that's what she claims. I know the truth: Noelle wanted to trail her boyfriend like a comet's tail. They've been together since ninth grade and her whole personality revolves around being the perfect girlfriend, the perfect daughter, the perfect student. She's never lived her life just for herself.

Even with Theo's hand in hers, Noelle's attention drifts across the quad. If I was holding his hand, I wouldn't be able to think about anything else. Not about my mounting workload, not about the classes I'm failing, not even about Hunter.

I yank a handful of grass from the dirt. *No.* I'm not thinking about him. Not now.

A guy in a black T-shirt with messy blond hair saunters down the sidewalk that separates the grassy slope of the quad from the brick bookstore. The front of his shirt reads SECURITY in all caps, and despite the heat, he's wearing a leather jacket. Pretty sure that's not part of the uniform, but he's the kind of guy who doesn't give a shit.

Beau Grayson. Most people call him Grayson, though the girls who fawn over him call him Mr. Grayson or sir to his face and daddy behind his back, even though he can't be more than twenty-four or twenty-five.

According to Addison, he got fired from his last job as a corrections officer because he'd roughed up one too many inmates. Piper heard he sells coke to students, but Addison swears it's pills. All I know is the scowl permanently etched into his face and the scar over his eye makes me stay far away from him.

Not every girl feels the same way, though. If the rumor is true, he's shacking up in a different girl's dorm every night.

My fists clench when I spot Noelle's gaze still following him. If I didn't know any better, I'd think she'd happily have him in her bed too. But she'd be an idiot to throw away someone like Theo St. James for Beau Grayson.

"You know he's an ex-con, right?" Addison's voice drips with derision even as her thumbs fly over her phone screen.

I roll my eyes. "I heard he's also got ten bodies buried in his backyard."

Theo gives an appreciative chuckle while Piper's doe-eyes fly open. "Oh my god!"

"She's being sarcastic," Addison tells her before her gaze lands on me. "You'll be glad I warned you when you don't end up the eleventh body."

"He's a security guard on a college campus. He passed a background check to be here," I point out.

Addison's gaze falls back to her phone, nails clicking as she types furiously. "Right, because a murderer has never managed to pass a background check before. Either way, he's creepy and weird."

Says the girl who threw herself at him when she drunkenly stumbled home the other night. Beau escorted us back to the house after she puked in the bushes. Sure, he makes me uncomfortable, but we made it home in one piece, not body bags.

"I did hear he stabbed a guy," Piper whispers. At least, her version of whispering. "And he's always wearing that jacket. Do you think he's hiding a bunch of knives under there?"

"Why don't you go ask him?" Theo teases.

"Oh my god, no way!" Piper squeals. She and Addison are both juniors, but she still talks and acts like a fifteen-year-old sometimes.

"A knife fight would explain his scar," Addison says.

The scar over Beau's eye stretches from his brow to his cheekbone. No one knows how he got it because no one's stupid enough to ask, but my money's on a fight while he was in a psych ward.

Noelle remains silent, eyes trained on Beau, following him as he heads down the sidewalk with his hands in his pockets. Theo watches her while I watch him, and it's like some sick love square except no one's eyes are on me. I'm invisible.

Except . . . someone's eyes are on me.

His eyes are on me.

Theo's.

On my bare thighs first. Then the blouse that hugs over my breasts. Before finally resting on my face.

And when our gazes lock, he smiles.

My heart stops.

"We should head to ECV," Noelle announces, breaking me out of my Theo-induced trance. At the mention of East Campus Village, my favorite dining hall, my mouth waters.

Noelle lets go of Theo's hand and stands, leading the way.

I get why she was the queen bee of our high school. Why Theo chose her. Why everyone chooses her. Because she is the sun, and when her rays shine down on you, you're the plant she breathes life into.

But sometimes, it's hard to live in the sun's shadow.

CHAPTER TWO

NOELLE

Someone is watching me.

I'm waiting for Theo on the steps in front of Arbor Hall, but I can't find the eyes on me in the sea of students who rush past on their way out of class. Maybe it's all in my head.

I return my focus to my sketchpad, shading in the newest drawing. Birds launching out of their pond and heading for the bright, blue sky. Searching for somewhere better.

Sometimes, I wish I could do the same. Find somewhere to hide out and pretend Perfect Noelle van Buren doesn't exist for a little while.

The hairs on the back of my neck stand up.

This time, I spot him. Twenty feet away, a man is watching me.

A security guard. The one with the unruly, white-blond hair and a jagged scar over his eye. The one who makes my heart skip every time I catch a glimpse of him on campus.

Beau Grayson.

He's leaning back against a low brick wall, arms crossed and gaze tracking my every move. Everyone thinks he's dangerous because of the scar on his face and the tattoos across his knuckles.

But the real danger is in his eyes.

"Hey!"

I jump at Theo's voice behind me. He chuckles and takes a seat beside me, and I flip my sketchpad closed. My sketches are like a diary, and Theo has long since learned not to ask to see them. "Hey. I figured I'd walk with you to practice before I head home. Family dinner tonight."

Not looking forward to a second of that.

I glance back at the low brick wall, but Beau is gone. I should be unnerved that he was staring at me like that, yet my stomach dips with disappointment at his absence.

The smile falters on Theo's face. "Actually, I was kind of hoping we could talk first."

Theo takes my hand and leads me to a bench beside the pond, the inspiration behind my drawing. He pats the spot next to him before hunching forward, folding his hands between his knees and refusing to make eye contact.

I know exactly where this is going, and hope flutters in my gut as I clutch the sketchpad to my chest.

"This is really hard to say." He straightens, rubbing his palms down his shorts.

"You want to break up."

His head whips to me, eyes wide. "Uh . . . yeah. How did you know?"

I smile. "Because I've been your girlfriend since we were freshmen in high school. I know you."

Theo has never really been into me, and my heart has never skipped at the sight of him. Sure, we're a cute couple on Instagram, but he's always felt more like a friend I take to school dances and kiss on the cheek. One awkward, failed attempt at sex last semester pretty much sealed the deal, but neither of us has had the guts to end it.

"Honestly, this relationship has always felt more like a friendship," I admit.

His hand lands on his chest and a heavy sigh rushes out.

"Thank god. I mean, I kind of figured you felt the same way, but I would've felt like such a dick if you didn't."

"Our moms are going to be in mourning for the next month, though."

He chuckles. "They're going to hold a memorial for our relationship. You know my mom's already been calling you Mrs. Theo St. James."

Our moms have been best friends since high school, and they've been planning my and Theo's wedding since they found out they were pregnant at the same time. We were destined to be together. That's why Theo asked me to homecoming freshman year. His mom knew I didn't have a date and told him to ask me. Our families were so happy, we just kept going to dances together and started calling each other boyfriend and girlfriend.

But now we're in college, and we both deserve more.

"We can still be friends, right?" Theo asks, like he's actually worried I might say no.

"Of course. You've been my friend since we were in diapers. You're stuck with me."

He grins and pats my knee before standing. "Awesome. Enjoy your family dinner tonight. I'll see you tomorrow?" He's already backing toward the sidewalk, late for practice.

"See you then."

On my way to the parking lot, I send a message to the group chat with Cassie, Addison, and Piper.

> I have news. Video chat tonight after family dinner?

If I tell them over text, I know they'll all flip out, expecting me to be far more heartbroken than I am. Worse, they may go after Theo with torches and pitchforks while I'm gone.

Home is only a thirty-minute drive away. Mother almost insisted I commute, but when I got accepted into Chi Omega, Dad pushed her to let me live on campus.

My parents aren't home yet, so Angel, my ancient Labrador, barks when I walk in. I scratch her head and give her a treat before dumping my backpack on the kitchen island and digging in the fridge for an open bottle of wine.

I'm pouring a glass of Merlot when heels click into the kitchen. "Really, Noelle?" Mother's voice is already icy. My spine goes rigid. "We agreed to a glass on holidays, not drinking like a fish. Being a college student doesn't make you an adult. You're still underage."

She snatches the bottle and pours a glass for herself, marking it with her ruby lipstick.

A daughter who has a normal relationship with her mother would want to spill all the details of her breakup, but my mother is the last person I want to tell.

"Freshen up your makeup before we leave. And for the love of god, fix your hair. Please tell me no one saw you looking like that."

I examine my reflection in my phone camera. Not a strand out of place. "I will."

She sighs, smacking her glass down on the island. "You need to pull yourself together. People will start to talk, and lord knows we don't need anyone looking too closely at us right now."

I scan the front entrance. My father should be following behind my mother. Maybe he's sneaking a cigar like he does when she's being particularly insufferable. "Where's Dad?"

"Don't worry about your father." She waves a hand. "Worry about yourself. You're going to embarrass this family."

The rage simmering in my blood comes to a boil, but I bite my tongue. I always bite my tongue.

The front door squeaks open, and Angel lets out an exhausted bark at my feet but doesn't budge. Thank god he's here. Dad is our buffer, the only one who can restore peace when Mother goes for the throat.

She sighs when she sees him. "Reason with your daughter. She's becoming a lush."

My nails bite into my palms. One glass and I'm a lush.

Dad examines the bottle. "It's Merlot, darling. Who could resist?"

I giggle, but Mother narrows her eyes at him. "I'm serious."

Dad's expression sombers and he takes my hand, elbows on the island. "You doing okay, sweetheart?"

Mother rolls her eyes behind his back.

I blink back the tears, at his kindness and her hostility. No matter how hard I try, I will never be perfect enough for her. "I'm going for a walk."

"You're not going anywhere. We have reservations." When I don't stop, she calls, "Where do you think you're going?"

"To the police station."

"Noelle—" Dad calls.

Mother's heels click furiously across the marble floor. She wraps her fingers around my arm like a viper in a death grip and spins me. This close, I can see the lines on her forehead and around her mouth that she's so desperate to hide. No matter how hard she tries, no matter how much money she spends, she'll never be the perfect woman that she's so desperate to be. That she's so desperate for me to be.

Now that ship has sailed, and she can't stand to be around me anymore.

"And what exactly do you plan on telling them?" she hisses.

"What we should've told them from the beginning. The truth."

"Absolutely not. You're not going anywhere. Your father and I have risked everything for you. Our reputation, our integrity, and don't get me started on the money it cost to—"

"I didn't ask you to do that," I challenge.

Her hold on me tightens. "We did this for you. You should be grateful, you little bitch."

I jerk back like she slapped me.

Dad steps forward. "Janice—"

But I don't get to hear her excuse before I'm yanking out of her grasp and flying out the door.

CHAPTER THREE

BEAU

*S*he's deadweight in my arms. A little chloroform knocks a girl out like a light.

She didn't even notice me watching her from my car as she strolled down the sidewalk, clutching her arms because she was the silly drunk college girl who forgot a coat in March. Her body shook like a terrified Chihuahua, but she was walking like she was on a mission and not just some drunk girl crying over a broken nail or whatever the hell spoiled rich girls cry over.

Dead of night, my headlights trailing a few yards behind her, and she only glanced back once.

As soon as my headlights flicked out, she forgot all about me. I pulled over, got out, and snuck up behind her. None of it was hard. Not a single person in that overblown mansion noticed a strange car sitting motionless across the road.

Didn't think it'd be tonight—just thought I'd stake the place out, figure out when she normally comes and goes. When my best opportunity would be. Then she handed it to me on a silver platter.

This girl is missing some vital survival instincts.

I've seen her around campus. Hard not to notice a girl like

her. Those startling blue eyes always glued to her sketchpad, the side of her hand permanently stained with graphite.

But every time I trail her around campus, it's never the art building she disappears into. It's the science lab or the University Center.

I've seen her sketches. Snuck a peek when she left her stuff on a table while she grabbed a sub ten feet away. She's good. Wasting her goddamn potential.

I adjust her in my arms. She shouldn't be this light. She's gotta be five-seven at least, and she's not much more than skin and bone. I like a girl's body skinny or curvy as long as she knows how to use it, but she's at least gotta take care of herself and this girl isn't.

Guess that doesn't matter now.

I lay her down in the backseat and dig in the front pockets of her jeans. Jackpot. I slide her phone out and toss it into the field. Should be obvious enough for the cops to find, not that it'll lead them anywhere. She's only a quarter mile from her house. For all they'll know, that brainless jock boyfriend of hers picked her up.

God, she looks fucking delicious laid out in my backseat. Perky tits that threaten to slide out of that tiny top. Her stomach exposed, perfect for a belly button ring, and sharp hips that jut out too much. One tug and I'd have those jeans off her in a second. She's the type of girl who wears a skimpy thong just to feel good about herself. I won't complain as long as I get to see it.

Little rich girl would probably lose her shit if she discovered she was in the back of a busted-up Dodge Neon from the nineties. Bet it's still got more thrust than that limp-dicked boyfriend, though.

I drive us on the back roads out of town. Under the cover of night, the houses soon disappear and we're alone with nothing but empty fields and dense woods. Let's see them try to find her out here.

When we reach the driveway, I throw the car in park and

scoop her back up into my arms, kicking the door shut. She doesn't even flinch.

I've got a job to do, but I'm not the kind of guy who does his work on someone else's timeline. The job will get done when it gets done. In the meantime, I'm gonna have a little fun.

There's something about a girl helpless in my arms that gets me going. Fuck, she's pretty, and I hate that about her. Her soft, flowing blonde hair. Her slightly upturned nose. Her pink little bowtie lips that make me wonder how she'd suck me off. How she'd look staring up at me with my cock in her mouth.

Shit. I'm getting hard, she's not going to be conscious for hours, and I'm not a sick fuck who takes advantage of girls when they're knocked out.

No, I'll wait until she's fully awake and aware of where she is, who she's with, before I see what she can do with that pretty little mouth.

CHAPTER FOUR
CASSIE

"Where's Noelle?" Piper half-shouts over the din of the dining room. Chi Omega is bustling this morning as the girls grab breakfast before morning classes.

According to Addison and Piper, Noelle spent the night at home, but she's normally back at the house bright and early to make tea before heading to the gym with us. I fucking hate gym mornings, but I don't want to give anyone another reason to think Noelle's better than me. If she's running a mile on the treadmill three days a week, so am I. No matter how much it makes me want to kill myself.

"Not sure." I grab three pancakes, and when Addison scrunches up her nose, I put one back. "I didn't see her in our room this morning."

"Maybe she spent the night with Theo," Piper suggests.

I stiffen until Addison snorts. "Does that girl ever spend the night with her man?" she asks me.

I shrug. "No." Now that I think about it, I guess it is weird that Noelle isn't spending as many nights as she can riding Theo's dick. God knows I would be if he was mine.

Addison picks a table for the three of us, waggling her fingers at a few seniors at the table nearby. "If I didn't know any better, I'd think she was his beard."

No way. I saw how Theo looked at me yesterday on the quad. The way his eyes lingered on my chest. "Theo isn't gay."

Addison shrugs. "Whatever. They have a weird relationship. They barely even touch each other. I don't get why they're together." I don't either. Especially when he and I would be so much better. "Did you see the way she was eye-fucking Grayson? I'm amazed Theo didn't notice. But who could blame the girl? Even if he is a psychopath."

"I heard psychopaths are sexy now." Piper says it like she heard bell bottoms are back in fashion.

"I am dying to know what her news is, though. She left us on a cliffhanger. Did she text you?" Addison asks me. "You two are besties and roomies. Aren't you supposed to check in?"

I pull out my phone. No notifications. "Nothing. I'll text her. She's probably just running late." Except Noelle doesn't run late. She's always punctual, with a perfect attendance record. A perfect everything.

I fire off a text to her.

> Are you on your way?

Addison one-ups me and sends Noelle a voice message before we pack up our stuff and head for the gym. On the sidewalk, under a cloudy sky, the baseball team runs by. Among the group, one of the guys spots us and waves above his head, breaking off from the pack and jogging over.

"Hey, Cass!"

My heart leaps into my throat at the voice from my dreams.

Cass. I love that he calls me by a name that no one else does.

Theo's beaming as he jogs toward us. In another life, he'd run right for me and close the space between us, pull me up into his arms, and kiss me. I'd dig my hands in his hair and play with those curls until I traced the hard edges of his jaw like I've daydreamed about for years. He'd press every inch of himself into me, slip his tongue into my mouth and let me taste him, run his hands all over my body.

But he's Noelle's. So when he's a foot away, he stops. He doesn't kiss me or touch me, even as I will him to with every cell in my body. Even as I scream in my head for him to put me out of my misery.

"Where's Noelle?" he asks.

"We don't know." Addison's eyes are exaggeratedly wide. "She hasn't gotten back to the house yet. You haven't heard from her either?"

"Nope. She must just be running late. I'll give her a call."

Theo steps away to call Noelle and we linger, even though we're already behind schedule. After a minute, he shakes his head. No answer.

"Hey, sexy!" A sleazy guy with too-long, greasy black hair leans out the passenger window, grinning at Addison. Kyle. I don't know what the hell she sees in him. "Want a ride?"

"On this dick!" Piper's boyfriend, Neal, shouts from behind the wheel, and they both hyena laugh.

"We'll take a ride to the gym!" Addison rolls her eyes and asks Theo, "You coming with us?"

"I'm gonna keep jogging." Theo nods after his teammates, long gone. "Thanks, though."

Even though he belongs to a frat too—Sigma Chi—he's not the biggest fan of Kyle, a member of Beta Theta Pi, a frat notorious for spiking drinks and executing campus-wide pranks. Theo is way too pure to be friends with an asshole like Kyle.

"I'm going to jog with Theo," I blurt.

Ice slashes through my veins when Addison lifts a perfectly plucked brow, but all she says is "whatever" before flouncing off to the car. The tires squeal when Neal slams on the gas.

Theo inclines his head to the sidewalk, hair flopping adorably. "Shall we?"

My heart is about to burst and we haven't even started running yet. I'm finally alone with Theo St. James.

CHAPTER FIVE

THEO

I shouldn't be this excited to be alone with her. Noelle and I aren't together anymore, but I'm not sure she'd give her blessing to date her best friend five seconds after we've broken up.

I can't lie that Cass wasn't at least part of the reason I chose to end things with Noelle, though. She's Noelle's best friend, so she's always been around, but since we came to Westbrook, I haven't been able to keep my mind off her. Can't stop staring at her. Can't help thinking that if I got to spend more time alone with her, I'd get hooked.

There's this spark that I've never felt with Noelle, a magnetic pull toward Cass.

Part of me wants to tell her to forget about our run and the gym, pull her into the cover of the woods, and kiss her. Tug down that shirt that barely hides how her incredible tits bounce and see what I've been missing.

She's so damn cute jogging next to me. A tiny five-foot-three to my six-two. I've shortened my stride for her, but she's still red-cheeked and huffing, pretending like she's not already winded and struggling to keep up. If she asked me to run the rest of the way with her in my arms, I'd do it in a heartbeat.

"How are you doing, Cass?"

"Just fine," she huffs, forcing a fake, cheery smile.

"I mean everything with school, your brother, your mom. How are you holding up?"

After we graduated, Cass seemed so excited about college. She talked about the classes we'd probably wind up in together as STEM majors and how we'd study together, fuel up on coffee, grab dinner.

Then her brother died.

She's been almost unrecognizable since September, the adorable, nerdy honor student gone and replaced with a hollow husk. A shell that shuffles from class to class, forgets exams, and doesn't turn in assignments. School and astronomy have always been her passions, but for a few weeks after Hunter's death, Noelle couldn't even get Cass to leave their room.

I miss her being happy, and I hate that there's nothing I can do to help.

"I'm okay. I've stopped crying myself to sleep." She forces false cheeriness into her voice. "I'm getting my grades back up, and Mom is . . . she's still another galaxy away, honestly."

"She'll come around," I reassure her. "Obviously I have no idea what you're going through. But it was really hard when my grandpa died. So if you ever need someone to talk to, I'm here."

I cringe as soon as the words are out. God, she probably thinks I'm such a tool, comparing my grandpa's death to her brother's. Sure, I was closer to him than I am to either of my parents and nearly every good memory I have from my childhood includes him, but that's still nothing compared to losing a sibling you were raised with. Losing him before he'd barely gotten a shot at life.

Still, she smiles, a real one this time, and the tightness in my chest loosens. "Thanks, Theo."

"No problem."

She must be able to read my mind because she adds, "You shouldn't downplay what you went through, though. Your grandpa was really important to you. We don't have to do the trauma-comparison thing. It all sucks."

Something in my chest twists. If I think about it too long, I can come up with a long list of all the things Cass and I have in common. We've both lost someone close to us, we're both science nerds who want to understand how things tick, and we've both got lofty ambitions and big dreams.

The difference between us is that Cass does her own thing. She lives her life exactly the way she wants to, not because anyone told her she had to. My parents made it clear that my options were law school or med school. Lucky for me, I've wanted to be a doctor since Granddad got sick. I was nine years old and wishing I knew as much as those doctors did so I could figure out what was killing him and eradicate it from his body.

I doubt I'll be curing cancer, but hopefully I can help some sick people and keep them around a little longer for the ones who love them.

"You're probably the strongest person I know," I say.

Cass snorts. "I'm a mess."

"You're not. You've been through a lot, and you've come out on the other side. That's impressive."

Another glance at Cass and she's beaming at me. I can't take my eyes off her. Off her bright smile. Her tits, bouncing up and down. Flashes of me shoving my hands up her shirt and my dick in her mouth have me swallowing down the lump in my throat.

Shit. She's going to notice me ogling her like a creep, but she doesn't flush or slap me.

And I can't help the words that come out of my mouth next. "I'm glad you're into running now."

Jesus. I'm an idiot.

She nudges me. "So am I."

CHAPTER SIX

NOELLE

At first, I don't realize someone stuffed a rag in my mouth. All I register is the pain in my head and the rough fabric on my tongue.

The mattress beneath me is hard and lumpy. Not my mattress at Chi Omega or the memory foam bed at home.

I try to sit up, and that's when I realize my hands are bound behind my back. Not handcuffs. Rope, maybe? I tug, but the knot is unmovable. My heart gives a hard thud as the first wave of panic slowly washes over me.

Through the tiny, singular window high above my head, gray light trickles in. Casting the empty basement in a dreary haze. The stench of bleach fills my nose, like someone recently cleaned the entire floor.

I'm in someone's basement.

The room has been completely cleared of everything but me and the old mattress. On the opposite wall, an open door leads to a small, dark bathroom with a toilet, sink, and glass shower.

By my feet, a giant mirror covers nearly the entire wall from floor to ceiling. My feet are bare. Whoever brought me here took my shoes.

My stomach twists.

The rest of my clothes remain intact—the same white crop top and jeans I wore to class yesterday. I nearly cry with relief.

Except something is off. My pockets are empty. My phone is gone. I take it with me everywhere, but maybe I forgot it in my rush to get out of the house and away from my mother.

I manage to flip onto my other side. A wooden staircase cloaked in shadow leads up to a closed door. If I can just get on my feet and make it up those stairs, I can get out—

Except someone is on the staircase.

Watching me.

A man with wild, white-blond hair slouches forward, elbows on his knees. His leather jacket is zipped only halfway up, revealing his bare, tattooed chest beneath. I swallow at the sight of it.

His gray-eyed stare is piercing, but the rest of his features are somehow neutral. No crease between his chestnut brows, a lovely contrast to his light hair. No curve to his soft lips. His cheekbones are razor-sharp, cheeks indented just slightly. He has the natural angles and highlights that Mother uses makeup to paint on me.

The only imperfection is the scar that breaks through his eyebrow and stops on his cheekbone.

Beau Grayson. The campus security guard.

And now he has me trapped in his basement.

I try to scream around the gag in my mouth, but the sound is little more than a muffled groan. No one will hear me down here. No one will know what he's done with me. What he's going to do to me.

I jerk upright and scramble back, head throbbing worse with the movement, bound hands smacking against the cool stone of the wall. I'm barefoot, bound, and gagged. He's between me and my only exit. I can only hope my thundering heart bursts before he does whatever he's planning on doing with me.

I always thought all the gossip about him was just that—baseless rumors. I never thought any of it might actually be true. That the guy hired to keep us safe on campus is actually the most dangerous one among us. A predator searching for his prey.

And he chose me.

He stands slowly. A low, guttural voice floating out and clawing down my spine. "Relax. In my experience, you girls like to be tied up and gagged."

I grimace. I don't know if he means with a rag or his cock. Probably both. But I can't retch because if I throw up, I'll suffocate on my own vomit. I gnash my teeth against the rag, try to spit it out, but it's lodged too deep.

He meanders over to me, moving silently. The panic boiling in my veins starts to scream. He's taller than I remember. Slender, with prominent collarbones and a hint of muscle beneath his jacket.

He crouches and reaches out, brushing his fingers against my cheek. My breath hitches. The slight touch of his skin against mine sends a bolt of lightning down my spine. Goosebumps prickle along my arms.

His gray eyes roam slowly down every inch of my body, lingering on my lips, my throat, my breasts, my thighs. Like he's a convict fresh out of prison after thirty years behind bars.

I've never been so terrified in my life. Not even that night with Hunter.

But for a wild, heart-splitting second, I'm not worried about what Beau Grayson is planning on doing to me. Maybe I want him to do it.

I jerk back, away from his touch, and shake the horrifying thought away.

His voice comes out in a seductive drawl. "You look like shit, princess." He grabs my arm and I try to scream again around the gag as he yanks me to my feet. "See for yourself."

He hauls me toward the mirror, the ice-cold concrete biting into my bare feet, every inch of my body aching from practically sleeping on the floor. His grip on my arm isn't a viper's deathhold like my mother's last night, but it's solid. Unshakable.

I face my reflection. The bleached blonde hair that typically falls in voluminous, perfect waves is untamed, erratic. My eyes are bloodshot, irises a dull, muted blue. Smeared makeup mars my cheeks. One of my diamond earrings is missing.

My eyes drop quickly from my reflection, like they always do.

Whenever Mother sat me in front of a mirror—before a pageant, before a shoot, before school—she'd point out all my flaws. All the parts of me that could be prettier, thinner, better. My button nose that curved too far upward. My blue eyes that were too puffy or spread too far apart. My lips that were too chapped or too pale. My eyebrows that were too thick or too thin. No part of me ever good enough.

Beau shoves me back toward the mattress and my foot catches so I fall flat on my face. I choke on the rag, scrambling back, trying to put any amount of distance between us. How the hell am I supposed to fight back? I can't bite; I can't claw. I can kick, but he'll pin my legs down.

When he reaches for me again, the scream comes out in a gurgle and I close my eyes. A toddler willing the monster to go away.

He pulls the rag from my mouth.

I blink, stunned. He's still crouched in front of me, a hard edge to his tight jaw. The way his eyes trace over the curves of my face, an outsider looking in might mistake this moment for intimacy.

Until I finally come to my senses and remember to scream.

He cringes but doesn't move away or slap me or stuff the rag back in my mouth. We sit in silence when I've screamed myself hoarse, and then there's nothing.

No feet thundering across the floor above us. No one hurrying to the door. No one asking if I need help.

No one coming to save me.

"You done?" He lifts a brow. "Or do you want this stuffed back in that pretty little mouth?"

The words should nauseate me. Instead, liquid heat spreads

through my body at those three words. *Pretty little mouth.* That's where his gaze lands now. Like he's imagining kissing it. Or stuffing his dick inside it. Gross.

"I know you," I breathe. "You work at the university."

He leans an inch closer, a hint of a smirk pulling at the corner of his mouth. "Yeah? How many times have you come thinking about me?"

Heat crawls from my neck to my face. What an arrogant piece of shit. . . . He's not wrong, though. I have come thinking about him. Only once. Maybe twice. Three times at the most. I couldn't help myself. He has one of those faces that once you see them, you can't get them out of your head. The kind of face that sends my hand itching to draw every line and edge. That sends my hand drifting down my panties. That makes me ache to see the rest of him.

"I haven't."

He smirks. "Liar."

"Why did you bring me here?" I mean for the words to come out like a demand, but they're small, weak.

The last thing I remember is getting in a fight with my mother, leaving the house in the dark, and heading down the sidewalk. Shivering, tears streaming down my cheeks. Texting my friends about the fight before stuffing my phone back in my pocket.

Then nothing. No memories between striding down the sidewalk and ending up here.

"Why do you think I brought you here?" A teasing lilt to his voice.

I swallow down the terror. "What do you want? Money?"

He wouldn't need to be a student to know the kind of wealth my parents have. They paid for my Mercedes, they're paying my tuition, and they're even paying Cassie's. After her brother died, they thought it would be a nice gesture to relieve my best friend of the burden of student debt. They gave her enough to cover undergrad, grad school, and to get her on her feet after graduation. One less burden weighing her down.

I pray that's why he brought me here. Because the only reasons to kidnap someone are money, sex, and murder.

He laughs, a sound that cleaves my heart and contorts the long scar on his face. "I don't need your money, princess. I'm a self-made man."

Fuck. I have no idea how a security guard on a college campus could be a self-made man, but if he didn't bring me here for money, that leaves only two other possibilities.

"Guess again," he commands.

I speak around the knot in my throat. "I've seen you watching me. You've been following me around campus."

His voice turns to melted chocolate. "So I'm your stalker?"

"You tell me."

He shrugs, a glimmer in his gaze. "Sounds like you already know."

Part of me was glad to be the center of his attention whenever our paths crossed on campus. I'd fantasize about him sauntering up to me, calling me beautiful, and asking me out. Taking me back to his place and making me feel things no man ever has.

But I never imagined he'd do something like this.

"So you brought me here for what? To live out your twisted fantasies?" Tears sting at my eyes and I bite down hard on my lip when it starts to tremble, copper coating my tongue. "You're sick."

"Don't pretend." His hand caresses my cheek and I want to lean in, but I pull away. That's when he goes for my throat and I freeze. He doesn't squeeze, but I know he feels my pulse thumping beneath his fingers. "You want to be here. Don't you?"

"I want to get the fuck out of here and away from you." I want to spit the words, but they come out in a cry.

"No, you don't." He leans in, his soft breath drifting across my skin with every word. "I've seen the way you look at me when you catch me watching. You want me to keep you tied up and ravage you."

My thighs clench involuntarily. The words nearly get lodged in my throat, but I push them out. "You don't know what you're talking about. You think just because you've been following me around that you know me, but you don't know anything about me."

"I know everything about you that matters." He brushes a strand of hair behind my ear. Almost a lover's gesture, except for the sinister tone in his voice. "That's how I know beneath the perfect princess façade, your secrets are just as dark as mine."

CHAPTER SEVEN

CASSIE

My best friend's eyes follow me all over campus from missing person posters.

While I was in my Bio 1100 class, Mrs. van Buren reported her daughter missing and organized a search. Now the whole town is looking for Noelle, less than twelve hours later.

The van Burens are one of the wealthiest families in Westbrook, and Noelle is beloved. Child beauty pageant winner for five years in a row, Girl Scout, senior class president, homecoming princess, prom queen, honor student, paid model.

When girls like Noelle van Buren go missing, everyone is devastated. Everyone wants to find her. And everyone is a suspect.

Piper, Addison, and I walk arm-in-arm, following the huge crowd scouting the acres of land and woods behind campus. The sun is descending past the mountains in the distance. Soon, we'll need to break out our flashlights and jackets.

Rumors are already spreading about what could've happened to Noelle. A car accident on the way back to campus. A spontaneous trip to a vacant beach that ended in her drowning in the ocean. Maybe she got blackout drunk and found herself lost in the woods. Maybe she hit her head and she's lying unconscious somewhere.

Perfect Noelle van Buren wouldn't be so reckless, but she has been drinking more. Wilder since leaving home, free of her mother's shackles. Maybe once she got a taste of freedom, she drowned in it.

Tears are already streaming down Piper's face, her mascara and liner running. She sniffles. "What do you think happened to her?"

"Don't talk like that," Addison snaps. "She's fine. She probably just got stranded in her car somewhere or her GPS malfunctioned and she got lost. We're going to find her any minute."

"I can't believe we just assumed she was running late," Piper cries. "We should've known that she would've texted us. If we told somebody that something was wrong sooner, maybe—"

"Don't play the what-if game." Addison shakes her. "We can't undo anything now. We just need to focus on finding her. And she needs you to stop crying so you can actually help."

But Piper keeps crying, silent tears streaming down her face.

"Is he even allowed on campus without his uniform?" Addison asks.

I follow her gaze to where Beau Grayson walks with other campus security guards, hands in his pockets. He's in his typical leather jacket and dark jeans, but he's abandoned his black SECURITY tee for a blood-red shirt. "Anyone in the community can participate in the search," I remind her. "He's just trying to help."

Leaves crunch beneath our feet as we breach the woodline. Even if Noelle somehow dropped her phone or an earring or a hair tie, how would we find it? Not to mention it's March in North Carolina. It can be sixty and sunny one day and snowing the next. And any clue about where Noelle went would be buried with it.

A voice calls out to us.

Theo jogs our way in long shorts and a zipped-up hoodie. He'd look ridiculous if he was anybody else. But he's Theo St. James. The only son in an old-money family. The lovable baseball star with a head for Harvard. He's so gorgeous, he could make a paper bag look hot.

He closes the space between us and wraps his arms around me. I know this hug is for comfort, to express our shared distress over Noelle's absence. We're closer to her than anybody on this campus. But for just a second, I imagine he ran up and hugged me simply because he wanted to touch me.

He's so warm, a welcome heat source in the brisk March air. I could stay wrapped up in him forever. I've never been able to tell him, but the only time I feel at peace is when I'm with him. Like I'm home. He pulls away too soon, and suddenly, I'm aware of Addison's and Piper's eyes on us.

"I can't believe this," he breathes.

"Me neither."

"It doesn't feel real," Piper says. "Like she can't actually be missing, you know?"

I know. Hunter's death still doesn't feel real. I wake up most mornings expecting him to pound on my bedroom door or to holler that he's going to eat all the cereal if I don't get my ass out of bed. Then I remember I'm not living at home anymore and my brother is dead.

This day doesn't feel real either. It all feels like a dream.

"I should've been worried sooner." Theo rakes a hand through his hair. "I should've done something when she didn't answer her phone. She always answers when I call."

I bristle but try to shrug it off before any of them notice. I hate imagining Theo and Noelle chatting and laughing together for hours on the phone, casually updating each other about their day.

I want to rub away the frown etched between his brows. Bring back the easygoing guy whose greatest worry was whether he'd hit the ball or strike out. Not whether his girlfriend is alive or dead.

"I know how you feel." I wrap my arms tight around myself and swallow. "I wish I'd started worrying sooner in those hours we didn't know where Hunter was. If I'd started looking earlier, maybe I could've found him before he . . ."

According to the report, Hunter likely lay on the side of that road for half an hour or longer, drowning in his own blood.

If I could've gotten there in time, I could've called an ambulance. I could've saved him. And I'd still have my brother.

Theo shakes his head, and when he steps forward, I think he's going to hug me again. But he doesn't. I try not to let the disappointment show. "You can't blame yourself for that. What happened to Hunter isn't your fault." He squeezes my hand and my heart takes flight. "Don't worry. We'll find Noelle. We're not going to lose her."

Addison's gaze lasers in on our joined hands, and even though I don't want to let him go, I do.

∼

BY ONE A.M., there's still no sign of Noelle. Our phones are silent except for worried calls and texts from parents making sure we haven't disappeared too. Mom doesn't call. She's been asleep since eight so she can wake up for work at four. She probably doesn't even know Noelle's missing. Even if she did, I'm not sure she has it in her to care.

Hunter's death turned our mom into a ghost of who she used to be.

First Hunter. Then Mom. Now Noelle.

The glow from Addison's flashlight beside me flickers out. "Shit. My phone died."

Piper's thumbs fly over her own screen. "I better go. Neal wants me to spend the night with him."

"Ugh, you're actually worried about fucking your boyfriend right now?" Addison says.

"He wants to make sure I'm okay," Piper snaps. All of our eyes widen. Piper *never* gets defensive, especially with Addison.

"We should all get back," I announce, stepping into Noelle's usual role of peacemaker. "It's been a long day and we all need to sleep so we have enough strength to keep searching tomorrow. If we need to."

"Yeah. You're right." Theo rubs the back of his neck, screening another call from his mom. She's been blowing up his phone, calling every fifteen minutes to make sure he's okay. "I gotta take this."

He swipes his thumb across the screen and ambles a few yards away, back to us.

"Cassie!" Mrs. van Buren calls, the beam of two flashlights hurrying toward us in the dark. "Officer Lee, these are Noelle's sorority sisters."

Mrs. van Buren is Noelle twenty years in the future if she cuts her bangs and becomes addicted to Botox. Bleached blonde, voluminous hair, eyes rimmed with dark liner, lashes thick with layers of mascara, and a dash of glitter across her cheeks. A remnant from her beauty pageant days. She's tall, regal, and catches the eye of just about every guy between the ages of twenty and eighty. The red tip of her nose is the only visible sign that anything's wrong.

Officer Lee holds out his hand to each of us, his features rugged but handsome. I stiffen. I hate being around cops—that's what happens when one of them shows up at your door in the middle of the night to deliver the worst news of your life.

"Nice to meet all of you, though I'm sorry about the circumstances. You're all close to Miss van Buren, correct?"

We nod, and Piper starts sniffling again. "We live with her. We're all in Chi Omega."

"Have any of you seen or heard anything from Noelle since yesterday?"

"No." Addison's eyes mist. "The last time we saw her was at lunch."

"And did she say anything concerning at that time?"

We shake our heads.

Officer Lee flips his notepad closed. A sigh of relief rushes from my chest like a popped balloon. "I want you all to know this is very serious. If you know anything about any plans Noelle might've had to run away or—"

"She wouldn't," I cut in. All eyes turn to me. My face warms, but I push on. "I'm her best friend. I know her better than almost anybody." I glance at Mrs. van Buren. The *almost* is for her benefit, but I know Noelle better than she does. "She wouldn't take off. She wouldn't hurt herself. That's not Noelle."

Mrs. van Buren nods, eyes wide. "She's right. That's not like Noelle at all. She's very reliable, dependable. She's a good girl."

A few beats of silence pass. "Okay," Officer Lee finally says. "Thank you for that information, Miss . . .?"

"Cassie," I tell him. "Sinclair."

"Thank you, Miss Sinclair. If any of you receive any contact from Miss van Buren or her phone, please notify us immediately."

"We will," Addison promises.

"Thank you all for your time," Officer Lee says.

Mrs. van Buren dabs beneath her eyes with a wadded tissue. Even with a missing daughter, she manages to remain a beauty queen. She waves the tissue at us. "You girls should head home. You need to get some sleep. There's nothing more any of you can do right now."

Piper hugs her before she and Officer Lee leave, either to keep searching or to head home to continue the search tomorrow.

Who knows what will happen to Noelle in the hours we stop looking for her. Who knows what's happening to her right now.

"You coming to Beta Theta Pi with us?" Addison asks me without looking up from her phone. I guess she's crashing there too now that she's managed to secure an official invite into Kyle's bed.

I shake my head. Why the hell would I go with them when they'll both abandon me the second we get there to fuck their boyfriends-slash-fuck-buddies while I'm stuck in the living room, watching frat boys drink themselves to the ER?

My eyes find Theo in the dark, still reassuring his mother on the phone. "I'll ask Theo to walk me home."

"See you two tomorrow then." Addison returns her attention to her phone, and Piper wraps me in a quick hug before taking off after a power-walking Addison.

I hurry over to Theo and tug on his arm. "Can you walk me home?"

"Hey, Mom, I gotta go." As soon as he hangs up, he smiles at me. "Sure."

I try not to let my smile grow too big. "Thanks."

I forgot a jacket, so I keep my arms wrapped tight over my chest and clench my jaw so my teeth don't chatter as we pass under street lamps and past glowing blue emergency call boxes.

"Here." Theo shrugs out of his hoodie and wraps it around my shoulders. I'm instantly enveloped in the masculine, citrusy scent of him.

I give him a grateful smile. He's the kindest person I've ever met. "Thank you."

Campus is eerily silent at this time of night. Just like that night Noelle and I were walking back late from the library, when she practically did my schoolwork for me while I kept my head buried in my arms and cried, the raw ache of Hunter's death still heavy on my chest. During the walk home, I made her stop with me so I could check out a car with a bent fender.

A fender with a human-shaped dent.

"We should get home, Cassie," Noelle called. But I had to know. I had to know if this was the car someone used to kill my brother.

After the funeral, I made it my mission to find whoever had hit Hunter and left him to bleed out and die. Let them feel half the pain he felt. Half the terror in his final moments. I fantasized about all the ways I'd make them suffer for what they did to him.

I must've stopped ten, fifteen, twenty times to examine cars with dents in their fenders. It didn't matter whether we were cloaked in darkness or exposed in broad daylight. Noelle insisted we couldn't be caught circling and inspecting strangers' cars. That someone would call the police on us or bring out a bat to chase us off themselves. But I couldn't stop. Couldn't let it go.

I had to know. I had to get my brother justice.

So I jotted down the license plate number, heart drumming with the certainty that I'd found a clue. That I'd found *the* clue that would answer the mystery of who murdered my brother.

Then Noelle got a call. "Hi, Dad."

Even with a few feet between us, I heard him ask, "Noelle, is Cassie with you?"

I stiffened. I couldn't handle more bad news.

"Yeah, she's here. Is everything okay?"

"The driver who hit Hunter . . ." Her father sighed. "He turned himself in today. He's been arrested."

My heart leapt to my throat. What if it was whoever owned the car I just found? I'd start by keying their car and slashing their tires—

"Wait." Noelle's voice went up an octave. "What?"

He let out a long breath. "It was Michael."

Michael. Their personal mechanic. Their maintenance guy. Pool guy. Gardener. Mr. van Buren's right-hand man.

My stomach dropped.

"Oh my god." Noelle pressed a hand to her chest, horrified eyes flashing to me.

"Remember how he took the Bentley to the shop? Said the thing needed a lift to fix it? Apparently, they finished the work early and he took it for a little joyride." I could practically hear Mr. van Buren shaking his head, and acid washed over me. The same way it did when I'd heard the news about Hunter. Like he was dying all over again.

Noelle's eyes widened. Her voice turned muffled, like I was drowning in the sea and she was above water. "Cassie?"

"Cass?" Theo asks now. "Where'd you go?"

I shake the memory away, even though none of them ever go far. "Sorry. It's just . . . a lot."

He nods, lips pressed together. I should be grateful for this rare moment alone with Theo. Instead, I'm spending my precious minutes with him wallowing over the past.

I wish I could kiss him. Help each other forget. Get tangled up in each other and enjoy a blissful few moments when we're not worried about Noelle or remembering loved ones we've lost or agonizing over the past or stressing about the future.

But I can't comfort him the way I want to. He's Noelle's.

"Can we talk about literally anything else?" he asks.

"Yes," I say quickly, searching the sky for something to talk about. "Um . . . did you know I'm named after a constellation?"

"There's a constellation named Cass?"

"Cassiopeia." I stop in the middle of the sidewalk and point up at the sky. The lights from Nohren, the freshman residence hall, obscure some of the stars but not mine. "See those five stars? They look like they form a *W*. That's Cassiopeia."

Theo manages a little smile, and I nearly cry with relief. I needed him to smile again. "Were your parents really into astronomy?"

"My brother." I swallow, and Theo waits patiently for me to get the words out. "Since we were kids, he wanted to be an astronaut. I wanted to be an aeronautical engineer, designing the spaceships that would carry him to the moon or Mars."

"I'm glad you're still doing that." Theo's voice is warm like hot chocolate on a cold winter day. "Your brother would want you to follow your dream."

"Yeah, he would." Somehow, Theo has managed to make me smile at the thought of my brother for the first time since he died.

"I've always liked that about you, Cass."

My heart skips. "What?"

"How smart you are." Theo stops and I realize we've already made it to the house. The compliment has me completely frazzled. If he called me beautiful, I'd probably combust.

Most of the lights inside the house are already off, the girls tucked away for the night. All of us safe and sound except for one.

I wish I could invite Theo inside. Spend the night together. Even if he wasn't in the mood to fuck my brains out and make me forget every shitty thing that's happened in the past six months, I know I'd sleep like a baby in his arms.

"I'll see you tomorrow," Theo promises and gives me another hug. This one longer, lingering. Maybe he needs it as much as I do. Maybe part of him wants it too.

When he pulls away, he briefly walks backward to wave to me before turning and heading down the sidewalk.

I clutch his hoodie tighter around me. Maybe he'll forget to ask for it back.

CHAPTER EIGHT

THEO

*B*y the time I get home, I'm beat. But Mom was hysterical on the phone, so I'm here.

She rushes at me the second I'm through the door. "Oh, Theo! You must be devastated!"

I pat her back. "It's all right, Mom. We're gonna find her." Just once, I'd like to be the one who's allowed to fall apart while she comforts me.

The house smells overwhelmingly of her essential oils. The scents that are supposed to keep her calm that never quite seem to do the trick. She's already in her pajamas, and Dad's still in his slacks and button-up like he just got back from the office.

He rests a hand on her back, his cologne nearly enough to overpower her essential oils. "Let him breathe."

Mom pulls back, sniffling and swiping at her eyes. "I'm just so glad it wasn't you."

"Mom." Jesus. If there's anyone in the world who's great at always saying the worst thing at the worst possible moment, it's her.

"Go calm down," Dad tells her. "Theo needs to get some rest."

She listens to his order like she always does. Like we both do.

I head for the stairs, ready to pass out so I can be up at the crack of dawn again tomorrow, but Dad plants a hand on my shoulder. "Hang on a sec, Theo." He strolls to the cabinet and pulls out two shot glasses, pouring from a bottle of brandy. "If there's ever been an occasion for a drink, this is it."

We clink our glasses together. Lubrication for whatever he's about to say next.

I've never seen much of myself in him. I got my hair and eyes from my mom. Everyone called me her doppelganger when I was a kid. The only trait I got from my dad is my height. His hair and eyes are dark, stern, his jaw always rough with a five o'clock shadow. I've never grown more than a few hairs on my chin.

He rests his hands on the counter, trying to act casual. "You talk to the police yet?"

"No. They haven't contacted me. You think they will?"

Dad rolls his eyes. "You're the boyfriend. Of course they will."

I reach for the brandy and he doesn't stop me when I pour another glass. "Actually, I'm not the boyfriend anymore."

Dad freezes. "What?"

"We broke up yesterday."

"Yesterday," he says slowly. For some reason, his eyes narrow. Like I'm either in trouble or an idiot. Could be both. "As in, the day Noelle went missing."

I swallow the shot in a single gulp. When he puts it that way, it sounds bad. Really bad. "Yeah. She took it fine, though."

He stares out the window, jaw clenched. "Did Noelle tell anyone about the breakup?"

I shrug. "I assume she told her friends. Maybe her parents."

His steely gaze flashes to me. "Do you assume or do you know?"

Now that I think about it, no one has mentioned our breakup. Not even Cass. I figured Noelle would tell her as soon as it happened. But maybe she never got a chance. "I'm not sure anybody knows."

Dad rubs at his scruff. "Let's keep it that way. Just between the two of us. Let everyone think you're still Noelle's boyfriend for now. At least until she's found."

"Why?"

"Let me ask you this: how do you think the media would react if they found out you and your girlfriend broke up right before she went missing?"

Not good. But the insinuation makes me stiffen. "You don't actually think I had something to do with this, do you?"

"Of course not, Theo. Don't be ridiculous. But I also know it won't look good. They'll already be looking at you as her boyfriend. Don't fuel the flames by making them think you're a jilted ex."

"But I'm the one who broke up with her."

"Don't be dense. A breakup is a breakup." He schools his features back to neutrality before clapping me on the shoulder. "Just let the media think you're the dedicated boyfriend and stay under the radar. No need to give them a reason to suspect you."

CHAPTER NINE

NOELLE

I'm tied to a chair when I wake again.

My head swims, vision blurry, as I slowly return to consciousness.

In front of me, Beau is shirtless, shuffling tools on a workbench with a quiet *clink, clink*. The only source of light a red candle flickering nearby. Even in the darkness, I can make out the swirls of tattoos over his bulging biceps, up his ribcage, down his back, across his knuckles.

For a moment, his beauty distracts me. Filling me with the urge to reach out and skim my hands over every inch of him.

Until I realize they're tied together behind the chair. My ankles bound to the legs. I give a weak tug and don't budge an inch.

The rag in my mouth is making my jaw ache. I don't remember him bringing this chair down or tying me up again. Whatever he did to knock me out, he must've used the same thing when he kidnapped me.

My heart starts to hammer, nausea churning in my stomach.

Rescue won't be long now. That's what I have to tell myself. The police will find me when they track Beau's movements across campus the day I disappeared and around town as he drove past gas stations and restaurants and homes. Everyone has cameras these days. There's no way somebody somewhere didn't capture Beau Grayson kidnapping me, shoving me into his car, and carrying my unconscious body into his house.

I just have to bide my time. Somehow prevent him from hurting me or killing me before the police find me here.

Except the tools in front of him tell me my time has already run out.

A pair of scissors. A wrench. A hammer. A knife.

Beau flashes a wolfish grin, and this time, I know I'll throw up. "Oh good. You're awake."

To my relief, he pulls the rag from my mouth and turns back to his tools.

"Please don't hurt me!" I cry, tears stinging, heart pounding. "*Please.*"

He tips his head back and lets out a seductive moan that somehow both makes my thighs clench and chills me to the bone. "*Fuck.* I love when they beg."

They. "How many girls have you done this to?"

He picks up the knife, and my heart stops as he waves it casually. "Depends on what you mean by *this.*"

I take a slow, deep breath, trying to keep my voice steady even as my heart is on the verge of bursting. "How many girls have you kidnapped?"

He plants his hands on the arms of the chair and leans in. I should be repulsed by him, but liquid heat spreads to my core as his lean, muscular body looms over mine. Even without his jacket, he still smells of leather. "You're the first girl."

"You've kidnapped men?" I'm genuinely shocked by this.

Beau straightens, poking the tip of the knife against his finger. "Yes, well, they're usually the ones causing the most trouble, aren't they?"

"I'm not causing any trouble," I say quickly. "I won't."

He chuckles. "You already have, princess."

My eyes flood with tears, and I try to pull at my restraints again. But it's clear he's not lying—he's done this before. "What did I do?"

I can't think of a single thing I could've done to make him want to torture and kill me.

He sets the knife down on the workbench and relief briefly loosens the tight knot in my chest until he begins flicking his finger through the candle's flame. "Your family's Bentley was involved in a little accident, huh?"

My blood runs cold. I shouldn't be surprised he knows. Everyone in Westbrook does, and if he's been following me, there's no way he wouldn't have heard.

He tilts the candle, hot wax flowing. I swallow down the hard lump in my throat, but it doesn't budge. "Guess your handyman went for a little joyride. What was his name? Michael?"

"What does that have to do with me?" I whisper.

"That's the thing about a hit and run, isn't it? Never know for sure who was behind the wheel. Could have been anybody. Mommy or Daddy or you. Or maybe that boyfriend of yours. Wanted to take the two-hundred-thousand-dollar car for a spin. Or maybe your best friend. What's her name? Cassie? You girls keep a lot of secrets for each other, don't you?" He tips the candle in the other direction, the light flickering across his face. "So are you going to rat them out? Or are you willing to take their punishment?"

My nails dig into the arms of the chair, but I can't break free of the restraints. "Michael confessed."

Beau sets the candle down and shrugs, strolling back over to me. "Apparently, somebody doesn't believe his story. Or your family's. And there's not exactly any proof, is there? Only thing we can prove is the car belonged to your parents."

A tear slips out and down my cheek. "So I should die because someone thinks Michael is innocent?"

He shrugs and reaches for the knife. "An innocent man died. Somebody's gotta pay the price. Justice must be served."

"And you're the one to serve it?" My voice shakes.

"It's my job. Since I got this"—He points at his scar with the knife—"I've been hunting down the people who leave scars and giving them a few of their own. Especially when they think they can get away with it. Another rich, entitled woman gave me this, and I had to hunt her down to pay the price because no one else would. You know what they say." He presses the tip of the knife against my brow and a scream builds in my throat. "An eye for an eye."

"Please," I whisper.

He grins. "You do love begging, princess."

I need to keep him talking. Distract him long enough that he doesn't hurt me before I can figure out a way to escape. "Does that make you a . . . vigilante?"

"A bounty hunter."

I fight against my pounding heart, trying to keep my voice steady. "If that were true, you'd be capturing criminals and turning them in. Not taking justice into your own hands."

He drops the knife from my face, gently gliding the edge of the blade along my collarbone. The cry ready to burst from my chest. "I do that too. But sometimes, justice isn't life behind bars. Sometimes, justice calls for much worse." He presses the blade against my throat. "This is going to hurt."

"What if the man who died wasn't innocent?" The words burst out of me as I try to scramble back, away from the bite of the blade.

Beau's head tilts. "Who?"

His name comes out loud, desperate, as Beau holds the knife to my throat. "Hunter."

CHAPTER TEN
NOELLE

*I*n eighth grade, I slept over at Cassie's house. I'd noticed how Hunter's eyes followed me down the hallway at school. Around Cassie's house. But I never thought he'd sneak into her room while we were sleeping.

Cassie and I were head-to-feet in her bed, and she didn't stir when the door creaked open. I stared into the darkness, trying to make out the figure creeping toward me.

"Noelle," he murmured in a singsong voice that still haunts my dreams.

He crouched in front of me, and I'm not sure if he knew I was awake or not. His hand reached out and stroked over my hip. I was frozen in terror.

Then his hand slipped under the blanket. He groped until he found my stomach. I clenched my eyes shut, trying not to feel his repulsive, oily palm on my skin. Willing him to stop, to go away, to disappear.

His hand slid up, up—

Cassie turned, and Hunter flew back and out the door. She never woke up, and I never fell back to sleep.

The next morning, I still couldn't shake off the slimy feel of

Hunter's hand on my body. Of his eyes, roaming over every inch of me. But every time I tried to tell Cass, I couldn't bring myself to voice the words. Too ashamed and disgusted by what he'd done to even admit that it happened. All I wanted to do was bury it down and forget about it.

I managed to avoid Hunter as much as possible after that. Things got better when he graduated, and I assumed Westbrook's campus was big enough that we wouldn't run into each other. That he'd be preoccupied with other girls and forget all about me.

In September, we attended a party at Hunter's frat, Beta Theta Pi. I woke up on a couch. A guy snoring on the floor, a couple with their tops off on a loveseat in the corner, a few people passing a bong around by the coffee table.

And Hunter. Standing above me with his phone up and a shit-eating grin spread wide across his face.

I blinked a few times, trying to make sense of where I was, what was happening. The strap of my crop top had slipped down, revealing the bright pink bra underneath. My skirt had risen high on my thighs. I was already nauseated, and when Hunter showed me his phone screen, I wanted to be sick.

He'd taken a photo of me. Drunk, passed out, and looking every inch the wild party girl that would horrify my parents.

"Perfect little Noelle van Buren isn't so perfect after all, huh?" he taunted, low enough that no one else could hear him. "I was hoping college would make you wild."

"Can you delete that?" I asked, trying to keep my voice calm. I sat up, head spinning.

"I'll delete it," he agreed easily, and I braced myself. Because with Hunter, there was always a catch. He leaned down, the stink of beer breath coating my skin, and nausea roiled in my gut. "If you let me fuck you."

I recoiled. *No.* This wasn't happening to me. Hunter was known for dealing drugs in high school and manipulating girls to blow him for their next hit. But I hadn't heard of him blackmailing anybody. The blackmail must've been bad enough to keep their mouths shut. How many other girls had he done this to? "I'm not doing that."

He crouched down, rubbing my knee, and when I jerked away, he squeezed so hard, tears sprang to my eyes. I froze, staying motionless like he wanted, and he went back to rubbing. An act for anyone who was watching. "You will, Noelle. You're going to let me shove my hard dick inside you and fuck you hard until I cum on your pretty face. Or I'm sending this innocent little picture to Mommy and Daddy. And then maybe whoever else wants to see it."

My heart plummeted to my feet. My parents couldn't see that picture. They'd disown me. They'd never, ever forgive me. I'd tarnish their precious reputation forever.

"Please don't do this, Hunter," I begged.

"I've wanted you for a long time," he cooed. "Haven't you noticed me watching you?"

The first person I wanted to find was Cassie, plead with her to talk her brother out of this. Finally tell her what he did to me all those years ago. But she adored her brother, and I didn't want to hurt her by revealing what kind of person he really was.

And part of me was terrified she wouldn't believe me. That she'd choose Hunter over me. I couldn't lose her.

"I've noticed," I told him, standing. I turned my voice as sweet as I could manage. "But can we do it another night? I'm too drunk. I want to remember it."

His cruel smile told me he didn't wholly believe me, but he liked the idea of me never forgetting the night he'd get what he wanted from me. "Fine. But I'm not waiting long, Noelle." He wiggled his phone in the air. "If those panties don't come off soon, I'm hitting Send."

Before I could scurry past him, he grabbed my hand and drew on the back of it with a marker. The same marker he and his frat brothers used to draw on the faces and bodies of unconscious partygoers.

When he finished, I examined the drawing he'd left on my

skin. A crescent moon. Cassie always said how obsessed he was with astronomy.

    He sneered. "So you don't forget about me."

CHAPTER ELEVEN

BEAU

The son of a bitch was a fucking predator. If he wasn't already dead, I would've put him in the ground myself.

Unless she's lying to me.

She'd say anything to get out of that basement. To get out of that chair I had her strapped to. To get me to pity the poor little rich girl.

"Fuck!" The girl sucking me off scrapes her teeth against the head of my cock, and I jerk her back by the hair.

Her eyes go wide, hands still gripping my thighs. "Shit, sorry! Did that hurt?"

"You never given a blowjob before? Don't use your fucking teeth."

She nods and returns her mouth to my cock, obedient.

Half the time, I don't know whether a girl wants to fuck me or my scar. I've seen this girl around campus a few times, eyeing me like a dog with a steak.

I've had blue balls ever since I locked the princess away in the basement. So when another blonde wanted to pull me into a supply closet, I wasn't about to stop her. Especially when I found her on Hunter's Instagram, her arm around his waist while she giggled like he wasn't a scumbag who blackmails and violates girls.

I'll ask her about him, figure out if Noelle lied to my face. And get a little head while I'm at it.

Too bad this girl has no fucking clue what she's doing.

I bet the princess in the basement would. Even if she didn't, I'd teach her how to do it right. She'd be a quick learner.

I try to focus on the girl on her knees in front of me. She keeps making these exaggerated slurping and choking sounds, but she's barely sucking down more than a few inches. There's no way I'm getting anywhere near deep enough to gag her. Don't girls know they can fake it all they want, but we don't really get off until it's real?

"Close your eyes," she murmurs. "Focus on nothing but how good your dick feels in my mouth."

I grimace at those three words. *Close your eyes.* I've learned not to trust anybody with my eyes shut.

Her face morphs into Noelle's. Her tiny body in nothing but black lingerie. Hands pinned and bound behind her back while she bobs her head up and down on my cock, using that pretty little mouth to swallow my pre-cum.

I push into the girl until she falls back, pressed against the wall, and drive my cock into her throat. She chokes for real this time, and her nails dig into my thighs, hanging on for dear life while I fuck the soul out of her body.

She gurgles when my cum spills down her throat, but she swallows every drop.

I'd smile, tell my princess what a good girl she is, but she's back to being the nameless chick in the supply closet.

She stands, grinning like she's the reason I came that hard. *Not even close, sweetheart.*

My thoughts drift back to Noelle again. Her at some frat party, a wide-eyed freshman, plied with roofied drinks until she passed out on the couch and that asshole thought he could take advantage of her.

If she's telling the truth, I would've killed him where he stood.

He's the exact blueprint of the men I hunt down. Scumbags who've assaulted women, children. Others who wiped out their entire families before going on the run. Bottom-of-the-barrel cowards who don't deserve to call themselves men.

Most of them, I turn in for cash. After I've roughed them up a bit. Law enforcement knows to look the other way when I hand them a gift. But some of my marks don't know when to shut the fuck up. Don't know when to stop telling me about all the sickening shit they've done.

Those are the ones that end up in unmarked graves.

I zip my pants while the girl buttons up her blouse. She actually unbuttoned it down to her push-up bra as if I gave a shit about her tits when her mouth was open for me.

She giggles. "You're way hotter than Hunter."

I play dumb. "Ex?"

She shrugs. "Not exactly. More like fuck buddies. He's just the last guy I blew." She covers her lips with her fingers, eyes wide. "I can't believe I've fucked a dead guy."

"He wasn't dead when you fucked him." I roll my eyes then add, "I hope."

"Ew, of course not! I'm not, like, a kleptomaniac."

Jesus Christ. How the fuck this girl has two brain cells to rub together let alone enough to get into college is a fucking mystery. They'll really let anyone into these places as long as they pay enough. "Did you ever hear about him blackmailing anybody?"

Her nose scrunches. "Yeah, *me*. He said if I didn't blow him, he'd tell my parents I spent the five grand they gave me on coke. That *he* sold me. He had a photo of me snorting it, so what the hell was I supposed to do?"

My hands curl into fists. That prick would've done the same thing to Noelle if he'd gotten the chance. The thought of her pretty little mouth wrapped around his dick makes me want to pull him out of the ground and kill him all over again.

He's lucky he's dead.

But now I've got another problem. A girl I can't kill, but I also can't let her go. Five minutes out of that basement, and she'll tell everyone exactly who kidnapped her.

Time to visit Michael.

~

AN HOUR. That's how long Michael gets every week with a visitor. The clock is ticking.

He's a sheep among wolves in this place. Six-one and built so nobody fucks with him, but if they did, he wouldn't swing back.

"How you been?" He crunches on the chips I bought him.

"Been worse." I clasp my hands together on the table. "I'm not here for a social visit. I've got a question."

Michael gives a single nod. "Shoot."

"What if I told you I had evidence that contradicted your confession?"

He sets the bag of chips down between us. "I'd tell you to keep quiet about it."

I didn't expect anything different. "Why?"

He gestures around him. "Look at this place. Three hots and a cot. A roof over my head. When I get out, I'll be set up for life. I'm not losing sleep over a two-year sentence."

"Seems like a long time for an innocent man to sit behind bars."

"It's a sacrifice I'm willing to make for my son." He swallows. "A better life."

I let the words sit between us for a minute. "So a bad deed goes unpunished?"

"Not everyone needs a punishment to learn their lesson."

All I know is punishment.

I stand, chair squealing. "All right, old man. If that's what you want."

He has his reasons, and who am I to judge? I leave the prison and head back for the house. Noelle will be hungry.

Maybe I'll keep her for a while longer. Until she proves to me she can keep her mouth shut about where she's been and who she's been with.

CHAPTER TWELVE

CASSIE

My best friend's disappearance has made me famous.

My phone is hot to the touch, notifications blowing up. The TikTok I posted last night is already at two hundred thousand views and climbing.

There's nothing exactly special about the video, but everyone loves true crime. Everyone wants a chance to play detective, especially if it means they help bring a pretty girl home.

I included a picture of Noelle and me posing together before homecoming our senior year. Even though she had Theo, she went with me so I wouldn't have to be the only one of our friends without a date.

I tried to keep my voice strong while I told the camera about how we haven't seen or heard from Noelle in two days, but I didn't bother holding back the tears. TikTok loves to watch girls cry. That's why I got two hundred thousand views. That's why two hundred thousand people now know the name Noelle van Buren.

Please help me find my best friend. My final plea.

"Holy shit, your TikTok is blowing up!" Piper bursts into the bathroom, holding up her own phone as if I've somehow missed the influx of comments and messages from people asking for more information and how they can help.

Classes are canceled today so we can all participate in a campus-wide search and I wonder if the administration would've canceled classes for anyone else or if this is the kind of treatment reserved only for pretty, perfect, rich girls like Noelle van Buren.

Addison follows closely behind Piper, and her lips pucker when she spots me applying makeup. "Really? Lipstick? Are we searching for a missing girl or hitting a strip club?"

I pop the cap back on. "You're wearing makeup," I point out.

Addison washes her hands, probably for the millionth time this morning. She's neurotic about germs. Another reason it's astonishing she's into Kyle. "Yeah, the basics. Eyeshadow, liner, mascara, foundation, concealer, and highlighter. Lipstick is for date nights. Who are you trying to impress?"

I suppress my eye roll. She's literally wearing more makeup than I am. "That hot cop, obviously."

"Ooh, so you're into older guys. I can get down with that."

My phone rings. The three of us freeze. What if it's the call? The call from the police or Noelle's mom telling us they found her body.

But when I spot the name on my screen, my jaw clenches. "Relax. It's just my mom." I swipe my thumb across the phone and leave the bathroom, Addison and Piper trailing behind me. "Hey, Mom."

Instead of her usual, exhausted *hey, hon*, she blurts, "Why didn't you tell me Noelle is missing?" In the background, her spoon clinks against her coffee mug. I hope she's not in her usual three-day-old pair of jeans and a sweatshirt with a stain below the collar. After Hunter died, I became the only one who did laundry because she'd simply forget she needed clean clothes.

I sigh. "I've been a little busy, Mom. We've either been searching or sleeping."

Silence. She's biting her tongue. Wanting to say a thousand different things to me, but now that Hunter's dead, we don't know how to talk to each other anymore. There are too many things to say, but too much time has passed, so now we don't say anything. "I wish I could help with the search, but I have to work a double tonight."

She's a CNA at an assisted living home. A mostly thankless job for little pay. That's all she does now—works and sleeps.

"That sucks," I manage. Sometimes, I want to remind her that she has another kid to live for. But all I want right now is to get off this phone call.

Luckily, an angel appears in front of me. Theo, his hands in his pockets as he waits in the foyer for us so we can all join the search together. He gives me a small smile, and my heart melts.

"I have to go. The search is about to start."

"Okay, let me know how it—"

"I will." I end the call and stride the rest of the way to Theo, gesturing to my green pea coat. "I remembered to wear a jacket this time."

He grins. "Smart girl. It's cold out there." His gaze rises from my coat to my red lips, pausing there. Imagining kissing me? Imagining my lips around his cock? I'd love to mark him up.

I shake the thought away. *He's not mine. He's not mine.*

"We're gonna grab our coats and we'll be right down!" Addison calls to us. She and Piper disappear into their room.

Theo lowers his voice. "I'm getting really worried, Cass."

I give a comforting stroke down his arm, but I don't linger. You never have privacy when you're in a sorority, even when you think you're alone. "We'll find her. Maybe today will be the day."

"You and I know her best." His green eyes bore into me, and I'm a puddle beneath his stare. "I bet if we put our heads together, we can figure this out. You want to grab food after the search?"

Butterflies burst from their cocoons in my chest. Under any other circumstances, in a parallel universe, I'd think Theo St. James was asking me on a date. "Sure. Sounds good."

"Your TikTok just hit two hundred fifty thousand!" Addison's too-loud voice grates against my ears. "I'm such a moron—

why didn't I think of that? True crime is so popular on TikTok. Let's make a video together." She pushes between me and Theo and lifts her phone to film, but I stop her.

"Let's wait until we're at the search."

"Ooh, good idea." She drops her phone, thumbs flying as she responds to a message. "That'll set a much better scene."

She acts like this is a movie, not Noelle's real-life nightmare.

"You guys ready?" Piper asks.

We nod, and this time, I'm the one to lead the way.

CHAPTER THIRTEEN
NOELLE

I'm still alive.

Beau untied me from the chair and threw me to the mattress after I told him about Hunter. The storm in his gray eyes told me he was torn on whether to believe me or not.

I lift my head, bleary-eyed. I've lost track of time, and the gray clouds and sprinkling rain aren't helping. It must be sometime in the afternoon because my stomach is growling.

When the door squeaks open, my heart leaps with hope, even though I know it shouldn't. Not when he emerges, shutting and locking the door behind him with a click.

He clutches a glass of water, setting it down on the floor beside my mattress before crouching in front of me and removing my gag. The ice cubes are already half-melted, a single drop of condensation trailing slowly to the floor.

But I know I'm not drinking that water, even if my throat is aching for it.

He rolls his eyes. "Relax. The water isn't poisoned."

"You'll drug me again." I'm not the idiot he clearly thinks I am. He was going to kill me last night. I have no reason to believe he isn't doing the same now. Slip something into my drink to make me pass out so I don't fight him.

"I didn't drug you," he says simply. "I used chloroform. Dipped a cloth in it and held it over your face. Didn't take long for you to pass out."

"Is that what you used to kidnap me?"

A wicked grin. "Always does the trick. Now drink up."

"You drink it."

He snatches the glass and takes three long slugs, Adam's apple bobbing. Watching a man drink shouldn't turn me on. Watching *this* man drink should repulse me. I'm ashamed that it doesn't.

Beau holds the glass out to me.

"You'll have to untie me first," I remind him. "I can't exactly drink with my hands bound."

"Trust me." He smirks. "You can do a lot with your hands bound."

My turn to roll my eyes.

He brings the glass to my lips. "Open." I shake my head, but he doesn't move. "Open your mouth or soak your shirt. Doesn't bother me either way, but I'm not getting more." His gray eyes fall to my chest, his scar shifting with the movement. "Actually, I wouldn't mind seeing you wet."

I can't help but growl before opening my mouth for him. He tips the glass slowly, pouring the water with surprising tenderness. I'm amazed he doesn't waterboard me.

He sets the empty glass on the floor, and already, my throat aches for more. The words claw and scrape as I force them out. "You didn't kill me."

"Did some research. Your story checks out." Beau leans close to me, staring so intently into my eyes, I stop breathing. "He shouldn't have done that to you. Any of it."

Relief pierces through the balloon of panic in my chest. Words I've needed to hear for months. Years.

Even from the mouth of my kidnapper, they reassure me.

In the distance, a siren wails.

Oh my god. They're finally coming for me.

Finally. Finally, they've found me. They're coming to rescue me. This nightmare will be over.

I lurch to my feet and race for the stairs. Surprisingly, Beau doesn't bother stopping me.

The siren blares as it approaches, and I try peering through the tiny window, but I'm too short to see anything.

I scream. Loud enough that if anybody's out there, they'll hear me. They'll get the police to stop and come find me.

Beau sits on the mattress, back against the wall.

The siren reaches its peak and fades.

No. My heart flips. They're passing me.

The siren grows quieter. And quieter.

Something in me snaps. I lurch up the rest of the stairs to the wide landing and kick at the door until my toes ache, screaming myself hoarse.

"Bad idea." Beau's low, seductive voice in my ear. I didn't notice him climb the stairs. "No one's going to hear you. We're in the middle of nowhere. The only person who's going to hear you is me." He grips my hips and flattens me against the wall, his erection pressed into my ass. My mouth goes dry. For a split second, I want to grind into him. Then I come to my senses and the terror sets in. He leans in, breath caressing my ear. "And I like hearing a girl scream."

I jerk back against him, shoving him off me the best I can with my hands still bound, and spin so I'm facing him. But he pins me to the wall again. Towering over me with a wolfish grin.

"Let me go." My voice cracks.

"I can't do that, princess."

Tears blur my vision. "Please don't kill me."

"Whether you live or die is up to you." His fingers trail down my cheek. They should make me want to vomit. Instead, my breath catches. "See, if I let you out now, I can't trust you not to tell anybody who kept you here."

"I won't tell anyone," I blurt. "I promise."

He tsks, gray eyes glazed and traveling over every inch of my face. "You lie so fucking easily. I don't know how I'm ever supposed to trust you."

"You can. You can trust me."

My mind scrambles, trying to come up with a way out of this. To make him think I'm complying.

I can't wait for my parents or the police to save me. I have to escape on my own. And to do that, I need to play Beau's game. I need to convince him that I won't try to run or leave. That he can trust me.

As soon as his guard's down, I'll take my chance.

"Untie me. I promise I won't try anything. Then you'll know you can trust me."

He smiles at me like a parent to their stupid child. "That so?" He shrugs. "I'll untie you. But if you try anything, if you try to run, you'll be punished."

Of course I'm going to run. I'll do anything I need to do to escape this psycho. "I won't try anything."

"Good. Because if you run, I'll find you before you get anywhere there's someone to help you." He skims his fingers tenderly behind my ear, across my jaw. "And you won't want me to find you."

I can barely form the words, heart galloping. "Because you'll kill me?"

His hand drifts from my hip and travels slowly across my thigh. Goosebumps race down my limbs. "Because I'll make you scream."

He's getting dangerously close to the spot between my thighs. Where I'm aching for him.

I break free of his grip and race down the stairs, cowering in the corner on my mattress like a caged animal. He saunters down the stairs while my heart hammers wildly.

Up close, the sharp edges of his jaw, his cheekbones, come into focus. The terrifying mixture of glee and danger in his gray eyes. His skin is smooth, lips full and promising to be the only soft part of him.

If my hands weren't bound, I might reach out and skim that flawless skin. The sharp edge to his jaw. The jut of his cheekbone.

If I were sane, I wouldn't dare.

"Did you fuck him?"

The question throws me. "What?"

"Hunter."

I shake my head. "No. I bought myself enough time, apparently. He... died a few days later."

Beau nods once, almost as if my answer satisfies him. As if he actually cares.

Like that's even possible for someone like him.

"You said you'd untie me if I promised not to run," I remind him, turning to reveal the rope around my wrists.

He slips his hand into his pocket and the glint of a blade flashes. "One wrong move, and you won't like how I tie you up next time, princess."

His knife slashes through the rope, freeing me. I nearly cry with relief, clutching my hands to my chest like they're my lost children returned to me.

Beau leans close, the musky scent of his leather jacket flooding my nose. "Try to run, and next time, you'll be spread eagle and naked."

CHAPTER FOURTEEN

THEO

*A*fter the police let me leave the station, I head back to Sigma Chi. Word about Noelle's disappearance has spread across the nation, and even though Officer Lee and Garcia told me I'm not in trouble or a person of interest, their questions sure made it sound like I am.

When was the last time you saw Noelle?
After classes and before practice.
How did she seem when you saw her last?
Fine. Normal.
Does she have any special nicknames?
No. Garcia didn't like that answer. What kind of boyfriend doesn't at least call his girlfriend babe or baby?
Does she have any distinguishing marks? Birthmarks, scars? Secret tattoos her parents wouldn't know about?
Not that I know of. They assume I've seen her naked plenty of times in the years that I've been calling her my girlfriend, but I've only seen her without clothes once and I can't think of a single distinguishing mark on her, not even on the skin she shows everyone.
What type of alcohol does she drink?

A multi-choice question I knew I would get wrong. *Um. Rum, maybe. Or vodka.*

Does she use any drugs?

I don't think so. Noelle was never into drugs in high school, but some people experiment in college. Maybe she has and never told me.

Does she typically pay with cash or cards?

Uh. I'm not sure. Credit card, I think?

Did she mention having any plans for that evening?

I think she had plans with her parents for dinner.

Did she have any plans after?

Not that I remember.

What was she wearing when you last saw her?

I don't remember. Was she wearing a dress or jeans? I have no idea. I can picture exactly what Cass was wearing that day—that short gray skirt that climbed up her thighs and the black shirt that swooped low over her chest.

You can't remember anything?

No.

There seems to be a lot you don't know about your own girlfriend, Mr. St. James.

Part of me longed to tell them the truth, but Dad's warning rang in my ears. *Don't fuel the flames by making them think you're a jilted ex.*

I had a pretty good feeling that even if I told the police the truth, it wouldn't do me any favors.

Officer Garcia scowled at nearly every one of my answers. Throughout the interview, I kept kicking myself for not paying closer attention to Noelle the last time I saw her.

Doesn't help that Dad lawyered me up as soon as Noelle went missing. That same lawyer's gonna be pissed when she finds out I talked to the police without her, even though they said I could have her present when they called me. I'm the one who didn't call her. Even though it's my right, having a lawyer makes me look guiltier.

Except I might've managed to do that all on my own.

I can only hope the police don't dig any deeper into my relationship with Noelle.

The first person to greet me when I walk through the door of Sigma Chi is my mother. She didn't tell me she'd be dropping by, but I can tell by the salacious grin on Colin's face behind her that he's glad she's here.

And by the grin that falls away from her face, she was enjoying the attention.

I'm her excuse, but she's been coming around more and more lately. Something tells me it's about more than her usual helicopter-parent tendencies. When she's here, the guys give her all their attention, and she basks in it. The way she glitters under their stares turns my stomach. Every guy in here is my age, and she looks at them like a hungry lion.

She rushes toward me and clutches my face in both hands. "Oh, sweetheart. I wanted to check in on you. You must be worried sick. I'm so sorry you're still going through this."

"Don't worry about me, Mom. Worry about Noelle. She's the one going through this, not me."

"You don't have to be so strong all the time, Theo."

That's been her line to me since I was nine and Granddad got sick and she and Dad started fighting more. They'd always fought, but Granddad was the glue that kept us all together, and if we lost him, we'd all fall apart.

So when they decided on a "trial separation," I started leaving Mom flowers every day, telling her they were from Dad. I made breakfast every morning before Dad left for work and let him think Mom got up early just for him. I did everything I could to keep them together, and it worked.

Sometimes, I wish I'd let them get a divorce. Maybe then we'd all be happier.

"Thanks, Mom."

"I know it's killing you not to have her here."

I nod. "Yeah, it is." I wake up every morning sick to my stomach, imagining all the horrible things Noelle might be living through. "Listen, Mom, I've gotta go. I'm meeting up with Cass and the girls. We're gonna go through our messages from Noelle."

Mom nods vigorously. "That sounds like a great idea, honey. Let me know if you kids find anything, and we'll go right to the police."

"I will."

Despite everything, a flicker of excitement ignites in my chest at the anticipation of seeing Cass.

∼

CASSIE

THEO, Addison, Piper, and I head to ECV to comb through our messages and DMs from Noelle for any clues. Did she plan to run away? I know she wouldn't, but there has to be a hint about something.

We each grab a slice of chocolate pie, today's dessert, but none of us have the appetite for it. Not even Theo, who's usually a bottomless pit. He pokes at his slice, managing to swallow down two bites before he drops his fork.

A small bit of chocolate flies from his fork when he does and hits me right on the boob. My top is low-cut today, and when Theo spins to apologize, he can't take his eyes off my chest.

I suppress my smile so Addison and Piper don't notice how much I'm enjoying the attention.

God, all I want is for him to take me back to the house, rip my top off, and squeeze and suck on my tits as long as he wants—

He snatches his napkin, and before thinking better of it, wipes the chocolate off. He drops it suddenly, realizing his mistake. You don't touch another girl's boob when you have a girlfriend, even if it is with a napkin. "Shit . . . sorry. Here."

Most of the mess is already gone, but I take the napkin anyway and swipe at the small remaining streak of chocolate.

Thank god Piper and Addison don't notice the exchange. They're both absorbed in their phones.

"Remember the news Noelle said she needed to tell us?" Addison gasps. "What if she was going to tell us that she was planning to run away or something?"

Theo's gaze drops to his plate, and I shake my head. "She wouldn't do that. I know her."

"So what news could she have had?"

That's the one question I can't answer. There wasn't a hint in her text of what news Noelle might've wanted to share.

"Guys!" Piper whisper-shouts, leaning onto the table. "The night before her parents reported her missing, she messaged the group chat about a fight with them."

"She said it was just a little argument," I correct, and open up the group chat. "Did she say what the argument was about?"

Addison shakes her head. "No, nothing. I asked her, but she didn't answer. Did anybody get any other messages about it?"

"No," I say. Theo shakes his head.

Piper lets out a gasp so loud, heads turn. Addison shushes her. "She said she was going for a walk. Look, she sent the message after eleven. So if she went for a walk at night, somebody could've grabbed her—"

"I *highly* doubt that," Addison says. "The odds of that happening are practically zero. No, we need to focus on the fight between her and her parents."

"You think she ran to get away from her parents?" Piper asks. Addison shrugs, casting all of us a meaningful look. Piper's eyes widen. "You think her parents *did* something to her?"

I don't realize I've been bouncing my leg until Theo's hand lands on my thigh.

I freeze, but he doesn't pull away.

His palm is rough with callouses from weightlifting in the gym. I glance at his face. He's completely casual, eyes on his plate. Addison and Piper don't notice.

Theo's hand is on my thigh. Right under the table. In public. In front of our friends.

Adrenaline courses through me. Holy shit. A giggle builds up in my chest like a lovesick schoolgirl, but I stuff a bite of pie in my mouth to swallow it down.

I've been in love with Theo since eighth grade. He never noticed me back then, but he was friends with Noelle, and I got the stupid idea in my head that he might somehow finally notice me and ask me to homecoming freshman year.

A week before the dance, students were shouting to friends and heading to the buses after the final bell. Out in the parking lot, a half-circle had formed. At the center was Noelle. And Theo.

Noelle was smiling at Theo, who was down on one knee and holding up a sign that said *Homecoming?*

My stomach dropped. All the air was sucked out of my lungs.

No. They'd known each other since childhood, and Noelle said they'd never been anything more than friends. She wouldn't want to go with him.

But then she nodded. "Sure!"

He stood and they hugged while everyone around them cheered, whooped, and clapped.

Except me.

I ran for the bus and let Noelle's texts go unanswered. It wasn't her fault—she didn't know about my crush on Theo. I'd harbored the secret in my chest, too afraid that if I spoke the words out loud, they'd find their way back to Theo and he wouldn't want to be my friend anymore. But part of me hoped that Noelle and I were close enough that she knew without me having to tell her.

The next day, she pulled me into the restroom after lunch. "What's up with you today?"

"Nothing." I tried heading for the door, but Noelle pulled me back.

"Cassie, I know you. Something's up. Tell me."

I hated the stupid tears that blurred my vision. "Theo asked you to homecoming." She waited for me to continue, not understanding. "I . . . I wanted him to ask me."

"Then I'll tell him I changed my mind," she said simply.

"What? No." I shook my head, trying to blink back the tears. "I don't want you to hurt his feelings."

"But it's hurting your feelings if I go with him." She stepped closer, grabbing my hand. "You're my best friend, Cassie. I don't want to hurt you."

I sniffled and composed myself. "It's really okay. I promise. Theo chose you. I don't want to be a second choice or whatever."

"You're *sure*?" she asked.

I nodded, and when she told me Theo asked her to be his girlfriend after homecoming, I said that was okay too.

Theo chose Noelle. Not me.

But now I'm the one he's touching. Maybe he's not choosing Noelle anymore.

When his thumb drifts lazily back and forth across my skin, warmth floods between my legs.

God, if he can have this effect on me with just his hand, imagine what he can do with his—

"We need to get into her parents' house," Addison says, breaking me out of my trance. "Who knows what they're hiding."

CHAPTER FIFTEEN

BEAU

The search efforts for Noelle van Buren have finally recovered her phone. Took them fucking long enough. The cops are supposedly combing through it now for any clues about her whereabouts.

They're not gonna find shit on that phone. Nothing that points to me, anyway. Hopefully they're already targeting her shitty parents. Who lets their drunk, sobbing daughter stumble down a sidewalk in the middle of the night alone? Don't they know that any creep could be out there, watching and waiting for their opportunity?

They do now.

"How old are you?" Her quiet, musical voice floats up from the mattress, barely reaching me even in the silence.

I've got my back against the basement door, not that I think she'd dare to make a break for it. She's smarter than I thought she'd be. Hasn't made a move since I cut the restraints from her wrists. Not sure if she's biding her time or her spirit's already breaking.

"Twenty-five."

She sits with that information before she dares to ask another question. "You said a woman gave you that scar. Who was it?"

I smirk. Princess is just like every other girl wanting to get in my pants. Pretends she gives a fuck about getting to know me when all she really wants is to tell her girlfriends about how she rode the guy with the scar over his eye. The guy who's damaged and broken and all it took was her perfect pussy to grow his heart three sizes.

I've seen the way she looks at me on campus. The way she looks at me here, trapped with me. Scared but intrigued. Wary but wanting to know more. Exactly the type of girl who gets wet for a little danger.

I head down the staircase, every step creaking beneath my feet.

Her big, pretty blue eyes blink up at me, putting on an act to convince me that she's not shitting herself. She should stick to art—she's a shit actress.

I pull my shirt off and sit beside her. She scrambles to the corner, as if she'll ever be able to get far enough away from me. I flick out my pocket knife and she grimaces before I point the blade at my scar. "This one? Was from Mommy Dearest."

Her eyes pop. "Your mother did that to you?"

"That was the last one." I point to the tattoos swirling and cresting along my torso. "What do you think these are covering up?"

Horror etches into her face. A sheltered princess with parents who ground her from her phone as punishment. They don't extinguish their cigarettes on her skin or whip her with belts or chase her around the house with a knife.

My mother raised me to lie and steal and cheat to get what you want. To not care who you step on. She'd do anything for a fix, whether that was a drug-induced high or crime-fueled adrenaline.

The first body she made me help her bury showed up in our kitchen when I was ten. Even with the crimson knife in her hand and the man facedown on our floor, blood pouring from his back, she called it self-defense.

She was always the victim, even when she was burning or

cutting me. *You made me do this. You see what you do to me? You see what you make me do?*

She had me so brainwashed that even when I turned eighteen, I stayed. Helped keep her hands clean while she stuck mine in the mud.

Then I fucked up a drug deal when I found out her dealer had a predilection for little kids. I beat the dude within an inch of his life, and when my mother found me with his blood on my hands, she came at me with that knife.

Close your eyes.

"I'm sorry she hurt you." A small voice in the dark, bringing me back to myself. Words I've never heard from anyone.

"She certainly gave it her best effort. Real fucked-up part is, sometimes, I didn't mind her hurting me because it meant she was around to do it."

"She'd leave you alone?"

"Any time she went on a bender. Or had a mess to clean up."

"For how long?"

I shrug. "Few days. A few months."

Silence settles between us. Her fault for asking. Don't want to know the ugly truth, don't ask the question.

"What about the tattoos on your knuckles?"

I grin, holding them up so Princess can see each of them clearly. "I guess you could call them . . . souvenirs."

A cross for the priest. A diamond for the dealer. A hook for the sex trafficker. A spider for the bar owner. A blade for my mother.

"Did you kill them?" she whispers.

She wants to know how afraid of me she should be. How far she should hide from the claws and fangs of the beast keeping her in a cage.

"They deserved it." Sex crimes can't be justified. Because of me, the priest can't target his choir boys, the dealer can't go after his clientele's kids, the trafficker can't brutalize innocent women and girls, and the bar owner can't spike his customers' drinks.

Noelle swallows. "Where's your mother now?"

I tap my first tattooed knuckle. My first kill. "Let's just say she can't leave any more scars."

She'd disappeared as soon as she sliced me open. Turns out, she had a rich mommy and daddy and an inheritance I never knew about. They paid to sweep everything under the rug, wipe her filthy slate clean.

Her first mistake was teaching me how to track down someone who doesn't want to be found. Her second was giving me a reason to find her.

When I did, I didn't drag it out. Didn't torment her the way she'd tormented me from birth.

But I finished the job.

Once her blood was on my hands, what was a little more?

Hunting down fugitives for bail bond agents pays the bills. Getting rid of the worst predators walking the earth cleanses my blackened soul.

"What about your father?" Noelle asks. "He didn't protect you from her?"

I chuckle. "Nah, he's the reason I'm in this shithole town. Mommy Dearest told me he didn't want anything to do with me my whole life. Figured he was just another lowlife. After I got good at tracking people down, I added him to my list. He needed to pay for abandoning me with my psychotic mother."

She doesn't nod or say a word. She might not even be breathing. Hanging on to my every word, every syllable.

"Found him, and first thing he told me was that he'd been trying to find me for years. He'd wanted to know me, be part of my life, be a father, but she kept me from him. A way to punish him. And me."

Years of my life I'll never get back. Memories he and I will never make.

Noelle huffs out a sigh. "I thought my mom was bad. All she does is control me and make me feel worthless."

"Sounds just like mine."

Her blue eyes flash to me. Something new sparking in her gaze. Like someone finally understands her.

"She's why you're not an art major."

A flicker of surprise, but she should know by now that I've done my research. I know everything about her. "Yeah. She wants me to go to med school. I guess because Theo is pre-med and she has this weird competitive thing with his mom. Who can get engaged first, married first, pregnant first. Who has the biggest house, the priciest car, the most successful child."

"Pitting you against your boyfriend?"

Her pale brows pull together. "You know about Theo?"

I lean toward her with a smile. "I know your major. Of course I know your little boyfriend's name."

The side of her pretty mouth quirks up. My heart stutters. "But you don't know he isn't my boyfriend anymore. Guess your stalking skills are a bit rusty."

I scoot toward her and the cocky smirk slips from her face. But she doesn't move. Not even when my hand drifts to her throat. She doesn't let out another snarky comment. The panic building up, her pulse jumping beneath my thumb. I squeeze her neck. Not enough to hurt, but enough to make her wet for me. Her blue eyes stay wide and fixed on my face when I lean toward her, lips brushing her ear. "Princess, none of my skills are rusty."

I drop my hand when her heart can't seem to take it anymore, but I don't scoot away and she's frozen in place.

"Not the boyfriend anymore, huh?"

She shakes her head, clears her throat. "We broke up."

I tilt my head back against the wall and smirk. "Shame."

A little shrug. "We're better as friends."

I couldn't give less of a shit about the kid. One night in my bed and she'd forget all about him. "What are you always drawing?"

"Um. It depends. What I see, sometimes. Other times, I have an image in my head."

"You ever draw people?"

She drops her gaze to her hands clasped in front of her. "Once." She peers up at me through her lashes. "I drew you."

She's full of shit, but I like it. "I bet you did. You like painting too?"

The question throws her. "Uh, yeah."

"Screw what your mother tells you to do. If you want to be an artist, go be an artist."

My mother wanted me to terrorize the world, just like her. Tried to make me her reincarnation. She'd roll over in her fucking grave if she could see how I've turned out.

"Kind of hard when I'm a captive in someone's basement." There's that snark again. I want to fuck it out of her mouth.

"This isn't new to you. No part of your life has ever been your own. You're not in charge of any of it. You've always been someone's captive." I stand, and she doesn't argue again. "Now you're mine."

CHAPTER SIXTEEN

CASSIE

While the van Burens are being interviewed at a press conference, the four of us sneak into their house. I memorized their door code years ago—1-2-2-8. Noelle's birthday.

Angel barks twice before she flops on her back for belly rubs. Theo obliges her while I rush upstairs with Piper and Addison. We have to hurry. The van Burens could return any time and we have no idea what their housekeeper's schedule is like.

Addison plops in Noelle's pink desk chair and turns on her expensive desktop with the triple-monitor setup. "Any ideas on a password?"

"We can look around," Piper suggests. "Maybe she wrote it down somewhere."

"Please. No one's been dumb enough to write down their passwords since 2005."

Piper's cheeks flush to match her bright red hair.

"There is no password," I say.

Addison clicks Sign In and finds I'm right when the desktop screen loads. "Who doesn't have a password on their computer?"

"Her mom won't let her," I explain.

Addison lifts a brow. "Wow. Controlling much?"

Piper and I comb through Noelle's room while Addison digs

through the files on her computer. Her room is spotless—a result of their housekeeper's hard work. All these years later, and I still can't believe Noelle's family employs a housekeeper. How they have enough money to hire staff in their home, while my family barely has enough money for groceries.

Just as I suspected, our search is fruitless. Even Addison's search of Noelle's computer turns up empty.

"How does somebody just vanish into thin air?" Addison asks.

We sit in silence. Noelle has been gone for a week, and we're still no closer to finding her.

"We're just getting started," I tell them. "Let's try their computer in the office."

Piper and I look through the room while Addison attempts to hack into the van Burens' computer. After a few attempts, she cackles. "Seriously? They used Noelle's birthday."

Of course they used Noelle's birthday for their computer password. Just like they programmed her birthday as their door code. Their whole world revolves around her.

From downstairs, Theo's jovial laugh echoes in the near-silent house. I can't help but smile. I love hearing his laugh. I wish I was down there with him right now.

Addison hisses through her teeth. "Get over here. You need to check this out." She's pulled up a window filled with bank transactions. "So everything looks normal until you get to a few months ago. All of a sudden, they start sending huge sums of money to some isolated checking account they just opened. And none of the money in that account has been used yet."

"What do you think that means?" Piper asks.

"They're transferring over money for Noelle to spend. Her parents must've planned this whole thing with her. They know where she is."

I shake my head. "Why would they report her missing then? Why would they be going on the news? They wouldn't be trying to draw attention to her or themselves if they know where she is."

"Of course they would," Addison argues. "What kind of parents don't report their daughter missing? They have to play along and make it seem like she disappeared."

"I don't know . . ." Piper bites her lip. "Why would Noelle even want to leave? She wouldn't want to just vanish and start a whole new life somewhere. She likes college, and it's not like she ever said anything to us about wanting to run away."

Addison considers this. "Maybe they're paying somebody off."

Piper gasps. "Like a coverup? Like they . . . did something to her?"

"They wouldn't kill their own daughter," I object. "They're basically obsessed with her."

"What if it's to protect her?" Addison suggests. "She's probably living a whole new life in Cabo or something."

"Find anything?" Theo strolls in, Angel in his arms. He manages to make carrying a Labrador appear effortless.

Theo looks best in bright colors that match his personality and his shiny green eyes, yet I can't help but drool over him in black too. The dark T-shirt outlines the hard ridges of muscle on his shoulders and biceps and chest. His jeans curve around his perfect backside. God, athletes have the best asses—

"Come here." Addison gestures Theo over, and he sets Angel down. "Tell me what you think of this."

All of these wild theories are making my head spin. "I need some water."

Theo flashes me a warm smile before I head downstairs. My heart flutters in my throat all the way to the fridge.

As soon as I close the door, a bottled water in hand, I scream.

Mrs. van Buren stands in the kitchen, Berkin in hand and frown pulling at her lips. She's perfectly put together like always, her hair blown out and fingers manicured. "Cassie." Her voice is tight. "Why are you in my home? And my refrigerator."

"Mrs. van Buren!" I stutter. "Um . . . I'm so sorry! I . . ."

"Found her!" A low voice calls. Theo pounds down the stairs,

Angel cradled in his arms again. "She's ready for a walk—Oh! Hi, Mrs. van Buren."

"Theo." Her smile is still strained. "I was just asking Cassie what you two are doing here. You *four* are doing here," she corrects when she spots Addison and Piper behind him.

"Yeah, sorry to barge in on you. We came to check in on you two and heard this girl barking like crazy, and we wanted to make sure she was all right." He coos down at Angel and I've never loved him more.

Mrs. van Buren relaxes, tossing her thousand-dollar bag carelessly on the island. "Well, thank you for checking on Angel." She digs in the fridge for her own bottled water. "But please call or text first next time."

"Absolutely." Theo clips Angel's leash on. "We won't let it happen again."

"Would any of you like anything to drink?" Mrs. van Buren asks it like she resents her own hospitality.

I start to say, "We're fine," but then Piper asks for a Coke.

Addison taps her nails on the island, trying and failing to appear casual. "Hey, Mrs. van Buren? Do you remember if anything happened the night Noelle went missing?"

Mrs. van Buren stiffens, a slight crease between her brows breaking through the Botox. "Excuse me?"

The tension in the room mounts. Piper's huge doll eyes dart back and forth between Addison and Mrs. van Buren, the can of Coke clutched in her hands.

Even Addison looks afraid. "Just . . . she mentioned an argument. That's all. We were just wondering what it was about. Maybe she threatened to run away or something—"

"There's nothing to talk about." Mrs. van Buren has morphed into an ice queen. I've never seen her like this before. She's always the perfectly polite, pleasant woman everyone adores, respects, admires. "That's family business. And if you want to stand in my home and insinuate that I'm involved in my own daughter's disappearance, you can leave."

Addison and Piper briefly make eye contact before scurrying out of the house without another word. I stay crouched petting Angel until the door shuts behind them.

Mrs. van Buren rubs her temples before she pops a pill and chases it with water.

"I'm gonna take Angel outside," Theo says, breaking the awkward tension. He aims a pointed look my way, a gesture for me to follow him, but I stay behind.

As soon as he's out the door, I say, "I'm sorry about Addison. She shouldn't have said something like that."

Mrs. van Buren manages a tiny, tired smile. "Thank you, Cassie. You're really such a sweet girl. Noelle's lucky to have a friend like you. I hope college is going well for you, in spite of everything."

She's invested in my education—literally. She and her husband offered to pay for my tuition at Westbrook after Hunter died. Mom told me not to take it, but there was no way I could turn down the gift. "Very well, thank you. But really, I'm the lucky one. Noelle's always doing whatever she can for me. She helped me with all my studying after Hunter's funeral and she's been driving me everywhere."

"Well, her Mercedes has just been sitting in the driveway. The police examined it. No evidence. You can take it until she comes home, if you'd like."

I shake my head. "Oh no, that's too generous. I couldn't."

"I insist." She digs in her purse until she finds Noelle's keychain and hands me the key to the sleek Mercedes I've coveted since Noelle's sweet sixteen.

"Thank you. That's really kind of you. I promise I'll be careful with it. I'll go check on Theo and Angel, and we'll get out of your hair."

She nods, forcing a small smile before popping another pill.

Outside, I shade my eyes against the bright sunlight. Angel is sprawled on her back, tongue lolling out of her mouth while Theo rubs her belly.

"We better go. She's about to be on her third pill and I'm pretty sure that's the stuff that either makes you sleepy or loopy."

Theo straightens, towering over me in a way that always makes my heart skip. "Addison and Piper already left. Can you call them so they can come back and give us a ride?"

"No need." I pull the key out of my pocket. "We're taking the Mercedes."

Theo frowns. "Noelle's car?"

"Yeah, Mrs. van Buren said I can borrow it until Noelle comes home."

Theo lets Angel inside and hangs the leash by the door before jogging back to me. "Hey, is that my hoodie?"

My hand rushes to the zipper. "Oh, yeah. Sorry. I wore it to give it back to you—"

"Keep it." He shrugs, his signature grin turning me into a puddle. "Looks better on you anyway."

CHAPTER SEVENTEEN

NOELLE

*B*eau Grayson has murdered five people. Including his own mother.

Some depraved part of me can understand why, though. She covered his body in scars. Caused him pain, physically and emotionally, by burning him, abandoning him, manipulating him.

I shouldn't be able to empathize with a serial killer. But I feel bad for the child he was. Lost, hurt, lonely. For a second there, it almost felt like we were bonding.

When I ask him for soap and shampoo so I can rub the stench and grease from my body, he surprisingly brings them to me without argument. The hot water soothes the tight knots in my shoulders and back, stiff from days on a lumpy mattress on a cold, unforgiving concrete floor.

Too late, I realize I forgot to ask for a razor. The hair on my legs has grown in prickly and uncomfortable. I step out of the shower, towel wrapped tight around my body, and stick my head out the door.

Beau's standing right there. I jump. "I want to shave my legs."

He shakes his head. "Forget it. I don't trust you with a razor."

"I'm not going to kill myself. I just want to shave." Even

though it's such a stupid thing to cry over, my eyes well. I want to feel like this body is still mine. Like I have control over what happens to it.

"Then I'll shave you." He heads for the stairs.

"What? No." I don't trust him coming anywhere near me with a razor. Not after he pressed that knife to my throat.

"That's the deal, princess," he calls.

When he returns, he has a jar of men's shaving cream and a metal razor. I sit on the toilet seat and hold my hand out for the shaving cream, but he pops the lid off and lathers up my shin himself. I hiss at the cool cream against my skin, but his hand rubbing over my leg is somehow soothing. Despite him being my kidnapper and captor.

I stiffen when he picks up the razor with his other hand.

"Relax. If I was going to kill you, it wouldn't be with a razor blade."

"How would you do it?" I ask, even though the answer is obvious. That knife in his pocket. He'll use it to slice my throat before stabbing me and cutting me into ribbons.

He smirks up at me. At his startling gray eyes peering into mine from this angle, something deep in my gut stirs. "You gagging on my dick."

I roll my eyes. "People don't die from that." Although . . . I don't actually know that for sure. I've never given a blowjob.

"Wanna test it?" he asks.

I grimace. "No."

The smile still lingers on his face when he drags the razor up my shin. He shaves my entire shin and calf in silence, and it's almost . . . romantic. Kind. If the circumstances were completely, utterly different.

Still, a nonsensical, idiotic part of my brain convinces me the gesture is sweet.

When he's finished with the bottom half of my leg, he wipes a damp washcloth over my skin and presses a kiss to my shin. My spine goes rigid. "There," he murmurs. "Perfect."

Fuck. His lips against my skin shouldn't feel this good. Shouldn't make me want more.

He put a chloroform rag over my mouth to knock me unconscious and lock me away in his basement. His touch should repulse me, nauseate me.

How does it have the opposite effect?

He has me stand so he can shave my thighs, a feline grin spreading across his face every time he goes too high under my towel and I push him away, even as heat pools in my core.

I'm shivering by the time he's done, the cool air from the basement dissipating the hot air from the shower.

"Where else do you want me to shave?" he asks, staring pointedly between my legs.

"Absolutely not," I tell him. "Can you just let me shave under my arms? Leave me with a little dignity, please. That's the least you can do."

He stands. "You've got shelter, water, and food in your stomach, and you're not dead. I've done far more than the least I can do. Lift up your arm."

I concede, even though I hate him seeing me like this. That's another one of Mother's rules—never let anyone see your imperfections.

"What kind of people do you hunt?"

"Could be anybody who skips bail. Everybody from fraudsters to murderers."

"What about the people you kidnap?"

He keeps his gaze on the razor's sharp edge gliding over my skin. "The worst of them."

I stiffen. "You think my family is the worst of them?" Or Theo. Or Cassie. I can't believe he actually accused them. Theo's too good a person to commit a hit-and-run, and Cassie would've never left her brother behind to die.

Beau snorts. "No. Your situation is . . . unique."

"How so?"

He keeps his lips shut. He doesn't trust me with all his secrets yet.

"The people you . . . killed," I manage. "What did they do?"

He sets the razor down on the sink behind me. "Things that can never be justified. They left the kind of scars that can't be covered up."

I picture the tattoos etched into his skin beneath his jacket. Beautiful and entrancing, making my hand itch for a pencil. Covering nearly all the scars his mother gave him, except one. "Why do you go after them?"

His gray eyes turn stony. "Because when I was a kid, I wanted someone like me to show up."

Impossibly, a part of my heart aches for him. I can feel bad for the helpless kid he was and disgusted by the serial killer he's grown up to be.

He may not trust me with all his secrets yet, but he does trust me enough to let me walk around with my hands free. Now is the time to put my plan in motion. I need to get out of here—no matter what it takes.

"You said I'm the first girl you ever kidnapped?"

Those gray eyes land on mine. "Yes."

I swallow. "You're my first too."

His chuckle reverberates down my spine as he plants his hands on either side of me. Caging me in. He leans forward, breath whispering across my neck as he twists a strand of damp blonde hair around his finger. "So you are a virgin."

My hands grip the towel around me, terrified that at any second, he's going to rip it from my body. "Yeah. I've been waiting for someone like you."

He leans back, fixing me with a knowing grin. "You think you're going to play games with me?"

Shit. I should've known he'd be too smart for this. He sees right through me. My mind whirls, trying to devise a way out of this.

I brush my fingers against his cheek, startled by how soft his skin is. He leans into my touch on reflex before his eyes flash to mine. Suspicious but intrigued. "You were right before, you know. I have come thinking about you."

A half-smile pulls at one side of his mouth. "I love how stupid you think I am. But if you want to play games?" Beau grabs my hips and shoves me against the wall, pinning me there. "Hey. I'll bite."

He lunges at me, sinking his teeth into my shoulder and flattening us both against the wall. I cry out and adrenaline shoots through my veins. *Shit*. I try to shove his shoulders without dropping my towel, but he doesn't budge. Part of me panics while another melts, the pain and terror mixing with desire.

I shouldn't want him . . . but I do.

I should want him to stop . . . but I don't.

When he releases my shoulder, his gray eyes blaze, staring at me so intently, the towel might as well be on the floor.

His gaze falls to my mouth and my heart stops. He's going to kiss me.

I brace myself. Knowing I won't be able to stop him. Unsure whether I want to.

He closes the space between us, stopping a mere inch from my mouth. His soft, sweet breath curls over my skin when his lips part. "Remember, princess. You started this."

∼

BEAU

I ALMOST KISSED HER. Almost couldn't fucking help myself. She was trying to pull some mind-game shit with me. Telling me everything I want to hear like I'm a fucking idiot who can't see right through her pretty little words.

Her lips were right there, looking soft and delicious. It took all my willpower not to push her to her knees right then and pull out my throbbing cock, watch her swallow every drop.

She's asleep now, still wearing my sweats and shirt. They're way too big on her. Her panties and bra are drying in the bathroom where she washed them after her shower. Maybe I'll take them upstairs so she'll have to go without them. One less layer to fuck with when I yank those clothes off her and take what she's dying to give me.

I like her in my clothes. She looks like she's mine. Now, I suppose, she is.

For once, she doesn't feel my eyes on her or stir in her sleep. I'm tempted to walk down these steps and push that strand of blonde hair out of her face, but then I wouldn't be able to stop touching her and I like to wait to touch a girl until she's begging.

When my eyes start falling shut, I head down the stairs and leave the sketchpad, pencils, paintbrushes, and can of paint on the concrete. She's been treating her art like some dumb little hobby for too long. Like it's not what she was born to do. But that's all she should be doing. That, and riding my cock when she's ready to beg for it. She'll go insane in here if she doesn't have a distraction. I can't always be around, and she might be here a while.

She's clever, but I've been at this a lot longer. Princess isn't manipulating her way out of this basement.

If she's as smart as she thinks she is, she'll figure that out soon enough.

Or she'll be here with me forever.

CHAPTER EIGHTEEN
THEO

*C*ass is making herself impossible to resist. She keeps wearing those low-cut tops and short skirts that make my mouth water. I can't keep my hands off her, let alone my eyes.

When she was sitting next to me in ECV, nerves jiggling her leg, I couldn't help myself. I reached out and put my hand on her thigh, and she froze instantly. Her skin was so soft and smooth, I nearly pulled her onto my lap right there. Somehow, she didn't shake me off or push me away. She let me touch her.

I've thought of a hundred other places I want to touch her since.

Maybe she does know about the breakup. If that's the case, I wish she'd mention it so I'd know for sure. I'm too deep in the lie to come clean now, and Mom and I know better than to go against my father.

He makes the money, so he has the final say over everything. What we do, what we say. His livelihood relies on our family's reputation. Can't exactly get away with bribing judges and burying evidence when everyone's got you under a microscope.

Tonight, Cass is in a bright pink dress that doesn't suit her at all, but she makes it look good. Maybe it's a size too small, but I love the way it hugs over her hips and thighs. Her tits are practically busting out the top and I imagine burying my face between them until my roommate, Colin, punches my arm.

"You getting on stage tonight?" he asks.

The university is holding a vigil in Noelle's honor at the football stadium. Soon, we'll be lighting candles in her honor and listening to speeches from her parents and the faculty about how her disappearance has rocked the community.

"Nah. Just family and faculty," I tell him.

"You sure you don't want to get up there and clear your name?" Colin teases.

"Maybe not a bad idea."

He chuckles. "That's what I'm saying. Always the boyfriend."

My body temperature goes up, even though I have nothing to feel guilty about. "What matters is everyone focusing on finding Noelle."

"Dude, I can't imagine going that long without pussy. You must be losing your mind." Colin nods down to Cass, where she's walking into the stadium. She spots us up on the bleachers and waves. And damn if a big, goofy smile doesn't break across my face. "Especially with her friend looking like *that*. Did she get hot all of a sudden?"

I guess I'm not the only one who's finally noticed Cass when she's been right under my nose this whole time. Part of me wants to tell him to back the hell off, but I bite my tongue. Colin's not exactly a Boy Scout, but he's mostly talk and if he thought I wanted to cheat on my girlfriend, he'd call me on my bullshit.

Even if the whole world knew Noelle isn't my girlfriend anymore, I still wouldn't be able to date her best friend less than two weeks after her disappearance. Everyone will point the finger at both of us. The boyfriend who got rid of his girlfriend for her best friend, and the best friend who helped him get rid of the body.

Worse, it would distract them from Noelle. All our resources need to go toward finding her.

"She single?" Colin elbows my ribcage, nodding down at Cass. "You should put in a good word for me."

My jaw clenches. Not if he was the last fucking guy on Earth.

∽

CASSIE

EVERYONE IS WEARING PINK—NOELLE'S favorite color. I post three videos of the vigil to social media to show the huge crowd that turned out for her. All the students, staff, and members of the community wearing pink shirts, hoodies, coats, ribbons, and even some pink pants in her honor. Even Beau Grayson, posted by the entrance with another security guard, wears a pink hat.

But no one else is wearing a pink dress or the pink heels straight from her closet, hand-me-downs she passed along to me when she grew tired of them. Items that would've cost me two weeks of tips at my old waitressing gig that meant nothing to her.

When I spot Theo in the bleachers with some guys from his team, I wave and run up to him. Or, at least, run as well as I can in heels. I've only been in them for half an hour and my feet already ache.

"Hey, Cass!" He grins at me. "You look great." He takes in every inch of me, from my high ponytail to my heels. His gaze sets me on fire.

I could melt. Exactly the reaction I was hoping for.

He runs his hand over my ponytail and my breath catches. "I kind of miss your hair down, though."

"You've never said you like my hair before," I remind him.

He gives an easy smile. "I didn't think you cared what I thought."

"Why wouldn't I?"

"Why would you?"

Because I love you, Theo. I've been in love with you for years.

"Because you're a guy, and I've never had a boyfriend. How am I supposed to know if I'm attractive to the opposite sex if none of them ever say so?"

His smile dips. I said the wrong thing. "Oh. Well, in that case." He glances behind him at his teammates a few feet away, ignoring us, before turning back to me. "You're gorgeous. Every guy here thinks so."

My heart stops. Theo's sparkling green eyes are glued on mine, and I can't remember the last time we've ever held eye contact for this long. Maybe we never have.

He could've chosen any other word. *Cute*. *Pretty*. But he chose *gorgeous*. That's not a word you reserve for your girlfriend's best friend.

A voice calls out to me. Addison and Piper at the bottom of the bleachers.

"Save me a seat?" I ask Theo.

He flashes me his winning grin. "You got it."

He thinks I'm gorgeous. He wants me to sit with him. And I've thought of nothing but his hand on my thigh since that afternoon at ECV. What if Theo St. James actually wants to be with me? Butterflies take flight in my stomach, even as I remind myself he already has a girlfriend.

When I reach my friends, Addison's eyes narrow on my heels. "Why are you wearing those? It's, like, forty degrees out."

"Because they're pink. For Noelle."

Piper spots Neal sauntering over from the parking lot, late as usual. She runs to him, and Addison's gaze finds Kyle beside him. They make eye contact, but her mouth pinches and she turns her attention back to me. So they're off again. We'll see how long it lasts this time. I'm guessing until eleven o'clock tonight when he texts her asking if she wants to come ride his dick.

But Addison isn't tracking Kyle from her peripheral vision. She's staring up at the bleachers. At Theo.

He's oblivious to our eyes on him, leaning back and chatting with his teammates.

"Be careful with Theo," Addison warns.

"What are you talking about?"

Her face scrunches. "I know you see the way he looks at you."

Shit. So she has noticed. "Don't you think it's weird that his girlfriend goes missing, and all of a sudden, he wants to bang you?"

"Who says it's all of a sudden?" There's a high, defensive edge to my voice. "Maybe he's been into me for a while."

The way he looked at me that afternoon on the quad. Noelle was still beside him, he still had his hand on her. But he was looking at me.

"If that's true, that's an even bigger red flag. What kind of guy lusts over his girlfriend's best friend? I know he acts all nice and charming, but that's exactly the type of guy who does shit like this."

"Shit like what?"

"Kills his girlfriend," she hisses.

I scoff. "Do you hear yourself, Addison? Theo's not a killer. He feels guilty when he accidentally steps on a bug."

She steps closer, chin dipping. "Cassie, I know you're into him. But please keep your eyes open. I'm just asking you to be careful. That's all."

I should deny that I'm into him. But there's no point. She knows the truth. "I'm being careful."

"Good." Her gaze drifts to Theo again, and this time, he spots us and waves. That smile, those eyes, those huge, incredible hands that show up in every one of my fantasies. There's no way he'd do what Addison is accusing him of. "I hope you know what you're doing."

CHAPTER NINETEEN
NOELLE

I'm still in Beau's clothes, a pair of sweats and a T-shirt I swim in. I hate that I have to wear his clothes. That I'm reminded of him every time the scent from the threads finds its way into my nose. That wearing his clothes makes me feel like I belong to him.

Worse, I hate that I love it.

He left a sketchpad, pencils, paintbrushes, and a can of wall paint for me. When I woke up and saw them waiting for me, I couldn't help the grin that spread across my face.

Mother practically banned art supplies from the house when she decided I was spending too much time "doodling" and not enough time perfecting my poses. Even living on campus hasn't given me much time to focus on my art. All I have are the fleeting moments between classes to draw another line or two—the rest of my time is devoted to lectures, studying, school work, community service, parties, family dinners, and campus events with my sorority sisters.

Beau left a note in the sketchpad for me: *Go crazy, princess.* So I have been.

The click of the lock echoes in the silent basement, followed by the squeal of the door opening and the creak of each of Beau's footsteps down the stairs.

"Ham and cheese, princess."

"Thank you," I murmur, keeping my focus on my sketchpad and shading in a gray eye.

He crouches, setting the plate down. "You're drawing me?" His voice is strangely hopeful. Light and soft.

"What do you think?" I hold the sketch up to him.

He skims the tips of his fingers along the edges, careful not to brush the graphite. "I think you're doing exactly what you're meant to be doing."

My heart flutters. He scans the pages scattered across my mattress, most of them in the early outlining stages still, but I had to get all the images in my head sketched before they disappeared.

I've never let anyone look at my art, not even Cassie. Too ashamed by how my mother made me feel about it, like all the time I spent pouring my soul onto the page was completely worthless. Like I was completely worthless.

But I like letting Beau look.

He examines each drawing the way someone might view a Picasso or a van Gogh. Studying every line. Viewing my soul on the page, in awe of it.

He taps the corner of the sketch in my hands. His portrait. "Don't ever stop doing this."

I can't help but smile. Perhaps the first real, genuine smile I've ever given him.

"I want this whole room covered."

"That would take me a long time."

"So?"

I clutch the sketchpad to my chest. "If I cover the whole room . . . will you let me go?"

Silence falls between us. I've said the wrong thing. He's going to punish me—

"Maybe by then you wouldn't want to."

He leaves me with the ham sandwich on dry wheat bread and heads back up the stairs and out of the basement.

Without the unmistakable click of the door locking behind him.

My hand scrawling across the page stops. There's no way he forgot to lock me in here. He's been doing it day and night since he kidnapped me.

He'll return any second to lock the door behind him.

An insane part of me doesn't want to move. Doesn't want to attempt escape.

Maybe by then you wouldn't want to. Maybe I already don't.

I'm surrounded by sketches. My hand and wrist ache from drawing for so many hours, but I can't stop. My mind is whirring, this obsessive need to get everything out of my head onto paper. I haven't felt like this since I was a kid, when all I wanted to do was draw, whether I was in my room, playing outside, sitting at a modeling shoot, waiting for the casting director to call my name, or eating the carefully selected, calorie-deficit meal my mother laid out in front of me.

I can't remember the last time this feeling filled me up. This feeling of... joy. Hope. Freedom.

But I'm trapped in someone's basement. This isn't freedom. Beau must be getting in my head, that's all. I won't let myself succumb to Stockholm syndrome or brainwashing or gaslighting or whatever other shit he's trying to pull on me.

When nothing but silence follows, no sound but the ticking clock in my head, I move with feline stealth. Setting my sketchpad and pencil on the mattress, stepping onto the frozen floor.

I brace myself for the inevitable squeak on each wooden step. Three tiny creaks mark my ascent, and I'm sure he'll come flying through that door any second.

He doesn't. It remains shut. Silent on the other side.

My breath shudders, heart jackhammering. I have a chance. I might actually make it out of here.

Beau's warnings ring through my head: *If you run, I'll find you before you get anywhere there's someone to help you. And you won't want me to find you.*

Try to run, and next time, you'll be spread eagle and naked.

He must've been lying. Trying to scare me so I wouldn't try to escape. More likely, we're surrounded by houses full of people who've been searching for me, who will jump at the chance to call 911 after they find missing Noelle van Buren dirty and barefoot with a story about a psychotic security guard who decided to kidnap a girl and hold her captive.

I twist the knob as slowly and quietly as I can. And pull the door open.

The hallway is empty. No one to observe my movements except the paintings on the wall and the fake, leafy plant sitting on a dark glass shelf. Surprisingly tasteful decor for someone like Beau Grayson.

To my right, huge swaths of sunlight pour into a massive open floor plan. A connected living room and kitchen.

All leading to the front door.

I glance around one last time for Beau, and when I know my path is clear, I run for it.

Heart in my throat, beating a thousand times a minute, a second, I dart across the carpet. I'm halfway through the living room, my escape so close, I can taste it.

I brace myself for Beau to materialize from the shadows and throw me to the floor. But nothing touches me as I reach the front door and fling it open, not bothering to shut it behind me.

Shit. He wasn't lying about us being alone out here. I take in all the nothingness that surrounds us. No other houses in sight—just us and acres of smooth grass that turns to woods. A peaceful, tranquil home off a quiet road.

The air is brisk, cutting right through Beau's flimsy T-shirt and sweats. My feet are still bare, but I don't care. There has to be somewhere for me to run. To hide.

I take off for the woods, his warning ringing in my ears like a chant.

You won't want me to find you.

~

BEAU

SHE LEAVES WITHOUT A WORD. Just like my mother did so many times. I chased her too, following my mother's car down the driveway and up the gravel road. But unlike my mother, Noelle isn't getting far.

No shoes and no clue where she is. She'll head for the woods, thinking she can hide from me. Forgetting I've tracked more desperate people than her across states through deserts, swamps, and forests.

I slip on my shoes, letting her get the headstart she thinks will help before I take off after her. She's halfway to the woodline, glancing over her shoulder every few steps.

When she spots me, she starts screaming.

I smile.

I told her what would happen if she ran. If she tried to get away from me. She's supposed to be convincing me I can trust her, but some lessons take a while to learn. Some require punishment.

When she breaches the treeline, I lose sight of her long blonde hair swaying back and forth with every step.

Her feet crunch through the dim woods in front of me, guiding me right to her. She's stopped screaming now, finally coming to her senses that there's no one out here but the two of us. Exactly why I brought her here.

"Princess," I call. Haven't even broken a sweat, but I'd bet my life she's already breathless.

Twigs and leaves crunch beneath my feet until I stop. Silence. She's not running anymore.

She's hiding.

Not sure which is worse—her thinking she can run from me or thinking she can hide from me.

I follow her obvious trail between the trees. Once you've hunted before, you never miss the signs. The scratch across the bark where her nails dug in, the divide between the leaves where her feet ran past, the trickle of blood where she cut her foot.

When I plant my palm against the bark and lean around the tree, certain that's where I'll find her, something sharp and heavy strikes the back of my skull.

CHAPTER TWENTY

NOELLE

I expect Beau to fall flat on his face, unconscious. But he spins, totally steady on his feet, and snarls at me.

Then he lunges.

The branch flies out of my hands, and Beau slams down on me like a brick wall. Branches and roots dig into my back, making me gasp at the pain.

I don't know what I cut my foot on, but once I started hobbling, I knew I couldn't run any longer. I had to fight.

I should've known I could never win a fight against him.

He plants his hands on either side of my head, pinning me down. Fury rages in his eyes in a way it never has before. In a way that terrifies me. In a way that excites me.

Beau leans down, his cheek brushing mine when he whispers in my ear, "You're not getting away that easy, princess."

I should be horrified, screaming and fighting against him with every ounce of strength I have left.

But his deep voice in my ear, his breath on my skin, makes my thighs clench.

Every inch of him presses into me. Every long, hard inch.

He tsks. "And I thought we were starting to get along. I give you everything you need—I bring you art supplies, I feed you, I shave you, I spare your life. But nothing's good enough for a spoiled princess."

"You locked me in your *basement*. Of course nothing's going to be enough."

Except I'm not entirely sure that's true anymore.

My heart pounds. I was just running away from him. I just attacked him. But somehow, all I want now is for him to press his lips to mine.

Beau has never been more dangerous, not even when he had a knife to my throat.

I'm in danger of giving in to him. To my own darkest desires.

I wiggle beneath him, desperate to escape both his body holding me captive and the desire for him burning low in my belly.

"Quit writhing or I'm going to fuck you." A low, sensual warning.

I freeze. I must be deranged because part of me wants Beau to tear off my clothes and fuck me right here in these woods. Pound me into the dirt where no one can hear me scream.

"I thought you hunted sex predators," I gasp.

"You would be begging for it, princess." He rubs his hard length between my legs. Pleasure sings through me, and I know instantly that he would be right.

He stops moving and glowers down at me. Involuntarily, I grind against him, trying to relieve my pussy of the dull, throbbing ache.

His gray gaze drifts down, the long scar over his eye smoothing while he watches me rub desperately against him. "I told you you wouldn't want me to find you," he growls.

Warmth spreads between my legs.

He was wrong. I'm glad he found me.

An impossible smile flutters across my lips.

Suddenly, he pushes off me and scoops me up, making me yelp. My back and foot sting, but somehow, he seems completely unfazed by the hit he took to the head.

As he carries me back to the house, I don't bother trying to escape, even when he kicks the door shut behind him and descends the staircase to the basement.

He sets me down on the mattress gingerly, my drawings scattering, and I can't tell if I've made my situation here better or worse.

Until he starts twisting the rope into a loop.

My heart races, breath shuddering. "Please don't tie me up again."

He doesn't say a word as he approaches with the rope.

I stand and back up to the wall. "Leave me alone."

He doesn't grab me and wrap the rope around my wrists. Instead, he lies on the mattress, propping himself up with an elbow casually. "I'll leave when I want to leave," he says simply. "Get naked for me."

No. No, no, no. I won't let him leave me naked and spread eagle.

"Either you take your clothes off or I will." He flicks his knife out, skimming the blade along his lip. An obvious threat.

Against every instinct, I pull up the hem of his T-shirt, peeling it off as slowly as I can.

His gray eyes stay glued to my face until I drop the shirt at my side. Then they fall to my breasts heaving beneath my bra and down slowly to my navel.

I burn under his gaze, savoring the way his eyes feast on me.

"Keep going," he commands.

I slip off the sweatpants next. Until I'm in nothing but my bra and thong before him.

A smile creeps over his face now as he takes in my thighs and the flimsy bit of fabric that keeps him from seeing the rest of me. "Good, princess. Now the rest."

Part of me wants to be naked in front of him. To unleash the beast he's holding back and get his mouth on every inch of me. But my stomach churns at the thought of him leaving me here alone, tied up and vulnerable, and never coming back. "Please don't tie me up," I repeat.

His gaze turns cold. "Do what I said."

Objecting won't get me anywhere. And I don't want to anymore. I want him to see the rest of me. All of me.

I want to find out exactly what he'll do to me when he does.

I unclasp my bra, letting it drop. My breasts fall in front of him, and he swallows. The erection bulges in his jeans and makes my mouth go dry.

"Beautiful, baby," he murmurs.

The compliment should sicken me, but I fight a smile. A psychopath tells me I'm beautiful and all I want is to hear him say it again.

Beau tracks my movements as I hook my fingers through my panties and slide them down my legs. I watch his face as he stares at me, throat bobbing and eyes hungry.

I've never felt more beautiful in my life.

"Good girl." He grabs the rope from the floor. "Now hold out your hands."

∼

BEAU

I SHOULD BE PISSED she tried knocking me out with a fucking tree branch, but I can't help smiling at the memory, even as my skull throbs. She's got spirit. She's got more guts than I expected of a princess torn from her tower. Can't help but admire her for fighting.

How could I forget to lock the fucking door? At least it gave me an excuse to watch her strip.

She's naked and spread eagle in front of me now. I brought her a blanket, but I'm not covering her yet.

Her body is more perfect than I imagined. Her tits small enough to fit in my hands, her nipples pink and peaked, her hips sloping down to slim thighs, and between them, her perfect little pussy that I know is wet and aching for me. Every inch of her soft and supple, begging me to taste.

The way she ground her pussy against me in the woods, I could tell how badly she wanted me to fuck her. Resisting her was damn near impossible, but I won't give her what she wants just yet. I can't let her little escape attempt go unpunished.

Not everyone needs a punishment to learn their lesson.

Michael was wrong about that. Every mistake needs a consequence. Within every punishment is a lesson to be learned. Noelle is learning hers.

She hisses when the soap meets the cut on her foot and tries to pull away from me. Doesn't get far with her ankle tied down.

"I need to clean it," I warn her. "You were just running through dirt."

"Have you ever tended a captive's wound before?" she teases.

I can't help but smirk. "Another first, princess." I swipe antibiotic ointment across her cut and cover it with a bandage before standing.

She looks fucking delicious splayed out before me. I want nothing more than to eat her pretty little pussy until she comes hard in my mouth and begs me to fuck her. Slip my cock past those perfect lips before shoving it inside her tight cunt, dripping for me. Imagining the sounds she might make as I thrust inside her while she's unable to move make my cock twitch.

"I'm cold," she whispers.

I grab the blanket and spread it out over her, covering her from her toes to her neck. A barrier to help me resist her. "Better, princess?"

"Thank you." Despite being tied down, she actually sounds grateful.

I pick up her portrait of me. Maybe she wasn't lying when she said she drew me before I brought her here. The sharp lines and hard edges of my jaw, my cheekbones, my nose, are practiced. Steady. Sure. Even without her inspiration in front of her.

Either she's drawn me before or she's memorized every inch of my face. Maybe mine shows up in her dreams too.

I hang her portrait of me on the wall by her head, directly in her line of sight. The drawing is incomplete, only one of the gray eyes shaded in, but I like that no matter where I am, she knows my eyes are on her.

CHAPTER TWENTY-ONE

CASSIE

"Your boyfriend is an idiot!" Addison shouts to Piper over the music. The thudding bass practically rocks the Beta Theta Pi house. The first frat party since Noelle went missing.

Neal performs a ridiculous, drunken jig on the couch. The three of us giggle, already well past inebriated and it's only eleven.

"I know, and that's why I love him!" Piper yells, taking another gulp from her cup before her delicate features scrunch. "Should we feel guilty?"

"For what?" Addison calls.

"Having fun while Noelle is missing."

"We can't put our lives on hold forever," Addison tells her.

Piper shoots me a look like we should be troubled by Addison's response, but she's right. Noelle's been missing for a month. Classes, exams, and sorority life have gone on without her. Now we're drinking and partying without her. We can't expect Earth to stop spinning just because Noelle's disappearance has thrown our little world off its axis, even if I do feel a pang in my chest at her absence.

"Where's Theo tonight?" Addison asks, an eyebrow arched while she peers at me over the rim of her cup.

"The library. He has to study." Between baseball and his rigorous courseload, he doesn't have time to party like we do. And maybe part of him is worried about how it would look, to be the boyfriend who gets blackout drunk and hooks up with another girl while his girlfriend is missing.

Because I'd hope if we were both drunk enough, neither of us would listen to our inhibitions anymore.

I know he wants me just as much as I want him. We just don't want to betray Noelle.

Kyle runs up behind Addison, lifting her and spinning her around. She squeals in that super annoying way she only does when he's around, and he rips off his shirt when he sets her down, tossing it at Neal before dipping Addison into a sloppy kiss.

"I better go get Neal down before he hurts himself," Piper says. She's so lucky she has an excuse to break free of the world's most disgusting fuck buddies.

Kyle slips his hand in the back pocket of Addison's jeans. "We're gonna go fuck," he tells me, beer breath melting my face.

Somehow, Addison is absolutely enamored as she lets him lead her upstairs to his room.

I head outside and lean against the lamppost, wishing for the first time that I was a smoker or a stoner so I'd have something to do with my hands. If Noelle was here, we could bitch together or laugh at the frat boys' drunken antics.

Maybe I'll go to the library and visit Theo. I'll have to swing by the house first and grab my laptop, pretend like I'm actually there to study.

"Miss Sinclair?" a woman calls behind me. When I turn, a police officer with a round face, messy bun, and crow's feet chews a piece of gum loudly.

I freeze. Do I make a run for it? She's stout. I've been going to the gym enough now that I should be able to outrun her. Maybe.

She holds her hands up. "Don't worry, I'm not here to bust you for drinking or break up a frat party."

I relax a little, but I'm still on edge. Cops are allowed to lie to you. Maybe she's trying to lull me into a false sense of security.

"How are you, Officer?" I cringe as soon as the words are out, high-pitched and wavering.

"You got your phone on you?" She doesn't introduce herself, but under the streetlight, I can make out the name on her badge. *Garcia.*

My phone burns a hole in my pocket. It's my lifeline. I don't want the police to take it, and I have no idea what she thinks she'll find on it. "Um. I actually forgot to charge it, so I left it at home."

Officer Garcia's face pinches, but she drops her hand and pulls out a notebook and pen. "Is there anything you know about Noelle that you're not telling us?"

"No." My voice goes up an octave, and I will my racing pulse to slow. What could they possibly think I know about Noelle that they don't?

Her dark eyes lift. "You sure? No secrets you may be keeping for your best friend?"

I nearly heave a sigh of relief. She thinks I'm covering for Noelle, not that I did something to her. I shake my head. "No secrets. I have no idea where she is or what happened to her."

Officer Garcia presses her lips together and flips her notebook shut. "Well, if you remember anything, even an offhand comment Noelle might've made about wanting to run away or sneak off with somebody or anything, let us know."

"Ask the van Burens."

Garcia cocks a brow. "Excuse me?"

My heart hammers. "Did you know they got in an argument with Noelle right before she went missing?"

Her mouth sours. "We're aware. We're not concerned that the van Burens were involved in their daughter's disappearance, if that's what you're insinuating."

"Did they tell you what the argument was about?"

"Miss van Buren's drinking habits. Again, this—"

"They're lying. And they're hiding things from you. She wouldn't have left the house on foot in the middle of the night over a little argument about her drinking." Garcia opens her mouth, but I keep going. "We were in their house the other day—we found a random bank account. They started funneling money into that account right before Noelle went missing. The van Burens have plenty of secrets, and they'll pay a lot of money to keep them that way."

Callahan flips open her notebook. "Can anyone verify your story? Who was with you when you found this bank account?"

"Addison, Piper, and Theo."

She jots down their names before nodding and snapping the notebook shut. "We'll look into it."

She stuffs her hands in her pockets, shifting like she's about to turn back and head the way she came. An image of Noelle's pale, lifeless body finds its way into my mind, and I blurt the words before I can think better of them: "Do you think she's still alive?"

Garcia narrows her eyes and I wish I could shove the words back in my mouth. "You don't?"

I search the front of the frat house for anybody who can rescue me, but everyone stays inside. "Don't most missing people wind up . . . dead?"

"Most missing people come back all on their own, actually." Garcia folds her arms. "So again. If you know something else that you need to tell me, now's your chance."

I stiffen. There's no way I can ignore the subtext of what she's saying. Panic swells in my chest, making my hands shake. But I will my voice to stay steady. "I've told you everything I know."

I turn to walk away. They can't question me. They can't arrest me. They can't put words in my mouth.

I've already lost Hunter and Noelle. I won't lose my freedom too.

If they want my phone, if they want to interrogate me, they can do it at the station with a lawyer present.

"Failing to cooperate with law enforcement doesn't look

good, Miss Sinclair. Especially when your best friend's life is on the line." I ignore Garcia's dig and keep striding. "Unless she's not really your best friend."

∼

I'M HALFWAY through the parking lot in front of the library when Theo exits the sparsely lit building. Another girl might mistake him for a professor with his dark slacks and collared shirt with the sleeves rolled up to the elbows, his coat draped over his arm despite the chilly April night.

My skimpy black dress does little to shield me from the cold. My teeth have been chattering so hard for the past fifteen minutes on my walk here, my jaw aches.

"Cass?" He jogs toward me, concern contorting his features. "What are you doing out here? You're freezing." He drops his bag on the pavement and wraps his coat around my shoulders, rubbing my arms to coax warmth back into my frozen limbs. "Come on. Let's get you warmed up."

A hand on the middle of my back, Theo leads me to his blue Audi, one of the few remaining cars in the parking lot.

He opens the door for me and waits for me to climb in before shutting it behind me. I feel like a queen in her chariot. The interior still has that new-car smell, and when Theo climbs into the driver's seat, he cranks on the heat so warmth blasts against my face.

"Thank you," I manage, still shivering.

Theo tosses his bag in the seat behind him and reaches toward me. I anticipate his touch, but he places his arm across the back of my seat instead.

"What's going on, Cass? How drunk are you?"

His voice is so gentle, it breaks me. I shake my head. "I'm not that drunk. The police are blaming me for Noelle going missing." The words come out watery.

"Hey," he soothes, rubbing my shoulder. My skin electrifies at the touch, even through his jacket. "Don't cry. They suspect everybody. They questioned me too."

I sniffle, try to blink back the tears to see him clearly. "They did?"

He nods. "Yeah, they're questioning everybody. You're not in trouble."

Relief floods through my veins. I heave a sigh. "Good."

He laughs. "No one would actually believe you had anything to do with this. You're Noelle's best friend; you'd never hurt her. Or anybody."

I smile at Theo. At his soft, green eyes. His easy, reassuring smile.

He sees the best in me.

I wring my hands in my lap. "Theo . . . I need to ask you something."

"Shoot."

The question I've been dying to ask him since that day on the quad, the last afternoon we had with Noelle. The question that's been both squeezing my heart and clawing at my soul. The question I haven't had the guts to voice out loud.

Because it could ruin everything.

I inhale a slow, deep breath. "Do you . . . have feelings for me? Or is it all in my head?"

Silence falls between us. I finally manage to peer up at him, his green eyes soft even though his jaw is tight. "No," he admits.

My stomach drops. *Shit*. I should've known. How could I have been such an idiot? Of course he isn't into me. He's with Noelle. I've been imagining the smiles and the lingering gazes. Assigning an underlying meaning to every little touch. Stupid, *stupid*—

"It's not all in your head." He swallows audibly. So much tension fills the air, I almost suffocate in it. "I'm definitely into you, Cass."

My heart breaks free of its cage, fluttering with hope. "What about Noelle?" I whisper. I can't be the girl who goes after her best friend's boyfriend, especially while she's still missing.

He nods, a knowing look crossing his face. "She didn't tell you."

"Tell me what?"

"We broke up."

My stomach drops to my feet. "What? When?"

Theo grimaces. "The day she went missing. Right before she left campus."

Relief floods through me. Theo and Noelle aren't together. Wanting him doesn't make me a shitty friend.

That must've been the news she texted us about. The news she never got to share.

"Who broke up with who?"

"Technically, I guess I did. But it was pretty much mutually agreed on. She wasn't upset at all. We've both been feeling it coming for a while, I think."

My heart pounds. Theo is single, and Noelle isn't bothered by the breakup. If she were here, she might even encourage me to go for him. "So why did you choose that day to end it?"

He returns his hand to my shoulder, massaging soothing circles again, and I want to drop the jacket so he can touch my skin. "Because of you."

"Me?" I can't breathe.

"I couldn't stop staring at you whenever you were around." His Adam's apple bobs. I want to run my finger over his throat. "I knew I couldn't stay with Noelle anymore when it was obvious I was into somebody else."

I grin. But then I remember the reality of our situation. "So, wait, why is the media still calling you her boyfriend then?"

He presses his lips together. "Because they think I am."

"Do the police know you're not?"

"Outside of Noelle and my dad, you're the only one who knows."

"Why haven't you told anyone else?"

"My dad said I shouldn't." Theo rubs his hands over his pants. "He thinks it'll make me look more suspicious. We broke up the same day she disappeared. It was still so fresh, so he figured... why say anything?"

I bite my lip. "What if the truth comes out? Won't you look guiltier for hiding it?"

He runs his hands through his hair. "That's what I've been thinking. I wish I'd been honest from the beginning, but now it feels too late to come clean. And you know my dad. It's his way or nothing."

I nod, mind spinning a hundred miles a minute. Theo's father wants him to continue pretending to be the perfect boyfriend who would never hurt the love of his life. A perfect boyfriend is a lot less suspicious than a bitter ex.

"I know it doesn't need to be said, but I would never hurt Noelle, Cass. Never."

"I know you wouldn't." The thought has never even crossed my mind. I shrug his jacket off. "So what do we do now?"

"What do you mean?"

"You broke up with Noelle because of me. But you want the public to think you're still together. So where does that leave us?" My heart is in my throat, hoping he tells me the words I want to hear.

"I guess... we wait until she comes home."

Disappointment deflates the hope in my chest. "I hate to be the one to say this, Theo. You know I don't want to believe it's a possibility, but... what if she never does?"

His face falls and he turns away from me, rubbing a hand over his mouth to keep the sob in as his eyes turn glassy. My heart breaks for him. "I don't know. I don't want to think about her never coming home." He lets out a broken laugh. "What's the customary waiting period for moving on after your girlfriend disappears?"

His dad might be right. If Theo moves on too quickly, he'll

look like the killer boyfriend who jumped in another girl's pants the second his girlfriend went missing and I'll look like the jealous girl who snatched her best friend's boyfriend the second she disappeared.

But I've spent years wanting Theo, and now that I can finally have him, I'm not letting anything stand in my way.

Even if it means we have to keep this a secret.

I make a show of scanning the empty parking lot. "No one's around, and it's dark. Even if someone happens to leave the library, they won't see us."

He swallows, shaking his head, but his conviction is wavering. "No one can find out."

Before he can protest again, I swing over onto his lap. "No one will."

Through his pants, I can tell he wants me just as much as I want him. The cold is long gone from my bones, and this time when I shiver, it's for a totally different reason.

Theo's hands drift to my hips like he's going to gently move me off him. "Cass—"

"I won't tell anyone, Theo," I plead. "I promise. I just . . . I want to kiss you. I've wanted to kiss you for a long time. I can't stop thinking about you. I can't stop wanting you. I've been trying so hard to stop, but I can't do it. I want you. I want to be with you."

His eyes fall closed, like my words are crushing him. But when they open again, his green eyes are different. Unmasked. He's not hiding himself anymore. What he really wants. "I can't get you out of my head either." He sweeps a strand of hair behind my ear. "*Cassiopeia.*"

My heart sings. The words I've been wanting to hear from him for so, so long.

This time, it isn't just me closing the space between us. We lean toward each other, eyes searching the other's face. His citrusy scent fills my nose, and his hands drift from my hips up to my cheeks in the tenderest caress.

We meet halfway, lips brushing in a perfect kiss that makes my heart explode. The moment I've been imagining, longing for, for years.

I'm kissing Theo St. James.

And he's kissing me back.

CHAPTER TWENTY-TWO

BEAU

She's so peaceful when she's sleeping.

On the wall behind her, she's started painting a blue mural of me in beast form. Thick brows, wolfish grin, dripping fangs. She did it to piss me off, thinking this is my house. I snort. She really thinks I'm stupid enough to bring her to my own place.

Even if this was my place, I wouldn't give a shit what she's painting on as long as she's painting.

She's finished the sketch of me. Both gray eyes shaded in and so startling, the scar is muted. Almost fading into the background.

The exact opposite of how I see my reflection every time I look in a mirror.

But maybe that's how she sees me.

I left her spread eagle that first night, just like I promised. The next morning, I removed the binding around her ankles. Her hands are still bound together in front of her a week later. Some lessons need to be learned the hard way.

When she finally allows herself to give in to everything she wants, she'll never run from me again.

She's happier here. She won't admit it, to me or herself. Not yet. But she will. She'll realize being here gives her a chance to focus on her art. To stop trying to be who everyone else wants her to be. To do what she wants, without shame.

To be exactly the girl she longs to be. To face her deepest, darkest desires.

And give in to them.

∼

NOELLE

HE'S IN THE SHOWER, water pouring over every inch of his naked body.

His back muscles are taut, ass round. A hand braced above his head while he uses the other to stroke himself. Slow, careful strokes. As if he's imagining the way he'd fuck me. He dips his head back in pleasure, water raining down on his neck and sculpted chest.

"What are you doing?" I shriek.

He stops stroking and turns to face me, full frontal. The sight of him, hard, dripping, and waiting for me . . . I can't swallow. He grips the shower above his head and smirks. "Want to join me?"

I jolt awake.

"If that's supposed to be me," Beau drawls from his perch on the staircase, nodding at the painting on the wall, "you nailed it."

His leather jacket is gone, leaving nothing but tattooed skin in its wake. An unhinged urge to draw a tattoo for him hits me. His shoulder muscles and biceps stay relaxed as he leans back, knees spread apart. Until he catches me staring and flexes his abs.

My mouth goes dry and I stand, pressing my back against the cool mirror before he catches me drooling.

Behind my mattress, I've started a huge, mural-style painting of Beau on the white wall with the blue paint he left me. He bound my hands in front of me this time, which made my strokes unsteady but left me free to vandalize his house. I also managed to get his sweatpants back on, but I'm still topless, my hair just barely covering my nipples.

I knew with every stroke of my brush that I was asking for punishment, but I couldn't bring myself to care.

Let him punish me. Let him pull my hair, squeeze my throat, gag me.

Maybe I'll like it.

Ever since he pinned me down in the woods and made me strip in front of him, I haven't been able to think about anything else. My memories twisting the moment from an attack to an affair. From punishment to praise. From revenge to reverence.

I've always thought my first time would be with someone who loves me. But maybe I don't need that. Maybe I don't need love or tenderness or validation.

Maybe I just need to get fucked.

The mural of Beau has fangs, pointed ears, and a wolfish grin. A beast with human eyes. "It's my best work," I tell him. He's smiling. I expected him to yell, throw shit, throw *me*. "You aren't pissed?"

"I told you to go crazy, didn't I?" He stands, swaggering over to me, muscles rippling with every step. I can't take my eyes off him. "Don't you feel better? This is what you're meant to be doing. Not the bullshit mommy and daddy tell you to do."

For a psychotic kidnapper who spoke his first words to me a mere month ago, he somehow understands me better than anyone. "Actually, yeah."

He examines the ripped-out pages from my sketchpad strewn across the floor before crouching. His long fingers pick up the drawing carefully, gaze roaming over it before turning the page to me. "What's this one?"

I give him a small smile, even as a lump forms in my throat. "The sun eclipsing the moon."

His brows remain puzzled for a few moments. But then understanding dawns on his face. Remembering the moon

Hunter drew on my hand the night he blackmailed me. "He's the moon, and you're the sun."

I nod.

Beau stands slowly, smiling. "You outshine anything he's ever done to you."

My heart nearly stops, and I can't come up with words to thank him.

His gaze drifts to the portrait of him, the ripped-out page from my sketchpad that he hung on the wall above my mattress. "I want to buy that one."

My chest squeezes. No one's ever been interested in my art before. "I can just give it to you."

"No. You'll sign it, and I'll buy it." He plants his hands on his hips, assessing the walls and ceiling. "This room would make a great art studio."

I let out a rough laugh. I asked my mother if we could turn one of the three guest bedrooms in our Victorian mansion into an art studio when I was thirteen and she looked like she wanted to slap me before telling me to stop wasting her time and get ready for my photoshoot.

Now Beau wants to turn this room from my nightmare to my dream.

"You know what's sick?" I tell him. "I like being here better than my own home."

I don't realize how true the words are until they're out of my mouth. I like being here. I'm trapped here, but I was trapped at home too. Under the control of my mother's thumb. Even as a college student, she's still controlling me. My major, my future, my whole life. The only reason I'm pre-med is because of her. Everything I do, every step I make is one she demanded from me.

I want to be an art major. I want my work to be about my creativity. I want to focus on my art again without guilt or shame.

Beau lets me do that. Encourages me to do that. My parents took away the one thing that gave me true joy. Beau Grayson gave it back to me.

"Of course you like it better here." A devilish, lopsided grin. "I'm here."

"Admit it," I challenge, uncertainty wobbling in my chest. "You're falling in love with me."

He steps toward me. A snake sizing up its prey before it strikes.

His gaze travels from my face to my collarbones, to my breasts swelling beneath my hair, to the flat plane of my stomach, to the long legs beneath his pants.

He smacks his palms against the mirror above my head, leaning toward me. "I'll admit it when you do."

My heart stutters. Wait. Does that mean . . . No. He's not falling in love with me. Someone like him, who stalks and torments and kills, isn't capable of love.

When I don't answer, he smirks. "You want me. Don't you?"

Yes. Despite everything, yes.

He watches my face while I take him in—the smooth, sculpted chest. The flat stomach with a six-pack. The hips that disappear into his jeans. The bulge below his belt.

"Maybe it's a curse." He leans closer, cool breath skittering across my neck, and I shudder. "Beasts like me have a thing for princesses."

His hands fall from the mirror above my head and caress my cheeks. I only have one heart-stopping moment to stare into his intense gray eyes before they drift closed and he brushes his lips against mine.

His lips are surprisingly soft, even as he deepens the kiss, mouth moving over mine with an unfamiliar expertise. Pulling a whimper from me as I part my lips for him. Both his hands cradle my jaw, not allowing me to go anywhere. I've never been kissed like this before. My heart is in my throat, breathing impossible.

Until he finally breaks the kiss, his eyes still shut and hands holding my face. Like he's glued to me and can't wrench away.

"Untie me," I breathe.

His gray eyes spring open. "What are you going to try this time?"

"Touching you."

He smirks but doesn't make a move.

"Trust me, I'm not going anywhere."

And I mean it this time. I want to keep making my art. I want to keep hiding from the outside world and doing exactly what I want, not what anyone else wants or expects of me.

Mostly, I want to fuck Beau Grayson.

With that, he flicks out the blade of his pocket knife and slices through my binding, releasing me. He slips the knife back in his pocket and returns his hands to the mirror above my head.

I swallow the lump in my throat and try to control my breathing. His collarbones jut out, and I sweep my fingertips over them. Soft skin covering hard steel. Then my palms graze over his shoulders dipped in ink. He's so gorgeous without even trying. The most stunning piece of art I've ever seen.

His hands remain braced above my head while I explore like he's a sculpture. My hands glide over his taut biceps, down to the hard wristbones and then his long fingers. Fingers perfect for playing piano or strumming a guitar or making me come.

Finally, I bring my hands up where I want them—to his chest. Smooth and hard. Solid muscle underneath. He exhales the softest sigh through his nose at my touch. My palms drift down to his abdomen, and he tightens the muscles there, bringing a small smile to my lips.

When my fingertips reach the strip of skin just above the waistband of his jeans, he catches my hands and pins them above my head with a crack.

"My turn," he growls not in anger or frustration but lust.

He crushes his lips to mine. My stomach flips hard, heart in my throat, and I can't budge, pinned against the cold mirror.

Beau opens his mouth for me, groaning, and that low sound from his throat makes the space between my thighs ache.

With his free hand, he traces the outline of my body. Until he latches onto my hip and yanks me into him, and I gasp. He's already rock-hard for me.

My body responds instantly to the roughness, goosebumps racing down my arms and the hairs on the back of my neck standing up. I whimper at the friction between my thighs, and he presses against me harder.

Fuck. I don't know what he's going to do next. What am I doing? He's a murderer, a *serial killer*. He nearly killed me.

But he's more than that. He protects women and children from horrible monsters. He admires my art and wants to devote an entire room in this house to it. He praises me, challenges me, comforts me, lusts for me. Understands me.

His mouth lands on my neck and he sucks. My knees buckle, and his body keeps me upright. I gasp, warmth and wetness flooding between my legs.

I've never wanted anyone this badly. Suddenly, I don't care if this is a decision I'll regret later. I know, right now, that I want this.

I want him. He's the only thing I know I want.

Beau nibbles on my shoulder and I jump. He lets out the sexiest rumbling chuckle I've ever heard, and it reverberates along my skin. "Sorry. Didn't mean to scare you." He licks the spot he just bit. All the way up to my ear. "You taste delicious, princess. I can't wait to get between your legs."

I nearly combust.

His intense gray eyes see past my irises and burrow into me. He drops my wrists and his hands drift to my neck, and my breath catches, remembering the knife he pressed to my throat. But he rubs soothing circles into my tight muscles. As the knots loosen, every inch of me slowly starts to relax. He does the same to my shoulders, down my arms, all the way to my hands. Like we have all the time in the world.

In here, maybe we do.

When he drops to his knees, I nearly gasp. He yanks the pants down in one swift movement. I step out of them and he tosses them over his shoulder.

I'm naked in front of him again, and I feel totally free. I don't care about anything except convincing him to never stop touching me.

He wraps his palms around my calves, slowly ascending as he continues his mouth-watering massage. He uses the perfect amount of pressure. I've never felt this good in my life.

"I know you work in hunting down criminals, but do you moonlight as a massage therapist?" I ask.

He chuckles. "No, I just know what you need. And my job does give me a certain . . . dexterity."

I can't wait until he shows me what else I need.

He kneads at my thighs, making me groan, until his hands slide up to my ass.

He tips his head forward and hisses, "*Fuck.*" Then he digs his fingers in, rubbing in circles, and I moan.

When he peers up at me, the sight of his gray eyes on me nearly makes me lose my mind. Our gazes are magnets. I can't look away from him. Can't stop watching every move he makes.

He stands and slips my hair behind my shoulder to suck on my neck. My legs tremble at the sensation, eyes rolling. He spins me again until I'm facing the mirror.

When I avert my gaze, he commands, "Look."

I expect to be unrecognizable—hollow eyes with bags underneath, dry skin, dull, lifeless hair.

Instead, I somehow look . . . better. Slightly fuller cheeks, dewy skin, clear blue eyes. I've been eating whatever Beau gives me and not obsessing over calories the way Mother taught me, and I look good. Healthy.

"Why don't you like looking at yourself?" he murmurs. "You're beautiful."

His words, his tender tone, make me swallow. My heart skip.

"Every time I bombed an audition or lost out on a modeling gig, my mother would sit me in front of the mirror and point out everything wrong with me. Once I realized I'd never be perfect like she wanted, I didn't want to look anymore."

Beau sweeps my hair out of my face so he can see me clearly. So he can see me like no one else has. "Fuck perfect. Real is better."

My heart thuds. Somehow, it's exactly what I needed to hear. Warm, happy tears spring to my eyes, and I don't bother blinking them away. Who cares now. Who cares if he sees the real me. He's seeing my body bare. He might as well see my soul too.

Beau presses his lips to my shoulder while his hands circle me and envelop my breasts. I gasp at the touch, and when he squeezes, I whimper. Adrenaline has never coursed through my veins like this.

"Imagine me fucking you against this mirror," he murmurs. "Your tits squeaking against the glass, watching yourself come."

Wetness floods between my legs at his words alone.

His palms scrape over my nipples, making them peak. I lean back against him and he bears my weight with ease.

"So. Fucking. Sexy," he whispers in my ear. Every hair on the back of my neck stands up.

Beau pulls the mattress fully in front of the mirror and guides me onto it. I'm vaguely aware of our reflection in my peripheral vision—me flat on the mattress, him on top of me. But I keep my eyes trained on his gorgeous face.

When he settles between my legs, I tense.

His brows furrow. "What's wrong, princess?"

"I'm . . . nervous," I admit.

"About?"

"The pain."

Theo and I never got that far in our singular, tipsy attempt at sex. And from what I've seen bulging in Beau's pants, I don't know if I can handle that.

"The key is preparation. The key . . ." He leans down to me, licking up my neck before sucking on my earlobe. Making my eyes roll. " . . . is making you come so hard, your eyes cross and you beg me to fuck you. And sometimes . . ." He flips us so he's on his back and I'm straddling him. ". . . the trick is letting you get on top and do whatever makes you lose your mind on my cock."

"Losing my mind, huh? Someone's pretty cocky."

He smirks at the pun. He thrusts his hips up, the friction from his erection between my legs making me moan. "You have no idea how cocky I can be."

I rest my hands on his chest. "I want you to make me come."

He grins and flips me onto my back. "Oh, I will, princess."

He pins my hands above my head again, and before I can protest, his lips wrap around my nipple and suck it into his mouth.

I gasp, the exquisite sensation unlike any I've ever felt before. Like fireworks going off in my brain. For a moment, I can't think about anything other than how good it feels.

Beau's tongue swirls around the sensitive spot before he sucks my nipple into his mouth again. Harder this time. Sucking like I'm a lollipop and he's trying to pull the candy off the stick. I squirm beneath him, but his body is so much heavier, holding me down, I barely move.

I can't go anywhere until he lets me. That shouldn't turn me on as much as it does.

His mouth latches onto my other nipple, repeating the movement, and I cry out. He can't help the cocky little grin.

Finally, when he's had his fill, he travels down my stomach. Kissing and sucking and licking and nibbling over every inch. When his teeth graze the sensitive spot just below my navel, I nearly convulse.

A chuckle hums against my skin, and he slides off my body, picking up one leg and pressing his lips to my ankle. He massages my foot while he sucks his way up to my thigh and I don't know which part feels better. My brain is mush.

"You're . . ." I don't know how to finish it. *Incredible. Amazing.* None of it seems like enough. "Wow," is all I can manage.

"You're wow too," he murmurs against my thigh.

I shiver.

When he sucks my soft, sensitive skin into his mouth, my back arches off the mattress. He goes harder, sucking me so far into his mouth that when he finally releases me, there's a small *pop*.

He repeats the delicious torture up my other leg until I'm a wet, whimpering mess beneath him.

His hand cups between my legs so suddenly, possessively, I gasp and clench my thighs together. "See what I mean?" he murmurs, feeling the wetness waiting for him. "Preparation."

That was all *preparation*? My heart is already galloping like I've run a mile, and we haven't even gotten started.

His fingers skim over my thighs. "You want me to make you come?"

My breathing is ragged and I can't form words. So all I do is nod.

"Say *yes, Beau*."

But I can't speak. I open my mouth, but no words come out. I nod my head more vigorously.

He tsks. "I want to hear you say it. I want to hear how much you want me. Say *yes, Beau, make your princess come*."

I manage to gasp the words, "Yes, Beau. Make your princess come." The ragged voice is foreign to my ears.

"Good girl." He presses a kiss so soft and tender against my lips, my heart melts. "You're going to love this next part."

Beau pulls away from me again, sliding down my body and stopping with his head between my thighs. He pries my thighs farther apart, taking in every inch of me. Even without his hand pinning my wrists down, I keep my arms above my head.

His hands find my breasts again and squeeze at the same moment his tongue flicks out.

A gasp wrenches from my chest at the shock, the pleasure. The warm breath from his chuckle heats the wetness between my legs. "Feels fucking good, huh, princess?" His tongue flicks out again. This time, licking me in one long stroke.

I groan and reach for his hair, tugging. He leans into me, licking with more pressure. When he reaches the apex, he lingers, rubbing hard with his tongue.

I cry out, not sure if it's pleasure or torture making me writhe.

"Told you you'd love this part," he murmurs.

My heart hammers so hard, I'm worried it's going to explode. "I don't think I can take any more."

"You will," he says simply, before returning his tongue between my legs. The sounds turn obscene as I get wetter with every stroke. His tongue swirls around my clit until I'm whimpering beneath him.

Then his finger nudges at my entrance. He presses harder with his tongue as his finger slowly eases in.

I gasp at the pressure, the foreign feeling of being filled.

He hisses. "*Fuck*. You're so tight. And soaked." His gray eyes find mine. "See what I meant by preparation? This is how ready I want you to be for me every time."

Every time.

He keeps his finger inside me without moving while he licks my clit, waiting for me to adjust and relax. After a few minutes, he pulls back and eases his finger forward. Back. Forward. Back. Forward.

Then he wraps his lips around my clit and sucks. I gasp and arch into him. *Holy fuck*. His finger thrusts faster, harder as he keeps sucking my clit.

I can't take anymore. I start to clench around his finger, dig my hands into his hair, and the inevitable crest approaches. I can't stop it now, even if I wanted to. I'm going to—

I cry out as the orgasm rockets through me. I spasm violently around his finger, and he sucks on me harder, slamming his finger into me through the throes of pleasure. My heart hammers, blood singing in my veins.

Tears of pleasure spring to my eyes as I try to squirm away

from the overwhelming intensity of his mouth on me, his finger inside me, but he doesn't let up. Not until I've collapsed onto the mattress, motionless and whimpering, pushing pathetically at his head. He eases up the pressure little by little, slowing the rocking of his finger until he pulls out of me.

I'm absolutely soaked, the mattress drenched.

He groans above me. "God, that's so fucking hot."

While I catch my breath, waiting for feeling to return to my limbs, he slides out of his jeans and lays on top of me, rolling us both over until I'm on top and straddling him like before.

His erection is rock-hard and intimidating. My mouth goes dry. There's no way that will fit inside me. No way it won't break my jaw.

"I can't fucking wait to make you come on my cock." He grips my hips and grinds me up and down his length, hissing between his teeth. When I take over, increasing the pressure and moaning at the delicious friction, a muscle in his jaw feathers and he squeezes my tits. His head falls back and eyes start to close, but he fights against them. Desperate to watch me.

I reach down tentatively, unsure how to touch him to make him feel good. He shows me, wrapping my hand around his cock and gliding it up and down. Squeezing harder, circling my thumb around his tip. "Be as rough with me as you want me to be with you," he rasps.

So I squeeze hard and jerk.

He gasps, eyes wide. I yank my hand back. "Sorry!"

He laughs. "*Damn.* I should've known Princess would want it rough. Patience. When I'm finally rough with you, you'll thank me for going easy on you your first time."

"Promise?" I slowly slide myself onto him, feeling the slight burn and pressure from his tip.

He groans, fingers digging into my hips while he watches me slowly take him in. "Promise."

I take slow inch by slow inch, getting accustomed to the

incredible fullness. I'm glad he used a finger to help stretch me, but I needed at least two to stretch this much. Maybe three.

When I've taken as much as I can, I whimper. His thumb finds my clit and circles it gently, helping me relax.

"I need to watch you come while I'm inside you." His voice is hoarse. "Lose your mind on my dick."

I rock up, then back down. He lets out a sound I haven't heard yet. Strangled, almost pained, but he drops his head back and his thumb rubs me harder.

The slight burn from the stretch is fading. I lean up and come back down harder, and *fuck*, that feels good.

When I reach the tip again, he jerks his hips up into me.

I cry out, collapsing onto his chest.

"Too much?" he pants.

I sit back up and shake my head.

"That's my girl." He grips my hips and thrusts into me again, faster this time. The slap of skin on skin fills the basement and pleasure mounts between my legs.

I moan. "Oh my god."

"Look," he breathes. His head is turned toward the mirror, so I follow his gaze. Both of us watch as he fucks me from beneath, my breasts bouncing. "Isn't that so fucking sexy?"

For perhaps the first time in my life, I like my reflection.

One of his hands returns to rubbing my clit while the other reaches up to hold my bouncing breast steady. Watching him fuck me... I've never been this turned on before.

He sits up and wraps an arm around me before scooting back and resting against the wall. Then he grips my chin between his fingers, squeezing to lock our gazes together. I rock again and a muscle in his jaw twitches.

This position is more intimate, our eyes not moving from the other's until Beau's gaze drifts to my breasts bouncing in his face and he can't resist catching a nipple in his mouth.

I gasp and ride him faster. He manages to slip a thumb

between us and rub my clit. The pleasure in my muscles mounts. And mounts. My mind is reeling, eyes rolling back in my head.

My pulse echoes in my ears. It's happening again. The tendrils of pleasure wind up from my toes to my head. That inevitable wave cresting—

"Come for me, princess," he rasps. "Go crazy."

I come apart around him, crying out and collapsing onto him.

"Fuck yes," he hisses.

He flips me on my back and thrusts into me so hard, my mind spins. My moans turn to screams at the pressure, the intensity, as he drives his cock deep inside me over and over.

"*Fuck*, princess!" He groans almost as loud as my screams before collapsing on top of me. His heart hammers against my chest, and I feel his hard length throbbing inside me as he cums. He groans in my ear, and it makes me shiver. The sexiest sound I've ever heard.

Beau gives one more half-hearted thrust inside me. I whimper. He stops the sound midway with a kiss, slipping his tongue in my mouth and luxuriating in me. "I've never cum that hard in my life," he murmurs.

"Me neither," I breathe. I still can't believe we just did that. I just fucked Beau Grayson. My kidnapper. My captor.

And I liked it.

No. I fucking *loved* it.

CHAPTER TWENTY-THREE
THEO

*O*n my way out of the gym, I call Dad. He'll be grabbing his second morning coffee, so I should get at least three minutes of his attention.

He answers on the first ring. "Theo? What is it?"

Hey, Dad. Doing great. Thanks for asking. "Hey. I've been thinking, and I . . . I think I should come forward to the police about the breakup."

Silence on the other end. Yep. Knew this was a bad idea.

"Theo." Dad's voice drops so no one overhears him eviscerate me. "The matter has already been settled. Your lawyer is perfectly capable of determining what is and isn't appropriate to say to the police right now. I am your father and an attorney. I know what's best. So next time you think about questioning me, don't."

Cass's words from the other night ring through my head. "But if they find out the truth, won't I look guiltier?"

"They won't find out the truth if you keep your mouth shut. You haven't told anyone, right?"

I told Cass. But she won't tell anyone. I know I can trust her. "Cass knows."

Dad huffs an impatient sigh. "And who is Cass?"

"Noelle's best friend." He should know that.

"Oh, yes. Sinclair. Make sure she knows not to say anything. And if you have any concerns about her, let me know, and she and I will have a conversation."

"Actually, I . . . I think I like her, Dad."

I want to be with Cass. Really be with her, not just sneak kisses in my car after dark. I want to take her on dates, hold her hand in public, comfort each other until we manage to find Noelle and bring her home safe.

Dad lets the silence linger between us for a full twenty seconds before speaking again. "I'm only going to say this once, Theo. Do not touch, speak to, or look at another girl until Noelle is found. Your ex-girlfriend is missing, and you sincerely have no idea how bad it would look for you if the media caught you with another girl right now. I will not have your indiscretions ruining the reputation of this family. Is that clear?"

Part of me wonders if he even gives a shit about Noelle in all of this. He cares more about our reputation. How we look to the public, to the media, to a bunch of strangers. All whose opinions matter a whole lot less than finding my missing friend.

"Is that clear?" he repeats.

"Yes." My thumb hovers over the button to end the call. "Crystal clear."

CHAPTER TWENTY-FOUR
NOELLE

I dip my finger into the blue paint again before tracing another line over Beau's chest. I've already painted each of his collarbones, trailing delicately over the hard bone beneath soft skin. He's my new favorite canvas.

Sunlight shines brightly through the tiny window this morning, turning the basement into a space that could actually be inviting if we added furniture and decor. Perfect for an art studio, just like Beau said.

"What are you doing?" he murmurs.

I swipe my finger through more paint and swirl it onto his shoulder. "I'm painting you."

"No, you're painting *on* me." But he doesn't move out of my reach or away from my touch.

I shrug. "Same thing."

He grabs my hand covered in paint. "You're my favorite artist." Then he lifts the back of my hand to his lips.

I nearly stop breathing.

He glances down between my legs. "How are you feeling?"

It's been a few days since we've had sex. I've been too sore to do it again, no matter how much we've both longed to. That hasn't stopped us from stripping and touching each other every night before falling asleep in the other's arms.

"Horny," I say, and he smirks. "But I want a long, hot shower first."

His gaze falls to the swirls of blue paint mixing with the dark ink on his chest. "Looks like we could both use one."

Without another word, he scoops me up in his arms. I squeal and he carries me to the bathroom, cranking on the shower. In the mirror, I catch a glimpse of my neck. A few hickeys mark my skin. Mark me as his.

He wraps his arms around me from behind, and for a wild second, it almost feels like we're a real couple. When his tongue makes contact with my skin, I forget for a second where I am. Who I am.

Beau tosses me on the sink and I plant my hands on his chest. My palms are coated with blue paint now, but I couldn't care less. His tongue dips into my mouth, swirling and flicking with the promise of what he'll do between my legs.

He spreads my knees wider and rubs his length against me, making me moan. "You ready?" he asks.

"I thought you said preparation is key."

"I meant for our shower. Give me some credit."

As far as I'm concerned, after the way he fucked me, he gets all the credit. Extra credit. AP credit.

I slip down off the sink and follow him into the shower. Another first. I have a feeling there are going to be a lot of those with Beau Grayson.

The water turns his platinum blond hair golden and flattens it against his head. Men are unfairly sexy with wet hair.

He grabs me, pulling me under the rain shower with him. The hot water soothes the tight muscles in my shoulders and back. I've been sore in more places than I realized.

With a washcloth, Beau rubs gentle circles over my skin. Starting with my shoulders and working his way down to my hands. Then at my collarbones and down to my navel.

"Turn around," he commands. I do as he says, and he washes the back of my neck, behind my ears, and down to my ass, where he rubs for a noticeably longer amount of time.

God, this may be even more incredible than the massage he gave me. The hot water running over us, the gentle exfoliation, his labored breathing as I turn him on just by letting him touch me.

He turns me again to face him. "Feel good, princess?"

I nod. He lifts an eyebrow, not moving until I tell him what he wants to hear. "Yes, Beau."

He flashes his lopsided smile. The one that turns my knees to jelly. "I love hearing my name on your lips."

He drops down and washes my feet, my legs. Then he stands and rubs the cloth between my thighs. My eyes roll back in my head. How am I supposed to take showers without him now?

When he sets the washcloth down, I nearly whimper and beg him to keep going. Until he drops to his knees in front of me. "Sorry, princess. You're getting dirty again."

He shoves his head between my legs, and I gasp. My thighs are pressed hard against his cheeks, but that doesn't stop him. His tongue drags over me, making my thighs clench tighter.

"Stop," I gasp. "You're going to drown."

He laughs. Perhaps the first real laugh I've ever heard slip past his lips. And it's the best sound I've heard from his mouth so far. "From you or the shower?"

I meant the shower, but . . . "Both."

"Then I'll die doing what I love."

Without another word, his tongue licks me again. Again. Before finally penetrating. *Oh my god.* I clutch at his head, slippery with water and soap. He pumps his tongue in and out of me, and even with the rain of the shower, I can hear how wet he's making me.

He brings a thumb up to my clit and presses, and I jerk into him. "Have you ever come standing up?" he asks.

"No." But I've never tried either. The shower has never been my preferred place to masturbate. I pretty much stick with my bed and my vibrator.

This is so much better.

"You're about to." His mouth latches onto my clit and I nearly scream, the sound echoing in the shower. I clap a hand over my mouth before I remember nobody can hear us.

Beau doesn't care. Doesn't stop. The pressure only gets more intense. He sucks my clit harder, flicking his tongue out at the same time, and my thighs quiver uncontrollably. I can barely keep myself upright. His fingers dig into my ass, pulling me into him even more.

When his gray eyes flash open and he stares at me, into me, I unravel, losing myself on his tongue, his mouth. I cry out, hanging onto his soaked hair. He slips his tongue inside me and keeps rubbing my clit through the throes of my orgasm, letting me ride his tongue and chase every ounce of pleasure.

Fuck.

He stands slowly with a cocky grin. "Good girl. Now how about I turn you around and we both come standing up?"

"Not yet. You still need to get clean." It's my turn to grab the soap and washcloth and drag it slowly over his chest. Most of the paint has already washed away in the water, but I'll take any excuse I can get to touch him.

He leans back against the wall, allowing me to do whatever I want with my new canvas. I want to paint him black and blue with hickeys like he did to me.

I don't get to scrub him as thoroughly, though, because when I wrap the washcloth around his hard length, he doesn't let my hand drift anywhere else.

He dips his head back, eyes falling closed, letting himself enjoy the feeling of me stroking him.

When I stop, his head jerks up and eyes flash open.

Until I drop to my knees in front of him. He gazes down at me with a wolfish half-smile. "You sure about that, princess?"

I answer with a flick of my tongue.

He hisses through his teeth and momentarily drops his head back before staring down at me again. He enjoys watching me too much to close his eyes this time.

Beau pulls my hair through his fingers, keeping it held back and out of my face. I almost smile at the unexpectedly sweet gesture. I've never wanted to give a blowjob before. But now I want to give as much pleasure as I've received.

I slip his tip into my mouth, not totally sure what to do, but I've watched some porn and heard enough guys talk about getting sucked off that I've got the idea.

When I swirl my tongue around his tip, Beau groans. His length jerks unexpectedly in my mouth and I gasp. He chuckles, loosening his grip on my hair like he thinks I'm done, but I'm not even close.

I slide my mouth over him again, taking in inch after inch.

"Fuck yeah, princess," he gasps.

He uses his grip on my hair to guide me up and down. Part of me always thought I wouldn't like a guy controlling my head, but warmth spreads between my thighs. I want him to fuck my mouth harder. To do whatever he wants to me.

I pull away momentarily to tell him so. "Harder."

He doesn't hesitate. As soon as my mouth's over him again, he steps away from the wall and fucks my mouth, thrusting in and out hard and deep. I start to gag, but he pulls back before it becomes too much.

"Do you like gagging on my cock?"

I nod.

So he thrusts in again until I choke. Then again. And again. Until he pulls out, still rock hard. He guides me to my feet with a smirk. "You're better at that than I thought you'd be."

I scoff, pretending to be offended.

"I didn't think you'd be able to take it that deep." He grabs my hips and pins me against the door of the shower, my breasts flattened against the glass. "Want to see how deep you can take it again?"

"Yes," I breathe, and he slowly slides into me from behind.

I cry out, but the pressure, the fullness, quickly turns to pleasure when he wraps his arm around me and finds my clit. "You set the pace," he tells me. "Slow, fast, gentle, hard. Whatever you want. What you can handle. I'd rather fuck you slow for two days than hard once and not be able to fuck you again for a week."

I'd rather that too. I don't want to go back to not fucking Beau Grayson every day.

I rock back into him slowly, carefully. Still, I whimper. His finger circles my clit harder, building that familiar pleasure back up, and I gradually stretch around him. Taking more and more of him.

"You've taken half," he murmurs into my shoulder.

"*Half?*" I practically screech. "There's more?"

He chuckles and gives one hard thrust that proves just how many more inches of his cock remain. I cry out. "Good or bad?" he asks.

I'm not totally sure, but I gasp, "Good."

He thrusts hard into me again, and this time, I know it's good. I back up into him, bending to give him better access, and he digs his fingers into my hips while he pumps into me faster. The smack of wet skin on skin mixes with my moans.

Beau snatches my hand from where I'm bracing against the shower and pushes it between my legs. To play with myself. I do as he wants, rubbing my clit and helping build to that crest of pleasure until he replaces my hand with his own, the pleasure from his touch driving me closer to the edge.

He's everywhere. On me. In me. All around me. His mouth sucking on my neck, breathing heavily in my ear.

"Come for me, princess," he begs. "I won't until you do."

God, that's so hot. I love how much he wants to make me feel good.

His hand between my legs grows more frantic. He's getting close, but I don't know if I'll finish before he does. He thrusts faster and lets out an almost pained groan.

"Fuck, Noelle."

It's the first time he's said my name, and my name on his lips makes the hairs on the back of my neck stand up. This is real. This is really happening. I'm not just Princess, locked away in the dungeon.

I'm Noelle van Buren, and I'm fucking Beau Grayson.

He thrusts into me over and over, so hard tears sting my eyes. But the pleasure of his fingers on my clit overwhelms the pain and I go over the edge, the sexy sounds of his groans filling my ears as I cry out and shake. He has to prop me up to keep fucking me, my tits squeaking against the glass with every violent thrust until he jerks out suddenly, panting and moaning. His cum hits my back, then my ass, and we're both left shaking and struggling to catch our breaths.

"You look so fucking gorgeous covered in my cum, princess." Beau grabs the washcloth. Before he can wash off his cum, I glance back to see it on my skin. His mark on me.

He cleans me again, trailing tender kisses down my back and to my ass while he does so.

I can't believe how comfortable I am with him already. How happy I feel when I'm around him. I've only been in this house about a month, and I already feel like he knows me better than anyone else on the planet.

Somehow, he's turned the worst thing that's ever happened to me into the best thing.

∼

BEAU

THE WHIR of the tattoo gun stops and the bearded bald dude inking my ribcage pats my shoulder. "All done, buddy."

Not the best place on my body to get a long fucking tattoo, but one of the few spots on my torso that wasn't already covered. The tattoo artist doesn't bother giving me the spiel about cleaning it and watching for infection—I've got more ink than he does.

I'm grinning like an idiot when I pull into the driveway. She's gonna love this.

I'm in unprecedented territory. Hunters aren't supposed to fall for their marks, but fuck if I'm not falling. Hard.

She's fucking *mine*. The way her eyes cross, her back arches, that strangled moan she lets out when she comes. She's finally giving in, taking exactly what she wants, and I'm happy to give it to her day and night.

In the basement, she's starting a new mural on the wall opposite the mirror. I've already brought her more paint. More colors.

She grins when she spots me, throwing down her brush and practically skipping over to me. Nothing like that fractured, terrified, hopeless girl she was when I brought her here.

"What's that?" she asks, meeting me at the bottom of the staircase. I hold out the paper to her.

Her brows fold together, head tilting. "Wait. This is my drawing. Why'd you take this?"

I pull my shirt over my head and show her my new tattoo. "Still inflamed, but it's your rose."

The wilting rose she drew, a single petal fallen off.

She presses her fingers over her mouth, eyes wide and glassy. "You . . . you got a tattoo of my drawing."

"Yes, princess. I want your art on me forever. You're my favorite artist, remember?"

She flings her arms around my neck and kisses me.

Yeah. She's falling fucking hard too.

"I wish I could've been there to see you get it." She smiles against my lips.

Right. That whole other world out there she's not allowed to see.

Upstairs, my phone rings. Her smile flickers for just a second before she kisses me. "I'll get back to work. When you're done with your call, can you make me dinner?"

"Of course, princess. Anything you want." I squeeze her ass when I kiss her and leave her to her painting. When I close the basement door behind me, it feels wrong to lock it.

The name on my phone screen is a familiar one, and I almost don't answer. Local bail bond agent. These guys only call when they've got an assignment.

I take the call, and as I suspect, he's got a fugitive on the run. Wants to know if I've got the time to handle it.

If I didn't have a girl locked in a basement, I'd take the contract.

It's been over a month now since I took her. She may be content with life in a basement creating her art and fucking me for now, but it won't last.

I don't want to let her go, but I can't keep her here forever. I have a job to do, fugitives to hunt down, and I can't be in both places at once. Not to mention this temporary security gig is turning into a long-term position, and I've gotta get out before the boredom kills me. The best part about that job was following her around campus without raising suspicions.

I'm not going to kill her, and if she leaves, I can trust her. She won't give my name.

So maybe it's time to let her out of the basement.

CHAPTER TWENTY-FIVE

THEO

I've been avoiding Cass. I take a different route on my morning run, skip the gym when I know she'll be there, and pretend I don't see her texts asking if I want to join her, Addison, and Piper at ECV for lunch. It makes me a pathetic little shit, I know, but I don't know how to be around her without wanting to rip her clothes off. I don't know how I'll keep up with the ruse of being Noelle's boyfriend when Cass is right in front of me.

I fucked up that night. I kissed her even though I knew I shouldn't. No one can find out about us, not while Noelle is still missing. Anyone could've walked by and seen us in my car. Her mouth on mine, her tits pressed against my chest, my hands on her hips.

But I have no idea how to quit now.

At practice, my heart nearly stops when I spot her in the bleachers. She waits while we run laps and bases, and her eyes are on me with every step. Every swing.

Before now, life has always been simple for me. Get good grades, go to college, become a doctor, buy a big house, start a family. Do what Dad says. Don't talk back, don't argue, don't have a thought of your own. He'll do all the thinking for you.

For the first time in my life, I have no clue what I'm doing. No idea what the right next step is.

Dad's a defense attorney—he knows what he's talking about. But following his orders means lying and pretending. What if Noelle was more upset by the breakup than she seemed? What if she did something reckless and ended up somewhere she shouldn't have? If I'm to blame for this, even in some small way, I want to own up to it. Want to tell the police everything they need to know so they have the best possible chance of finding her.

After practice, Cass runs down the bleachers to meet me. She's so beautiful. She's in jeans that barely stretch over her thighs and ass, her tits bounce with every step under her jacket, and I can't take my eyes off her.

If the guys don't see it yet, they will soon—I'm head over heels for this girl. I can't keep my mind or my mouth or my hands off her.

She steps in front of me, cutting off my path to the locker room. "Can I talk to you?"

I scan the faces around us, but none of my teammates give a shit. They're worn out from practice, and as far as they're concerned, we're not doing anything more than discussing Noelle.

Cass pulls me into the dugout, out of sight, and crosses her arms. "Why have you been avoiding me, Theo?"

Shit. I've screwed this up. I only got a taste of her for a night and I've already lost her. I squeeze her hand. I suck for letting her think I've been avoiding her because she did anything wrong. "We can't let anyone suspect anything's going on between us, remember?"

Her dark brows pull together. "And you think suddenly avoiding me out of the blue isn't going to raise any eyebrows?"

She's right. I'm an idiot. We have to keep pretending everything's normal. But doing that's becoming impossible when nothing has been normal since Noelle vanished. "You're right. I'm sorry. I just . . ." I drag a hand through my hair. "I don't know how to be around you and not kiss you. Now that I've had a taste, I can't go back, Cass."

She grins and steps closer, clutching at my sweat-soaked shirt. Relief rockets through me. "Good. I don't want you to."

She unzips her jacket, revealing a low-cut top. I can't help it—my eyes drop down right to her tits. When we were in my car, I didn't let my hands drift away from her face or hips. But I want my hands all over her now.

I grab her waist and push her up against the dugout. Then my hands are on her tits, squeezing, her velvety flesh pinched between my fingers. She gasps just as a groan escapes past my lips. God, I've been wanting to do that for so fucking long. They're perfect in my palms, but I want to rip off the layers between my hands and her soft skin.

I drop onto the bench, pulling her on my lap. "We can't get caught."

∼

CASSIE

Maybe I should've made Theo grovel more for ignoring me ever since that night in his car. But he's my weakness. He's a black hole sucking me in, and I'm never getting back out.

Theo grabs the back of my head and crushes my mouth to his. His hand slides into my hair, and finally, *finally*, his tongue slips into my mouth.

He lets out a groan that turns me on and makes me grind against the bulge in his pants. A strangled sound erupts deep in his throat that only makes me grind him harder and moan at the friction between my legs.

He buries his face between my tits, kisses frantic as his mouth moves over the exposed skin spilling out of my bra. I tug my shirt down and he moans, pawing my breasts through my bra. Luxuriating in me.

A gasp escapes me at his touch. Warmth pools between my legs. This is happening. This is really happening. I'm actually hooking up with Theo St. James.

He's mine.

His fingertips slip in my bra, and he gazes up at me with puppy eyes. "Can I?"

"Yes," I whisper. "Yes to everything."

He yanks the cups down. I gasp at the sudden release, the chilly air hitting my exposed skin and peaking my nipples. He groans, growing harder between my legs. "Is this your first time?" he gasps.

"Yeah," I whisper. "I wanted you to be my first."

He nods. "Good. I'm yours too, Cass. I'm all yours."

I would cry tears of joy if I wasn't so overcome with lust. Adrenaline courses through my veins. I'm finally getting what I've always wanted.

"Should we wait?" Theo asks, cradling my cheek. "Do it somewhere more special?"

My heart squeezes and I grin. He wants my first time to be special. *Our* first time to be special. "I've been waiting for you for years. I'm done waiting."

I kiss him, shoving my tits against him like I know he wants. He massages them, calloused hands scraping against my nipples and making me moan into his mouth.

"You're so beautiful," he murmurs.

I run a hand through his hair. Silky soft. "You're so sexy."

His mouth dips down to my breast and he pulls my nipple into his mouth, gently at first. I gasp, and when he tugs harder, I cry out.

"Tell me if I hurt you," he says before sucking on my nipple again. Pleasure zings down my spine. I let out a moan that echoes in the dugout. This isn't where I pictured my first time, but now I can't imagine a better place. We could get caught any second, and a rush flows through me at the thought of everyone finding out I was fucking Theo St. James in the dugout.

His hand squeezes my other breast while he sucks on my nipple. Then he switches, and I claw at his hair, pressing deeper into him. "Harder." He listens, pulling my nipple deeper into his mouth. The sensation of his warm, wet tongue on the sensitive spot makes my head fall back.

I find the bulge in his pants and rub with my palm.

He hisses between his teeth. "*Shit.*"

I slide off him, and his brows furrow. Until I drop to my knees and reach for his fly.

He scoots back. "Cass—" he objects.

But I palm him through his pants and he bites his lip, failing to suppress a groan.

"We can't do this. Not here. Let me take you back to my place." He's already breathless.

"It's okay," I purr. "You're not doing anything. It's all me."

I unzip his pants and pull down his boxers, pulling out his hard length. I wrap my hand around him and stroke down slowly.

He groans and drops his head back, eyes falling shut. This is all I've ever wanted—to make Theo want me.

I shove his cock into my mouth.

His eyes spring open. "Oh, fuck! *Cass.*" The strangled way he gasps my name makes my thighs clench. "You don't have to."

"I know." I slip him back in my mouth and suck the way I want him to suck on me. He lets out a long groan.

I bob my head up and down faster, sucking my cheeks in. He stiffens beneath me and hisses through his teeth. I'm certain I'm doing this right, that he likes this—*really* likes this—but he reaches down to stop me. My face burns. "Am I doing it wrong?"

He shakes his head, a smile across his face. "No, that was amazing. But I don't want to finish in your mouth."

"You want to finish inside me?"

"Hell yes." He pulls me up before he unzips my jeans, tugging the tight fabric down over my ass and thighs.

I shouldn't have worn jeans today. That was stupid. Now if we get caught, I can't just run off. I'll have to stick with skirts and dresses from now on. Chills race down my legs when I step out of my pants.

Theo notices the goosebumps. "Let's warm you up."

Liquid heat spreads through my body at the promise in his voice.

He stands, grabbing me by the hips and guiding me to the bench. He gently nudges my legs apart, running his hand down each before kneeling and draping them over his shoulders.

My breath hitches.

"I want to make you come, Cass." His voice and those words alone nearly undo me.

Theo trails a finger over the waistband of my panties, then under. I nearly beg him to hurry, to stop torturing me. "You're so gorgeous. I'm so lucky."

He thinks he's the lucky one? Theo St. James is on his knees before me, his face inches from my aching core. I've never been luckier in my life.

He hooks a finger in my panties and pulls them to the side. I don't have time to feel embarrassed, my first time nude in front of a man, before he kisses between my legs.

I jerk and hiss through my teeth.

He grips my thighs, keeping my legs in place when he goes back in. This time with his tongue. He licks tentatively at first, teasing me.

"More," I beg, pulling at his hair.

He gives me more, sliding his tongue slowly up and down before letting out a low "mmm" like I'm his new favorite flavor. "Wow," he whispers, and I think it's more to himself than to me.

When he licks up me again, I gasp when he reaches my clit, arching into him. He notices and stays there, swirling his tongue harder and harder. I'm soaked for him, throbbing for him. I want to come on his cock, not like this.

But before I can protest, he nudges a finger at my entrance. "Do you want this?" he asks.

I nod, and he laps at my nub while he slowly slides a finger inside me. I cry out at the stretch.

"You are *so tight*," he moans. God, how have I not fantasized a million times about those words coming out of his mouth? He rocks his finger in me slowly, and when I cry out again, he waits until I adjust and licks my clit.

"Suck," I tell him. He wraps his lips around me and sucks my clit into his mouth. *Oh god.* "Agh!" He's a good listener.

He pulls his finger back, and I spot my wetness glistening on his skin. He thrusts back into me, and this time, the sensation is pleasure. But I want his cock, not his finger.

A chorus of laughter reaches us from somewhere behind the dugout. A few guys—I can't tell how many. We freeze.

"*Shit*," Theo hisses, but he still doesn't move. Doesn't pull his finger out of me. A deer standing in the road waiting for the car to strike.

But then the laughter and shouts fade, and we're alone again. I feel Theo's shoulders relax beneath my legs.

He pulls his finger out of me. "We should leave."

No. We can't stop now. I'll be aching for him until I can get him alone again and who knows when that will be. We need this release.

I stand and push him toward the bench. "I'm not leaving until I come on your dick, Theo."

His face is almost pained. "We've gotta hurry. No one can find us out here."

He bites his lip, already throbbing in my hand. I know this won't last long, but I don't care. I'll have many more chances to fuck Theo St. James long and slow.

I straddle him again, reaching down and guiding his hard length toward my entrance. I bite down the squeak of pain as I nudge him inside. He hangs onto my hips, worried eyes trained on my face. He doesn't want to hurt me, and it makes me want to ride him so good, he cums harder than he ever has.

We both breathe heavily while I adjust, taking every inch of him in gradually. Theo whispers a kiss to my lips and rubs his thumb on my clit. I moan, arching into him, and he catches my nipple with his mouth. The pleasure and pain mix together, overwhelming, until the pain of the stretch fades and all that's left is the pleasure.

I rock against him, and thank god no one is out here because I can't even try to be quiet now. Desperate, Theo covers my mouth. Which only lets me moan and cry out as loud as I want into his palm.

"You feel amazing," he breathes.

"So do you. I love how hard you are for me. I want to feel you cum inside me."

His grin stretches from ear to ear. "God, Cass. If you keep talking like that, this is gonna be over in two seconds."

I bounce on him faster, breasts flying up and down until he grabs them to squeeze and hold them steady. "I don't care. As long as we get to do this at least a hundred more times."

"How are you so perfect?"

I beam at him. That's the first time anyone's ever directed that word at me. *Perfect*. The word usually reserved for Noelle. Perfect Noelle van Buren.

Perfect Cassie Sinclair now.

"I was wondering the same thing about you," I tell him.

He thrusts up into me, rubbing my clit again. The pleasure mounts, thrumming from my center down to my toes.

"Faster, Cass," he begs.

I drive my hips back and forth, getting both of us closer and closer to the edge. But apparently it's not fast enough because he flips us, planting my ass on the cold bench and pushing until I'm laying down. He plunges back into me.

"Agh!"

He thrusts into me like a jackhammer, hard and fast. The smack of skin on skin echoes in the dugout along with my cries and his groans. I've never heard a sexier sound in my life. I want to hear him make that sound every day.

He rubs between my legs just as hard and fast as he fucks me. "I want to feel you come," he pleads. "I want to see it."

My heart hammers harder than it ever has. Fuck running a mile on the treadmill—this is all the exercise my heart needs. I stare down at where our bodies meet, where Theo's hard length plunges in and out of me, glistening with my wetness. Where his thumb rubs frantically at my nub.

He's desperate to cum. Desperate for me.

Overwhelming pleasure barrels through me and I moan loud enough for the whole campus to hear.

"*Fuck, Cass.*" Theo comes down on top of me, almost suffocating, as he fucks me faster than I thought possible. He lets out a strangled groan before stilling, and I feel him throbbing inside me as he cums. We throb together, and it's the hottest thing I've ever felt in my life.

He kisses me once before collapsing on me again, both of us catching our breath.

Slowly, a laugh bubbles up and out of me. He joins in and we both laugh together breathlessly, deliriously, until he finally says, "We should go."

I almost whine. I want to go another round. Another five rounds. But I know he's right.

He slides out of me and I gasp, instantly sore. He winces. "Are you okay?"

I nod, straightening my clothes. I like the soreness. I like the reminder that Theo St. James was between my legs. "I'm great."

I'm better than great. I'm perfect.

CHAPTER TWENTY-SIX
NOELLE

I'm humming while I paint the wall when the basement door creaks open. Beau's usual footsteps don't follow right away. I bend, dipping my brush in the yellow paint again, stroking across my canvas.

When I peer up the staircase, the door is open, but I'm alone. "Beau?"

No answer.

I set my brush down carefully on the paint can and climb the stairs. I peer out of the doorway, not stepping a single toe over the threshold.

The last time I was up here, I didn't have a chance to take in the space—I was too focused on my escape. Now, I nearly gape at the stunning floor-to-ceiling windows that let sunlight flood the open floor plan. A stunning stone fireplace, an elegant chandelier hanging from the ceiling, a huge black sectional around a massive flatscreen perched on the wall, and a split staircase that leads to another level. His job must pay well. *Very* well.

From my position, I can just barely make out Beau on a stool, hunched over the kitchen island.

Panic squeezes my heart. He wouldn't leave the door open unless something was wrong. I rush to his side—

But he's not unconscious or bleeding out. He spins a small diamond earring on the island with the tip of his finger.

The diamond earring I lost that first night.

"You found my earring."

His gaze trails up to me slowly, like he's just now registering that he's not alone. That I'm not in the basement. That I'm standing in the kitchen, right in front of him. To my surprise, he doesn't leap up or yell at me to get back down there. He smiles.

"It fell out in the car." He delicately lifts the earring and holds it out to me, placing it in my palm. "You can go now."

I freeze, clutching my fingers around my earring. The sharp end stabs into my skin. "What?"

His gray eyes are resolute. "I can't keep you locked up here forever. You have school and friends and family. And you deserve a chance to share your art with the world. Even if it kills me to let you go."

Somehow, his words sound like a breakup. And the hurt I should've felt when Theo did the same finally shoots through me. "Why now?" I whisper.

"You said I could trust you. That you won't tell anybody who kept you here. I believe you."

I close the distance between us and set the earring back down in front of him. "And what if I want to stay?"

His gray eyes burn hot as coals. Somehow, he didn't expect that. Didn't expect that the last thing I'd want is to leave and be anywhere without him.

I've been happier here with Beau than I've ever been in my life. He understands me like no one else ever has. Pushes me to work on my art, admires it. Admires *me*. He gets having a mother you can never please. Who will never be proud of you or love you the way you wish she would. He makes me feel seen, understood, desired. Loved.

When he brought me here, all I wanted was to escape. Break free of him.

Now, that's the last thing I want. I want to be with him. Want to stay in this perfect little bubble we've created.

Beau stands and his hand fists in my hair. "Then I'll make you come day and night. I'll be your canvas. I'll give you anything you want." He grips my hair harder and pulls, jerking my chin up. "But if you stay, you choose me. No one else touches you. You're mine."

"That's what I want."

"You sure, princess?" His gaze could burn through concrete. He wants me here. But he wants it to be my choice this time.

"Yes," I breathe, clutching his shirt and pulling him close. "I'm not going anywhere."

CHAPTER TWENTY-SEVEN

CASSIE

Since it's a gorgeous April evening, the three of us eat dinner outside of ECV at an umbrella table. Addison flashes me a shit-eating grin. "Oh. My. God. You got laid, didn't you?"

My eyes pop open. "What? No, I didn't."

"Don't lie to us—I can see it written all over your face. You're glowing. Every girl looks like that after she's been with the first guy to make her come."

"Who was it?" Piper whispers, giddy.

"Uh . . ." I know I'm not getting away with denying it, so I scramble for a name and blurt the first one that pops into my head: "Colin."

Piper gasps before clapping while Addison's mouth falls open. "The ginger?" She swipes through Instagram to find his profile. "Hmm. I guess he has a decent jawline. And big hands. You know what they say about big hands."

"Big feet?"

Piper grabs my hand, squeezing. "So how was it? Was it romantic? Did he treat you right? Are you dating now? Give us all the details!"

I can't help the smile that sweeps across my face when I

remember kissing Theo in his car, fucking him in the dugout. "It was . . . amazing," I admit. "He treated me right. But we're trying to keep things quiet for right now."

Addison's face scrunches. "What for?"

"You know, just . . ." I wave my hand in the air, hoping it'll help me conjure an answer. "Theo. He's so sad about Noelle; we don't want to flaunt our new relationship in his face."

Addison's brows stay scrunched together, but Piper nods. "That makes sense. That's really thoughtful of you guys." She squeals and claps again. "Ahh! I'm *so* excited for you, Cassie! Finally some good news! Noelle would be really happy for you."

"Yeah." My smile wavers. "Too bad she's not here to see this."

Piper's right. Noelle would be happy for me and Theo. She'd take one look at our faces, at how happy we are when we're with each other, and give us her blessing. She's the kind of girl who wouldn't hold any resentment toward either of us for her and Theo's past relationship.

But she's not here to celebrate. We still haven't found her. With every day that passes, it feels like we might never find her.

On the sidewalk, Beau Grayson saunters by, hands in his pockets and shoulders back. Like he's going for a casual stroll around campus.

My stomach twists. His face is less rigid lately, less intensity burning in those gray eyes. A lightness to his step.

My eyes trail him until he's out of sight.

∼

THEO

After practice, most of the guys have cleared out of the locker room, leaving me and Colin behind. He rubs a hand through his damp hair. "Hey, man, you—"

The door squeaks open, cutting him off. Cass's stride comes to an abrupt halt when she spots him.

"You lost?" Colin asks.

Her eyes flick to me, panicked. Shit. What the hell is she doing in here?

Then her eyes flood with tears. "Um. I need to talk to Theo . . . about Noelle." Her voice breaks on the last words.

Colin's eyes widen and he snatches his bag, ready to bail. "Right. No problem."

Cass rushes to lock the door behind him before throwing her arms around my middle. I rub her hair and hold her to me as tight as I can.

"It's been over a month, Theo." She pulls back but still hangs onto me. Like I'm her anchor. "We still haven't found her."

"We will," I murmur.

"But what if we haven't found her body yet because she's being held somewhere?"

I swipe at the tears spilling down her cheeks. "You can't think like that. We have to stay positive. She's out there, she's okay, and we're going to find her."

Cass nods, wiping at her cheeks and sniffling. "You're right. Sorry. I just . . . the thought that somebody might have her somewhere, hurting her. It got to me."

"Maybe we can search her computer again. Search through her stuff in your room. Maybe there's something we missed."

Cass shakes her head. "We've been through everything. The police have been through everything. I'm telling you, Theo. I have a bad feeling that she's locked up somewhere."

I rub the back of my neck, preparing to put words to a thought I didn't think I'd ever voice out loud to anyone. "Honestly, I have a bad feeling she's not coming home alive."

Cass wraps her arms around her middle. "Wouldn't that be better, though? As awful as that is, it's better than being held captive and tortured somewhere. At least she wouldn't be suffering."

I unravel her arms, taking both her hands. "We'll figure this out, all right? We'll find her and bring her home. Together."

Cass presses her lips to mine, and I wrap her in my arms.

"You ready to go?" I ask.

She shakes her head and kisses me again, more urgently this time. "No one else is here," she whispers. "Let's take advantage of it."

I grab her hips, knowing she needs this. Comfort and distraction. "We just have to be careful, okay?"

She nods quickly. "We will. I promise."

I kiss her, slipping my tongue past her lips and stroking hers, long and slow. Our stress, our worries, our fears melting away with every shuddering breath. Her tongue grows more urgent in my mouth, and she pulls me closer.

I scoop her up with one arm and hold her up against the lockers, tugging at the buttons straining over her tits. But then I get impatient and tear open the rest, sending two of them flying before I fling her shirt off.

Her tears are gone now. All thoughts out of her mind, focusing on nothing but the present. On us.

My mouth lands on her neck, and I pin her into the lockers harder with my hips, my hard-on digging into her. *Fuck.* Even through layers, she feels so good. I don't know how I went so long without taking her.

She grinds on me, and I groan, hungry mouth traveling down to her perfect breasts. I kiss them while unclasping her bra and dropping it to the floor with her shirt.

Her body is perfect. Soft skin, supple breasts, every inch of her delicious and made for my mouth, my hands, my cock.

When I suck her nipple, she buries her hands in my hair, unable to hold back the loud moan. A smile pulls at my lips. I love every sound my lips elicit from her.

I clap my hand over her mouth, and the sight of my palm suppressing the noises she can't help making turns me on even more. I suck on her other nipple hard before dropping to my knees, keeping her pressed against the lockers before sticking my head under her skirt.

She's not wearing panties and I growl at the sight before latching onto her with my mouth. She's already soaked for me, and my cock twitches in my pants, straining at my jeans. She gasps, bending forward and thighs clenching around my head. I suck on her clit before dragging my teeth over the sensitive spot.

"*Fuck*, Theo!" I don't stop, even as she starts squirming. "I want to come with you inside me," she pants.

An agonized groan escapes my lips. Her words alone are making me painfully hard. I stand, looming over her, and spin her. Grabbing her tits and squeezing. "I love these," I murmur before I press her against the lockers.

I lift her skirt, massaging her ass. Her curves don't even fit in my hands, her soft flesh yielding to my rough touch. When I want to hear her moan for me again, I bring my hand around to rub between her legs. She shudders, grinding her ass into me, and *fuck*, I might just cum in my pants if she keeps doing that.

"Spread your legs," I breathe, desperate for her now. I need to be inside her. Need my hips slapping against her ass while she bounces on my cock. Need her walls clenching around me while she comes and I follow right after.

She does, peering over her shoulder at me. "I want you to cum inside me."

My eyes roll and fall closed, nostrils flaring while I force a calming breath through my lungs.

Then I pounce.

I grab her hands, pinning her palms against the cool metal of the lockers above her. Grind against her ass again before unzipping my jeans.

She arches her back more, lifting her ass so I can get a better angle. One of these days, I'm going to fuck her naked, but for now, I slip my cock out of my jeans and slide into her. She cries out, just as mind-blowingly tight as she was the first time. I flex my hips, jerking into her and savoring the sweet feeling of her wet pussy around my cock as she cries out again, slamming her hands against the metal.

I press into her harder so she's flush with the lockers and can't move. All she can do is let me fuck her.

The room fills with our sounds—the smack of my hips against her ass, the slick sound of my cock sliding in and out of her, our pants and groans.

I slide her hair from one shoulder to the other, baring her neck for me. I suck on her skin and rub her clit while my other hand digs into her hip. With my hand between her legs, she unravels, her moans echoing loud in the empty locker room. Music to my ears.

I pump inside her, chasing my own orgasm before we get caught. She pulses around me as I slam into her over and over, driving pleasure through every cell of our bodies.

When I ram into her one last time, she yelps, and I throb inside her while I cum, heart hammering and chest heaving. Her thighs clench when she feels me spilling into her. I can't peel myself off her until my cock gives one last twitch.

I pull out of her slowly, and my cum follows. *Jesus.* I'll never not love the sight of my seed spilling out of her. I spin her and kiss her deep. Gratitude and lust on her lips, on the tongue she sweeps into my mouth.

"You're incredible," I murmur.

She grins up at me, and I know it won't be long before I need to be inside her again. "So are you."

CHAPTER TWENTY-EIGHT
NOELLE

"So who decorated this place?" I ask Beau. "I know it wasn't you."

He snorts from his spot in the kitchen, where he's cleaning up after our morning pancakes. Why is watching a man scrub dishes with his sleeves rolled up to his elbows so sexy? "No idea."

"How do you not know who decorated your own house?"

"Not mine. It's abandoned. That's why I brought you here."

"Abandoned? Who would abandon a home this beautiful?"

The house is bigger, grander, than I thought it'd be. Stuck in the basement, I assumed the whole house was drab, dusty, gloomy. But it's a fully furnished, gorgeous colonial with three bedrooms and two bathrooms upstairs.

Beau shrugs. "Rich people who can afford to move to another country and keep the home they don't use."

What a waste. I can't believe someone wouldn't give another family the opportunity to have a home like this when they don't even want it anymore. "How did you get in?"

"I know how to pick locks." He puts the final plate in the dishrack and grins at me. "I'm good with my hands."

"I've noticed."

He sweeps me up and plants my ass on the kitchen island. A startling montage flashes through my mind—Beau and I five years from now, living here together. Having sex in every room, him coming home from work to find me in my art studio. I could be happy here. I could be happy with that life. I've never had this feeling before.

"What are you grinning about?" He smiles at me.

"Being here with you. I like it." I kiss him, and he deepens it, slipping his tongue in.

"I'll make you love it," he murmurs. Then he's pulling my shirt over my head and unclasping my bra.

My eyes flash to the windows, letting me see everything around us, but also exposing us to anyone who ventures too close. Not that there seems to be anyone in a five-mile radius, but—

Beau's mouth sucks hard at my neck, and I groan, forgetting about how exposed I am and knowing he'll leave a hickey there. I love seeing his marks on me. His lips move to the other side, sucking even harder, and I wrap my legs around him and clutch his shoulders.

When he pulls away, I nearly whimper. Until he reaches for the chocolate syrup we left on the island.

"I've never met someone who puts chocolate syrup on their pancakes," I tell him.

"Have you ever met someone who puts chocolate syrup on his girl?" He drizzles the chocolate onto my breasts, swirling it around my nipple with a finger. I gasp.

"Did you just call me your girl?"

"I'm fucking you," he says simply. "I'm about to lick chocolate syrup off your naked body. We're living together." He tugs me toward him by my ass. "I told you—you're mine now. You're my fucking girl."

I grin so wide it hurts. Being Beau's has made me happier than I've ever been in my life. "If this isn't your house, where do you actually live?"

He shrugs. "Nowhere, really. I go wherever the jobs take me."

"Where were you staying before you brought me here?"

"Told you. Came to town to find my pops."

"So you've been staying with him?" When he nods, I add, "He doesn't ask where you're spending all your time?"

"He knows about my job. The lifestyle. Better not to ask questions you don't want to know the answers to."

I swallow. There are so many questions I still need to ask him. So much more I don't know. I want to know everything about him.

But when he circles the liquid chocolate around my other nipple, all thoughts leave my mind. "What were you saying about licking chocolate syrup off my naked body?"

He smirks and his mouth travels down to my breasts. He licks up the mess before sucking on my nipple. I drop my head back and arch into him, which only makes him go harder. Right on the edge of pain. I gasp, wanting more. He moves to the other, repeating the tantalizing, tortuous movement.

Then he yanks my shorts off, flinging them away carelessly, and I'm bare before him. He grabs the chocolate syrup again, and when the cool liquid hits between my legs, I gasp.

His tongue chases it quickly, making my eyes roll with every stroke. He moves up and down agonizingly slow, savoring the chocolate and me. When he dips his tongue inside me, I whimper, clawing at his hair.

"I love when you're soaked for me, princess." He parts my knees wider, pulls out his hard length, and without warning, plunges inside me.

I cry out, gripping the edge of the island for support when he yanks me closer. The angle is deep, unforgiving, and I moan every time he slams back in.

His thumb finds my clit, driving more pleasure through every inch of my body as he fucks me hard. "Tell me how much you want to come on my cock," he rasps.

"I want to lose my mind on your cock," I breathe.

Abruptly, he sweeps me into his arms and carries me upstairs, kicking the door open to the master bedroom.

He tosses me on the bed. The soft white comforter is luxurious and I almost want to smack him for keeping me trapped in the basement on that dingy mattress when I could've been sleeping on this every night. With him. But somehow, I think sleeping on that mattress in that dark, dreary basement has made me appreciate this bed that much more.

He climbs onto the bed with me, opens a drawer, and reveals a crimson blindfold. "This is how I make you scream."

Beau slides the blindfold over my eyes.

Without any clue where he is, every brush of his fingers against my skin is a shock that makes me gasp. The feral beast that fucked me is gone, tamed and calmed for now. This time, I've got the prince. The man who takes his time, who touches me like he's savoring me, like he's memorizing every inch.

I squirm beneath the skim of his fingertips over my collarbones, my arms, my breasts, my peaked nipples, my ribs, my thighs. Then his mouth trails over the same path, kissing and tasting and sucking. He starts sucking and nibbling at random spots, on my shoulder, then my thigh, then my nipple, driving me insane. I can't tell where his next touch will land with the blindfold on, and the mystery makes every contact that much more delicious.

I'm a wet, trembling mess beneath him when his finger finally strokes up my center. I gasp just as he hisses at the slickness. His breath caresses the shell of my ear. "You have no idea how fucking sexy you are. I love every inch."

My mind catches on that word—*love*. Not that he meant he loves me; he loves my body. He loves fucking me, and I love it too. It's too soon for more. For that love to be for each other's soul.

But the possibility is there. I know I could fall in love with him, if given the time and the chance to do so. I'm already falling. Another first.

We are two magnets pulled together. It'll take an outside force to yank us apart now.

He takes my nipple between his teeth, making me arch and let out a sound that's somewhere between a gasp and a yelp. His chuckle vibrates down my spine. I clutch at him, trying to hang onto his hair or his shoulders or his back so I can track his movements, but he doesn't let me. He knows how much I love the surprise.

The first stroke of his tongue between my legs makes me cry out. He holds my thighs down when I squirm, pinning me to the bed so I can't go anywhere.

Beau's licks are slow and luxuriating before his tongue plunges inside me. I moan and search through the dark for his hair. His thumb drifts up to rub casually at my clit, and my hips buck beneath his touch. I've never been so turned on in my life. How did I go so long without Beau Grayson? It's like I've been sleeping my whole life until I met him.

Now I'm finally awake. The most alive I've ever been.

He presses harder when he senses my need. When he slips his tongue out, wetness follows, dripping onto the bed. He groans, and part of me wishes I could see his face, but another part of me likes being kept in the dark. Likes being at his mercy.

His finger replaces his tongue, stretching me. I groan, and he latches onto my nub with his mouth, sucking me. I whimper, heart hammering so hard, I'm worried I'm going to come before he's even gotten inside me again.

"I'm ready," I gasp.

"For what, princess?"

"For you."

"You've got me."

I smile. "Inside me," I correct.

He settles between my legs, laying on me and pressing me into the bed. He rubs his cock against me, the friction deliciously torturous. Then he pulls the blindfold off. His gray eyes are close, heady in the darkness. More intense than they've ever been.

"I want to look into your eyes while I fuck your brains out."

I swallow, and he slips a hand down between us, nudging at my entrance while his eyes don't move from my face for a second.

Then he slides into me, both of us letting out twin groans. "Oh *fuck*, princess."

I'm still sore from earlier, so he fucks me slow, kissing me and running his fingers through my hair with every lazy thrust. He circles my clit with his thumb, pressing harder and harder with each rock of our bodies against the mattress. As the pleasure radiating through my limbs climbs, I lift my hips and jerk down to meet his thrusts.

He groans. "Keep that up and you won't be able to walk tomorrow."

"Guess that means you'll just have to carry me everywhere," I gasp.

I'm not sure whether he takes that as permission or a challenge, but he slams into me, making me cry out. He jerks into me hard and fast, again and again. His hand has abandoned the slow circles around my clit and now both hands grip my head, pinning my body completely to the mattress with his full weight on top of me. I can't go anywhere. I can't move as he fucks me as hard and fast as he can, the intensity and pressure making me scream.

"Fuck, yeah," he breathes. "You're so fucking tight around my cock."

The friction from every jerk of his body into mine rubs against my clit, and the pleasure is too much. Too intense. I fall over the edge, screaming the whole way down.

He keeps fucking me through the throes of my orgasm, chasing his own until he gives one final thrust and spills inside me, breathing hard. "That's my good girl."

When he finally collapses onto the bed beside me, we're both limp and heaving. It takes me longer to recover, even though he did all the work.

He leans up on an elbow and presses a kiss as delicate as a

butterfly's wings against my lips. "How does a bath sound, princess?"

Before, I thought the universe was punishing me by putting me in Beau Grayson's path. By compelling him to kidnap me and bring me here. To put a knife to my throat with the intent to kill me.

Too bad for the universe, it sent me to hell and I fell for the devil.

CHAPTER TWENTY-NINE
CASSIE

Theo doesn't know when his roommate will be home, so we have to make this fast. In his closet, my knees are jammed against the wall and the door, his dangling shirts in my face, my hands braced against the thin plaster.

He rubs between my legs while I ride him, another hand squeezing and kneading my breast. "Faster," he urges.

Every time we fuck, it's a race against the clock. A quickie in his car between classes. A quickie on his hood on the side of the road after a game. At least this time I've made it into his bedroom, even if I'm stuck in the closet. I've lost track of how many times we've had sex now and I still haven't managed to fuck him in a bed.

Theo gets impatient with me rocking slowly back and forth on his cock and grips my hips before pounding into me from beneath. I like the way his face scrunches, the way he bites his lip when he thrusts into me hard. I might mistake the look for pain if I didn't know how much he loves being inside me. If he didn't groan at how tight and wet I am every time he fucks me.

My tits bounce wildly as he rams into me over and over. I cry out and he covers my mouth, even though the closet muffles our sounds.

"No one's going to hear us," I manage to gasp out. "It's a frat house. Let's finish this in your bed and be as loud as we want."

"Colin could be back any minute," he pants. His thumb lands on my clit, and it's all the persuasion I need.

He keeps fucking me, rubbing my clit wildly like he's begging for my release. Almost without my permission, it barrels through me, pleasure singing through every vein. He lets out a long, sexy groan, finally allowing himself to cum in me as I contract around him over and over.

As much as I want to resent him for relegating me to a closet, getting to ride him on the floor in a tiny room with every moan echoing around us was hot as hell.

I'm still weak with pleasure, but Theo is already moving us, sliding me off him and finding our clothes. I reluctantly slide my bra on when he tosses it to me.

Every time we're finished, all the thoughts I've managed to chase away, to push to some dark corner of my mind, come barreling back. Hunter. Noelle. Gone.

Gone, gone, gone.

I push those thoughts back down again. Focus on Theo. "Your family's Easter party is tomorrow, right?"

Every spring, his parents throw a lavish dinner party. Noelle always gets to go since their parents have been friends for decades. I'm not sure Theo's parents know my mom exists, and I've never been invited. Noelle always made the party sound stuffy, boring, she and Theo the only ones under the age of forty in attendance. But I want to be there, even if he can't parade me around or introduce me as his girlfriend.

Theo is still preoccupied with getting his shirt over his head. "Yeah, it is."

"Can I come?"

He halts his frantic movements for a second before slowly easing his shirt down. "I don't think that's a good idea."

My heart sinks. I'm still Theo's shameful secret. The girl he has to keep stuffed in a closet. The girl he can't bring to his family parties. The girl he can fuck behind closed doors but can't hold her hand in public.

This sneaking around used to be hot, but now there's a sour note to it.

"As your friend, Theo. Nothing more."

He gives me a small smile. "Is that possible?"

"I can manage not to jump your bones for one evening."

His smile slips into a grimace. "My father won't be happy."

"Why? He barely knows me."

"He told me to stay away from you. Because of the Noelle situation."

Even though it shouldn't, a flash of hurt pierces my chest. "I'm glad you didn't listen."

Theo takes my hand. "Me too."

A door slams. We both freeze.

Theo jumps to his feet, frantically yanking his jeans up and opening the closet door.

Colin lets out an easy laugh. "Were you getting dressed in there, man?"

"Nope. Taking a nap, actually. Something about cramped spaces makes me sleep like a baby."

I'm frozen in the closet, convinced Colin is going to call Theo on his bullshit any second, wrench the door open, and find me in here.

Part of me wants him to. Rip the bandaid off; get it over with. I want to be able to hold Theo's hand and kiss him in public. To put a sock on his doorknob and let him fuck me in his bed. Bring him back to Chi Omega and share winks with my sorority sisters as I take him upstairs.

"That's really fuckin' weird," Colin says. "But as long as you're not sleeping in my bed, I don't really give a shit. You coming to ECV?"

"Yeah, I'll be down in a sec."

The door shuts, marking Colin's exit, and I burst out of the closet.

Theo's already raking both hands through his hair. "That was way too close. What if he came in the room before we were finished?"

"Isn't that what the whole sock-on-the-doorknob thing is for?"

"I can't let him know I'm fucking a girl in our room."

I stiffen. "I'm not just a girl."

Theo's eyes soften, and he squeezes my arms. "Hell no, you're not. You're the only girl, Cass. But you get why no one can find out about us."

"Actually, I don't." I pull out of his grasp, heart in my throat. "You and Noelle broke up. I get that your dad thinks it'll make you look guilty or whatever, but lying is what really makes you look guilty. And you know you're innocent, so why should it matter what assumptions people make? You should be able to be with who you want. Maybe your dad isn't always right about everything, and you should try listening to your gut sometime."

He doesn't say another word and I crawl out his window the way I came in. I don't know if I've just screwed up my shot with Theo. The thought makes my chest ache. But I'm getting sick of being his secret.

∼

THEO

"Theo!" My mother calls, waving me over to where she stands in our stuffy living room with the van Burens. "Come say hello!"

Hard to believe Noelle's parents are attending a formal dinner party while their daughter is missing. Hell, I wouldn't even be here if my parents didn't insist on it. But I guess they can't put their lives on hold forever and there's nothing they can really do now except wait for answers.

I'm the only one who's been putting my life on hold.

Pretending I'm still dating my ex-girlfriend and blowing it with the girl of my dreams.

"Hey, Mr. and Mrs. van Buren." I flash them my best, charming-young-man smile. "Can I get you something to drink?" Anything to get me away from the men in suits asking how far I am in my doctoral program—still just an undergrad—and the women in their fifties squeezing my biceps while telling me I'm going to make a woman *very* lucky someday.

Mom waves away my offer. "You don't fetch drinks, Theo. Let the servers do that. The van Burens were just telling me there's an update in Noelle's case!"

My heart leaps with hope. "Really?"

Mrs. van Buren's lips purse for a second before she slips back into her polite, forced smile. "Somewhat. The police suspect someone close to Noelle may have been involved. They haven't given us any more information than that yet, despite my insistence." She snatches a drink from one of the server's trays as he passes and sips from it. "The law enforcement in this town are absolutely incompetent, I swear."

Someone close to Noelle. My stomach twists. Who could they be suspecting?

A brunette in a long, flowing red dress and trenchcoat strolls into the foyer, head swiveling like she's searching for someone. Relief loosens the tight muscles in my shoulders.

"Excuse me," I tell the van Burens, and head right for her.

Dad may not like it, but after our last conversation, I knew Cass was right. No one will think twice about her being here, and my father's not always right about everything. I need to start listening to my gut. If she wants to be here, I want her here. So I texted her an invite a few days ago.

She never responded. Can't blame her for wanting time to make her decision, to forgive me. But I'm so fucking glad she's here.

I can't help the grin that stretches across my face. All I want is to sweep her up in my arms, but I'm not sure that's what she wants just yet. "You came."

Cass slips her jacket off, draping it over her arm and revealing the crimson dress underneath. Her boobs nearly spill out of the top.

I swallow hard but force my eyes back up to hers. "I'm glad you're here."

She smiles, mouth painted red. "What are friends for?"

"Does this mean I'm forgiven?"

She grabs my hand and pulls me down the hall. "Give me the tour and I'll consider it."

Once we reach the half-bath, I pull her in and lock the door behind us, the smell of potpourri assaulting my nose. We keep the light off, but I can make out the outline of her features in the flickering light from the candles. Her big brown eyes, her raised brows, her perfect, pouty lips.

She grins. "I didn't think friends snuck around with each other like this."

I slip my hand between her legs. "They don't."

"There's a party going on in the other room," she pretends to protest. "Half the neighborhood is here."

"Then we better be quick. And you better keep quiet."

She grabs at my pants, finding the hard bulge she knew would be waiting for her. I grab her thighs and smack her down on the counter before yanking my fly down.

My cock has been aching for her pussy these last few days without her. I can't wait anymore. I place my hand over her mouth like duct tape, shoving her panties to the side and ramming into her.

Her cry is muffled against my palm. My hand grips her thigh to keep her legs apart while I continue slamming into her, harder than I've ever fucked her before. She moans into my palm.

I yank her dress down so her tits pop out and suck a nipple deep into my mouth before clamping down with my teeth. She moans again, but my hand is velcro over her soft lips. The only sounds that fill the room are my grunts and the slap of skin against skin.

Anyone could walk by and guess at the sounds coming from the bathroom. But I don't give a shit. My cock slides in and out of her easier, faster, as she grows wetter and wetter for me. She rubs between her legs, and my eyes fall to where she touches herself. I can't take my eyes off her, gaze darting back and forth between her hand working her sensitive nub and her breasts bouncing wildly with every thrust.

I lean into her, breath caressing her ear. "I'm going to cum inside you. Don't let anyone see it drip out."

She contracts around me and cries out into my hand, orgasm barreling through her and her pussy clenching around me.

I bite her shoulder to suppress my own groan as I slam into her once, twice, before spilling inside her. My cock twitches over and over with every spurt. Our hearts slam against our ribcages, heaving breaths filling the small room.

When I finally pull out of her, she grins and fixes her dress. "Was that makeup sex?"

"I'm sorry I made you feel like a secret. I really, really like you, Cass. I want to be with you." I take her hand. "I don't care who knows it."

She squeezes my hand. "I want to be with you too. But I'm okay with waiting to go public until we get your dad on board. I don't want him to hate me before I've even spoken to him. Just as long as you don't relegate me to the closet or make me climb through windows anymore. I don't want to feel like you're ashamed of me."

"I'm not ashamed of you. Not even close. I'm the luckiest guy on the planet to have you." I place my hand on the small of her back. "Let's go introduce you."

We find my parents in the kitchen, lost in a tense, hushed conversation. Cass stiffens beneath my palm, but we keep marching forward into the lion's den.

"Dad." I keep my voice light. "I want to introduce you to Cass Sin—Cassie Sinclair."

His stony gaze lands on Cass and she practically melts beside me. Shit. This was a bad idea. "Miss Sinclair." He holds out a hand, glass of scotch clutched in the other. "Nice to meet you."

Cass shakes his hand. "Nice to meet you too," she murmurs.

"Tell me, Cassie, have you ever had Romanee-Conti?" He pulls a bottle from the wine cabinet.

She gives him a small smile. "No, I haven't."

"Oh, it's delicious. You're twenty-one, right?" He winks at her, already pouring a glass. Then his gaze flicks to my mother. "Darling, why don't you give us the room?"

Shit. I stare at Mom, willing her not to go, but she knows an order when she hears one.

Dad hands Cass the drink, waiting for her to take a sip. Once she does, nodding and pretending she likes it, he swirls his scotch. "Listen, you two. I remember what it was like to be young. But you're making a big mistake." He's somehow keeping his voice light, conversational. Like every word isn't a threat. "The police have a lead, and Noelle could return any day. There's no point in ruining your reputation with the public before she does. If you keep your relationship quiet for now, you can skip around town together all you want when Noelle returns. If not . . ." He shrugs, sipping from his glass. "All eyes will be on the two of you. Not a great situation to be in, especially when you can't afford good legal counsel."

Tense silence crackles between us. He's talking directly to Cass now. An obvious threat cloaked in false concern. He's done his research.

Cass lifts her chin, even though the uncertainty is clear in her eyes. "I don't think Theo and I have anything to worry about if we're innocent."

A sinister half-smile pulls at a corner of his lips. "Innocent people wind up behind bars all the time. The police are already looking at someone close to Noelle. Let's just hope it's not either of you two. Because they may not like what they find."

CHAPTER THIRTY

BEAU

"You ready, princess?"

In the basement, Noelle stands in front of me, covered in goosebumps from my voice in her ear.

I loosen the blindfold from her eyes and gesture around the room with the biggest shit-eating grin. She lights up and her beautiful blue eyes brim with tears.

The basement has been transformed. Black shelves loaded with paint cans and brushes, wall-mounted easels, a sturdy workbench, storage baskets loaded with paper, and two lamps to make up for the little natural light that sneaks through the tiny ass window.

"Beau," she murmurs, and there's my name on her lips again. That sweet, delicious sound. "This is amazing."

I smirk. "Figured you could use me as your muse for your first piece in your new official art studio."

"Yeah?" She flashes a wicked grin with that pretty little mouth. The one that makes me want to shove my cock between her lips. "You're going to model for me?"

I wind my arms around her hips. "Not exactly. You'll paint me, I'll paint you, and then we'll fuck to make the best artwork you've ever seen."

"That sounds like fun. Now?"

I pull her in roughly. "Obviously." She gives a little squeak when I yank her hair back and expose her neck before sucking her soft skin into my mouth. I've already got her squirming.

I unroll the huge canvas, the paint already in position because I knew exactly how this would go. We watch each other strip, even though I want to tear the clothes off her myself. Sometimes the wait, the buildup, makes me cum harder.

Her tits fall from her bra when she at last gets that wretched thing off. They're bigger now that she's eating properly. So are her hips and thighs. Supple and delicious. When her panties come off next, I grin and can't restrain myself anymore. I want to taste her before I cover her body in paint.

She gasps when I suck her nipple into my mouth as hard as I can, my hand slipping between her legs so I can feel how wet she gets for me when I go at her rough. This is how my princess likes to be fucked, and I'm happy to oblige.

I latch onto the other one, and she whimpers, pulling at my hair. She fucking loves my hair. My girl loves everything about me, even the parts that scare her. Especially those.

I flip her onto her back, diving right into her pussy with my tongue. She squirms and cries out, and it takes every muscle to fight against the smirk that wants to spread from ear to ear. I love when she loses her mind on my tongue, my fingers, my cock.

"You're fucking soaked for me, princess." Just how I like her.

I lick and suck on her clit just long enough to get her heart racing before I pull away.

She whimpers, not ready for me to stop, but when I dip my hand in a can of blue paint and slide it over her tit, she doesn't complain.

She giggles and dips a finger in red paint, trailing a line from my sternum to my pelvis. "This is fun."

This will take way too long if she's planning on covering me one finger at a time. I toss a handful of blue paint at her and she gasps, staring down at her blue-splattered stomach with her mouth hanging open until she reaches in the red paint and flings it at me.

In seconds, we're both laughing so hard, our stomachs hurt, splattering and smearing paint on each other from head to foot. Until she suddenly stops, grinning at me. She looks ridiculous and beautiful covered in blue and yellow paint.

"I don't think I've ever heard you laugh like this before."

I grip her by the hips, leaving my handprints on her skin. "That's because I never have. Not until I met you."

She melts and pulls my face to hers, kissing me. Girls have made me hard before. They've made me cum. But none of them have made me laugh like she does.

When she pulls away, she dips her finger in the blue paint. "Close your eyes," she tells me, and I flinch.

The same three words my mother said to me before she came at me with a knife.

Noelle's mouth dips in concern. "What's wrong?"

"Nothing, beautiful. Paint me."

For my princess, I close my eyes.

I can hardly breathe when I feel the tip of her finger, cool and gentle, trailing over my skin. Through my brow, over my eyelid, and stopping on my cheekbone. When I open my eyes, she's giving me a small smile.

She painted my scar. Replacing my most painful memory with a soft, tender one. A loving one.

"You know, I think I'll just go out like this from now on."

She giggles and pushes me down gently, straddling me and ready to ride.

But I pull her up to my face and bury my tongue inside her. She hovers above me, bracing herself against the canvas and moaning. I dig my fingers into her ass. "Fucking *sit*."

"What?" she gasps, peering down at me with wide blue eyes.

"Stop holding yourself up. Sit on my face." I don't give her a choice—I grab her thighs and haul her down onto my tongue. She lets out a whimper. Exactly what I wanted.

That's right, princess.

I work her in broad, sweeping strokes. Painting her with my tongue.

"I don't want to suffocate you," she says.

"Princess, if I suffocate, I'll die a happy man."

When her wetness starts to flow down my neck, she gasps, "I want to come on your cock."

She starts to pull off my face. I shake my head. "You will, princess." I haul her back down, sucking on her clit, and she lurches forward, crying out. I keep her pinned in place and go at her like I'm sucking out her soul until she tumbles over the edge, thighs shaking as her moans echo off the walls.

I don't give her a chance to recover before I'm flipping her on her back and sliding inside her, wanting to feel her pussy throbbing through the throes of her orgasm. I nearly cum inside her that second as her walls clench around me over and over.

I pound her into the concrete, nothing between her and the floor except our canvas.

Her screams grow hoarse when I thrust into her again and again. She's so beautiful when she's getting fucked. Tits bouncing, thighs trembling, mouth open, eyes rolling.

"Beau!" she yelps.

I can't hold back anymore and my cock jerks, spilling inside her. I groan, her pussy making my mind spin. *Fuck.*

When we catch our breath and she finally sits up, we admire our artwork. Our canvas is covered in wild streaks of paint. It'll be the best fucking painting in this house.

She strokes a blue-streaked hand through my hair, a hint of worry furrowing her brows. "What are we going to tell everyone when we leave this house and return to our normal lives?"

"Easy. You fell in love with me." She smirks and opens her mouth, but I keep going. "You knew your parents would never let their little princess be with a beast like me. So you ran away so we could be together." I pull her onto my lap, kissing her. "And we lived happily ever after."

CHAPTER THIRTY-ONE

CASSIE

*A*fter dark, Theo drives me home in his Audi from the latest press conference regarding Noelle's disappearance. The police have officially named the van Burens persons of interest, which has the media up in arms.

I guess that's what the police meant by someone close to Noelle.

Theo's quiet, the press conference and thoughts of Noelle weighing heavy on his mind. The guilt he feels at not coming forward with the truth about their relationship.

I can't remember the last time I slept through the night. Even in the dim lighting, I can make out the bags under my eyes in the side mirror.

Though the police are focusing their investigation on the van Burens, what Theo's dad said at their dinner party has been circling through my brain ever since. If they start looking any closer at me and Theo, they won't like what they uncover.

We need to find Noelle.

In front of us, a Dodge Neon does sixty-five in a forty. My heart leaps into my throat. "Follow that car."

"What? Why?" Theo asks.

"That's Beau Grayson's car."

Theo's brows pull together. "Why do you want to follow Beau Grayson?"

"Let's just see where he goes."

He showed up to the search for Noelle on campus and the vigil. He's had a new swagger in his step for weeks. And Noelle's body hasn't been found, so it's possible she's still alive. My gut tells me she is.

And I think Beau Grayson is keeping her that way. Maybe if I figure out where he lives, I can know for sure.

Theo trails after Beau without any more questions. We make turn after turn, heading in the wrong direction now, until Beau pulls into a parking lot in front of a bar.

"Shit," I mutter. We can't just sit outside the bar waiting for him to drive home.

"Now what?" Theo asks, letting his foot off the gas.

I wave him on. "Let's just head back."

He takes the long way to campus, so I don't notice we're on the road until it's too late.

Too late to turn back. We're going to pass it—the spot where my brother was killed.

I hold my breath, the way little kids do when they pass a cemetery.

Theo notices me stiffen. "Are you okay?" When he spots the wooden cross staked in the ground in his headlights, he hisses through his teeth. "Shit. Sorry, Cass. I forgot."

"It's okay," I manage, hand clutching the door. "Actually, could you pull over?"

He does, coasting gently to the side of the road, the memorial for Hunter in the rearview mirror. I slide out of Theo's Audi and crouch in front of the cross. Someone pinned a Polaroid to the wood of Hunter flashing his big, cheesy grin with a group of his college buddies. Flowers surround the spot, some left here by mourners, others growing from the ground. New life springing up from death.

I skim my fingers along the soft, dark grass, the only light shining on me and Hunter coming from the red glow of Theo's brake lights.

"I wish you were here," I whisper to my brother. He'd be proud. He'd be happy for me. I'm with Theo now. I'm in college, pursuing the career we both dreamed of. Tears well in my eyes. He'll never get to see me fulfill our dream. But somehow, I think he knows.

Theo's hand lands lightly on my back, rubbing up and down. "You must really miss him."

I nod. I can't manage any words. I'm not sure when I'll be able to say Hunter's name again. Just thinking it is painful enough.

"You can talk about him, you know," Theo says. "With me. If you want to. I'm here for you."

I lean my head against his shoulder. He's everything I've ever wanted and more. Better than anything I've ever hoped for. "I know. Thank you."

We sit crouched like that in silence for another minute before I stand and hold out my hand to help Theo up.

He cocks an eyebrow when I lead him to the hood of the Audi. "What are you doing?"

I climb on top of it and spread my legs. He needs cheering up, and so do I. "You. I want you to fuck me on the hood of your car."

He chuckles and slides his hands up my thighs. "What if someone drives by?"

I unzip his pants. "Then you better be quick." Without another word, I slide him inside me. We both moan, and I feel the tension in him melt.

I slide my ass up and down the hood of his car until Theo starts thrusting into me. He yanks my hair the way he knows I like now, making tears sting the corners of my eyes. He's so hard and long, the angle deep and just on the edge of pain. I can't think. Can't remember anything or anyone other than Theo. *Theo St. James*. Inside my body. My heart.

The metal squeaks beneath me with each of his hard thrusts. He latches onto my neck with his mouth, panting against my skin. I clench my pussy on his cock because I know that'll make him cum faster and he groans.

He drives his hard length home, again and again. A small pinprick of headlights approaches. Theo's eyes widen. "*Shit.* Someone's coming."

"Fuck me faster," I gasp.

"We should stop," he says, even as he drives his hips into me.

I grab onto the back of his neck, pulling him closer. "You can stop after you make me come, Theo."

He groans, biting into my shoulder, humping me like an animal with his favorite toy. My hard nipples chafe against my bra, the approaching headlights making the adrenaline skyrocket, and pleasure bursts through me so unexpectedly, I scream out into the night.

Theo doesn't bother covering my mouth as he finds his own release, groaning and collapsing on top of me.

We break apart as the headlights get dangerously close, scrambling to get back in the car like a game of vehicular musical chairs.

Tires charge up the pavement and we slam our doors just as the Camaro whizzes by. We both break into a fit of laughter, and I want to take a picture of Theo laughing with my mind and imprint it on my brain.

"Holy shit!" he yells. Then he grabs my cheeks and pulls me in for a deep, adrenaline-fueled kiss. "You know what's crazy? It's like I was never really living until I kissed you."

I mirror his smile. "That's how I feel about you. Before this . . ." I wave my finger back and forth between us and try not to let the smile waver. Try to fight the tears. Try not to think about my dead brother in the rearview mirror. "I was . . . I don't know . . . empty. Like this empty cup, and you filled me back up."

"That's dirty, Cass." He gives me a wicked grin.

I swat him with a laugh. "That's not what I meant!"

He grabs the hand that smacked him playfully and presses it

to his lips. My heart melts. "I know. You filled me up too. You make me feel more alive than I ever have. I don't know how I could've gotten through all this without you."

"Me neither," I whisper.

Now that I've gotten a taste of what it's like to have him, I'll never be able to let him go. No one has a stronger gravitational pull than Theo St. James.

∼

THE NEXT MORNING, I trace red lipstick over my mouth to match the blouse that strains across my chest. Too small, but Theo will love it.

Addison texts me.

> You have a guest waiting for you.

I rush downstairs, a huge grin on my face—

Until I spot the guest standing in the foyer. I slow, the smile dimming. "Hey, Mom."

"Hello, Cassie."

Addison and Piper clutch styrofoam cups filled with steaming coffee, both of them wearing uncomfortable smiles.

"We're heading to class," Piper tells me, voice high. "We'll catch up with you later."

With that, they ditch me with my mother. We're used to moms turning up at the sorority house unannounced—a lot of the girls are legacies, which means alumnae drop in on a weekly basis.

But I'm not a legacy and my mom's not an alumna. She discouraged me from rushing because of the cost and the "hazing" that never happened. And she doesn't exactly look thrilled to be here now.

I grab my jacket and lead the way out the door. "Is everything all right?"

She purses her lips, falling into step beside me. "I was going to ask you that."

Here we go. I can't help but let out a sigh. "You're the one who showed up unannounced on my college campus, Mom."

She pulls me by the arm to a halt, forcing me to face her. Her brows are knitted together with frustration and something else. Almost . . . concern. "What's going on with you, Cassie? You've been ignoring my calls, and I haven't seen you in months. You know the van Burens have been named persons of interest?"

"Of course I know that." I lower my voice so anyone passing us on the sidewalk doesn't overhear.

"So you need to be careful around them," Mom whispers. "You didn't take that money they offered you, right?"

Of course I took the money they offered me. I won't tell her about the Mercedes either. Not that I've driven it in days. The thought of getting behind the wheel of Noelle's car makes my stomach churn. "Why would that matter?"

"The van Burens aren't a family you want to be indebted to," she warns.

I sigh. "They're not suspects. And if the police don't find Noelle soon, I will." I have to. I can't stand this sickening feeling in my gut anymore. "Now I've really got to get to class."

"Why don't you call me, Cassie? Why don't you tell me anything anymore?" Mom's eyes turn glossy and she covers her trembling mouth with her fingers, her voice watery. "I feel like I've lost both my children."

My muscles go rigid. She's the one who stopped talking to me. The one who forgot I existed after we lost Hunter. So I finally say the thing I've been wanting to say to her for months. "And I feel like I lost my whole family the day my brother died."

CHAPTER THIRTY-TWO

NOELLE

"Beau?" I whisper his name in the dark, unable to fall asleep.

He snores softly beside me.

I haven't been able to get my mind off my parents or my friends. Now that I'm not trapped in a basement and wondering if I'll survive to see tomorrow, the guilt from staying here of my own free will has been gnawing at me.

I try to nudge Beau awake one more time, but he's out cold. I slink out of bed and don't bother changing. I'll be back before he realizes I'm gone.

At the door, I slip on my shoes and Beau's leather jacket. I open the door as quietly as I can and hurry to the sidewalk. The rain has blessedly stopped, the only sound the slosh of my shoes through shallow puddles. I haven't been outside since that day I ran into the woods, and I didn't realize how much I've missed it. The fresh air, the cool breeze against my skin, the wide-open, midnight sky full of stars and possibility.

Down the empty sidewalk, the occasional streetlamp lights my way. By the time fat drops of rain begin to fall from the sky, I reach my house. Home. The towering three-story Victorian with a dark, pointed roof that juts into the sky and looms over the rest of the property like Ursula, waiting to destroy any ships that come too close. The night spring air mixed with the moisture of the light rain pierces through Beau's jacket like ice. I wrap my arms around my torso just as I spot my parents through the kitchen window. Smiling. Laughing.

My heart sinks.

They disappear momentarily until the front door opens. Angel leads four people out the door. Piper, Addison, Cassie, and Theo.

Piper clutches Angel's leash in both hands like my ancient Lab might pull her off her feet.

I can't hear anything they're saying from this distance, but they wave to my parents, smiling. They head for my car, and my parents shut the door.

Addison opens up the back door, and they encourage Angel to hop into the car. She stands there, tail wagging until Theo picks her up and lifts her into the backseat.

My stomach drops, tears pricking my eyes.

They're taking my Mercedes. They're taking my *dog*.

I've been gone for two months, and my parents are already giving away my belongings. Giving away pieces of me like they know I'm not coming back.

Like they don't want me back. They've already moved on.

The blow crushes my chest. Noelle van Buren, long forgotten. I'm standing right here, and none of them see me.

Because they're not looking for me anymore.

Addison and Piper climb into the backseat. Cassie heads for the passenger's seat, but not before she and Theo brush hands and exchange intimate smiles.

Everyone's happier now that I'm gone.

∽

BEAU

IN THE MIDDLE of the night, I jump awake. The hairs on the back of my neck stand up. Something's wrong. I search in the dark for an intruder, but there's no one. I'm alone with the shadows.

Noelle isn't beside me.

I fly out of bed, heading for the bathroom. That must be what I heard—the bathroom door shutting. But it's wide open, the room dark.

Downstairs. That's where she is. Got hungry for a midnight snack. My shoulder smacks against the wall, echoing with a loud *thud* in the silence.

The whole downstairs is dark.

I race down the steps and throw open the basement door, leaping halfway down the staircase to see if she's got a light on. Couldn't sleep and decided to come down here, draw what's in her head.

She's not here either.

She's not in this house.

She's. Not. Fucking. Here.

I pound back up the stairs, jerking the curtains apart and peering outside. There's no way someone could've gotten in here and taken her. Sure, I got in, but someone like me knows how to stop people like me.

She left on her own. Without a word.

She's fucking gone. She was just losing her mind on my cock hours ago, smiling with that pretty little mouth up at me, and she left.

She told me I could trust her. Got me to untie her. Convinced me she was falling for me, despite everything, and she slipped out the second my guard was down.

All of it a fucking mind game.

I yank my boots on and lunge for my leather jacket—

Gone.

She took it. A piece of evidence against the man who kidnapped her and locked her away.

I head for the door, not giving a fuck if it's cold enough to freeze my balls off because the blood boiling in my veins is hot enough to burn down hell itself.

But I stop in front of the door. Someone's hurrying up the driveway in the dark.

A blonde, swimming in my leather jacket.

My princess.

I brace my arm against the door, head falling while my chest heaves, breaths rattling from my lungs. She came back.

Thank fuck.

She came back.

Now I need to show her she can never leave me like that again.

CHAPTER THIRTY-THREE

THEO

"Is it bad to say I'm excited we're going to have a dog in Chi Omega?" Addison asks from the backseat.

Piper pets Angel, grinning, until her eyes widen. "Do you think they're going to get arrested?"

"That must be why they're giving us Noelle's dog," Addison says.

"They just don't want to take care of her." Guilt rushes through me. Noelle doesn't have the best relationship with her parents, especially her mom, but they've always been nice to me. I don't want to bad mouth them, but neither of them has the time to look after an aging dog.

"They're done with Noelle," Addison declares. "They don't want to deal with anything that was hers. That's why they gave Cassie her Mercedes."

"They didn't give me her Mercedes," Cass corrects. "They're just letting me borrow it until she comes back."

"It's been two months," Addison points out. "You still think she's coming back?"

Cass's eyes turn glassy. "I think I'm going to do my best to bring her back."

I squeeze her shoulder to comfort her without thinking of

Addison and Piper watching us in the backseat. But Piper's hand joins mine, rubbing Cass's arm, and neither of them seems to think anything of it.

We're still getting away with this. Still keeping this huge thing between us, a secret from everyone we know. I'm amazed her friends haven't suspected anything but grateful after that threat from my father. Even if the police wouldn't come after us, he might.

"I'm sorry, Cassie, but I really don't think this is a rescue mission anymore," Addison says.

Cass sniffles in the silence. Piper rubs Angel's head until she whispers to Addison, "What do you think they did to her?"

"I think we're going to find out what they did to her soon enough."

CHAPTER THIRTY-FOUR

NOELLE

*B*ack at the abandoned house, I sneak through the door and up the stairs into the silent bedroom. My eyes are still adjusting to the darkness, so I fumble a bit climbing back into bed, hoping Beau doesn't wake.

As soon as my head hits the pillow, the door creaks shut. Locks.

I sit straight up, Beau a looming figure approaching slowly.

He's up. He's been waiting for me.

My heart stops.

"Where've you been?" His voice is low, ghoulish. Like he's haunting this house.

"I tried to wake you up," I say quickly. "I couldn't sleep. I needed some fresh air."

"Don't fucking lie to me," he growls. I haven't heard him like this since he first brought me here.

I wring my hands together. "I'm not lying."

He comes closer and closer until he's a dark shadow towering over me. "Right. So you weren't headed straight for the cops to tell them where you've been the past two months?"

"No!" My eyes nearly bug out of my head. "I wasn't going to

tell them, I swear. I went to my parents' house. I missed them. I just wanted to see them—"

He whirls, punching the wall behind him.

The ear-splitting crack in the silence makes me jump, heart leaping to my throat.

"So you leave *me* for people who don't even give a shit about you?" Beau shouts.

Even though I know in my heart I can trust him, that he would never hurt me, I retreat. I'm watching his compassion for me unravel right before my eyes. And there's nothing I can do to stop it.

I don't know how, but he knows. He knows that he's the only one left in this world who still gives a damn about me.

I screwed up. I should've known not to sneak out. I should've waited until he woke up, told him what I wanted to do, and he could've come with me.

He thought I was abandoning him, just like his mother. Thought I was betraying him and turning him in. That I've never cared about him at all. That everything between us has been fake, a ploy to get him to release me. So I could stab him in the back.

Beau drops his hands on the mattress on either side of me, leaning dangerously close. "I gave you the option to leave. You chose to stay."

"I'm still choosing to stay." My voice shakes. "I want to be with you."

"Yeah." He straightens, mouth forming a flat line. "I'm going to make sure you don't forget that."

He drags me up by the hair, tears blurring my vision. Before my mind can catch up, he's yanking my shirt over my head and my pants down to the floor. He roughly pushes my panties to the side and shoves two fingers inside me. I cry out, shocked at the slickness already waiting for him there.

He pulls my hair, exposing my neck, and bites down. I whimper, more pain mixing with pleasure than usual but somehow not too much. Still making me want more of him.

His fingers move inside me in long, hard thrusts as he sucks on my neck so hard, I dig my nails into his arms. My panties grind against my clit with every movement, making me wetter and wetter on his fingers.

He shoves me down onto the bed, flattening me onto my stomach. His clothes are off in seconds, and he climbs onto the bed, lifting me up by the hips. I barely have enough time to catch my breath, to brace myself before he rams into me, making my pussy throb around him.

I cry out, my throat already growing hoarse. When he slams inside me again, pleasure like I've never felt before builds up all the way from my toes.

"You want to run away? You think you aren't going to miss this?" He grabs my hair, pulling my head back until I'm pressed up against him. "You only come like this on my cock. No one else can do this to you."

I back up into him so he knows I want this. Want him. I wasn't planning on leaving him. He smacks my ass hard, making me wince. "I don't want anyone else!"

"Prove it." After one final slam to the hilt, he jerks out of me, making me gasp. He lays on his back, arms behind his head. "Gag on my dick."

I pull my hair over my shoulders and he grips it in his fist but doesn't push or guide me. I wrap my lips around the head of his cock, taking him in slowly, keeping my tongue flat to stroke him all the way down. He doesn't make a sound.

I don't know how to read him right now. Unsure if this is a warning or a punishment or a reminder.

When I reach the tip again, I swirl my tongue around. He glares at me, gray eyes stormy and brows drawn low, scar crinkled. When I open my mouth to suck him down again, he thrusts into me.

I sputter when his cock hits the back of my throat, eyes instantly watering. But he doesn't give me a chance to recover. He keeps my head in place with both hands, jerking his hips up into my throat again and making me gag.

"That's it, princess. Take it like a good girl." He dips his head back, eyes falling shut. "Just like that. Such a good girl."

The tip keeps hitting my throat, and his cock fills my mouth, wrenching my jaw with every pump.

When I gag again, terrified that bile might come up this time, I jerk out of his grasp, coughing, heart hammering so hard, I feel my pulse jumping in my neck.

He leaves me on the bed, sputtering and gasping for air, and disappears from the room.

"Beau?" The word a strangled gasp.

Silence. Until he reappears with a chair.

The chair he tied me to in the basement. When he held a knife to my throat.

My heart stops. "You're tying me up?"

"You said you wouldn't run. I told you what would happen if you did. I warned you I would make you scream. Sit."

I do as I'm told, leaving the bed on shaking legs and taking a seat on the chair in the middle of the room. He binds my wrists together behind the back of the chair and my ankles to the legs.

Spread eagle and naked.

"Beau—"

"This is how you'll prove you trust me." His gray eyes are stony. "That you'll stay."

He doesn't bother waiting for my response. He grabs the crimson silk ribbon and covers my eyes.

I expect him to shove his cock inside me next, but a soft, slick sensation strokes up my pussy. His tongue. He laps between my legs and sucks on my clit, almost violently. With my arms and legs tied down, I can't move, even as I ache to move away from the overwhelming pleasure, to lessen the pressure from his tongue.

But he sweeps his hands under my ass, bringing me up to his mouth and taking me in deeper. I cry out and he thrusts his tongue inside me, not caring.

"I'm going to make you come over and over," he growls. "Until you're a sopping, simpering mess. Until you can't even speak. And then I'm going to fuck you senseless. You won't remember your own fucking name, princess. But you'll never forget mine."

CHAPTER THIRTY-FIVE

BEAU

My tongue strokes up her pussy, her thighs already trembling around my head.

The amount of pleasure I'll inflict on her will be torture. She'll regret what she did tonight. Regret the moment she thought she'd be better off without me. Thought she'd leave the man who saved her. Who makes her come so hard, she sees stars.

But she'll never regret meeting me.

I swirl my tongue around her clit, salivating at her desperate writhing as I dig my fingers harder into her ass.

I love her like this. Tied down, spread eagle. At my mercy. No place to hide. Nowhere to run. She trusts me, deep down. Even if she can't convince the rational part of her brain of that yet. That's why she let me knot that rope around her wrists and ankles. That's why she didn't push me away when I ripped her clothes off or try to escape when I fucked her mouth.

Her moans are music to my ears, and I lick at her clit hard until she starts to shudder. The movement that always precipitates her orgasm. When she cries out, pulling at her restraints, I dive in with my tongue, feeling her pussy clench around it over and over. God, she tastes so good.

One down. Three more to go.

She collapses against the chair and I almost chuckle. She has no idea what she's in for. "That was just the beginning, princess," I murmur between her legs.

"Beau," she moans, but she doesn't ask me to stop. She doesn't want me to.

With this one, I'm taking my time.

I slide a finger in, her pussy already soaked. She tightens around me and hisses in a sharp breath. I lap at her clit and she whimpers, trying to pull away. Still sensitive from the orgasm. "Don't pull away," I growl, and suck on her clit.

She cries out, but she stops trying to escape my mouth. She lets me take what I want. What's mine. My girl's a quick learner.

I go back to licking her gently, thrusting my finger in and out slowly. Letting her come down from the first orgasm before the buildup to the second. Next time, I won't be so generous.

When she's finally relaxed around my finger, I slide another in. We groan together. She's so fucking tight. My cock twitches, wanting inside her. But she's not getting that yet.

"Fuck," she moans, hands straining for my hair, but she's not escaping that knot.

"I know, baby," I tell her, before wrapping my lips around her clit and sucking her into my mouth. She arches into me, whimpering like she already can't take it. "Be a good girl and come for me."

"Yes, Beau." My name on her lips like a prayer.

I growl my approval and curl my fingers, hitting that spot that always makes her eyes widen with surprise pleasure.

"Oh my god," she hisses.

"Yes, I am, princess. Get ready to worship me with your tongue."

She's on the brink of another orgasm, and I slide my fingers out of her. She whimpers, bucking her hips and aching for the release.

I loosen the knots around her ankles and wrists. "Lay on the bed. Leave the blindfold on." She shuffles until she reaches the bed and does as she's told. "Grab the headboard."

I tie her wrists and feet to the bed this time. I climb on the mattress with her, and she's squirming, not sure what I'm going to do next.

"Now open that pretty little mouth."

Her lips part for me and I slide my cock in. *Fuck*, she feels good. Especially when she closes her lips and sucks in her cheeks. I fuck her face, savoring the feel of her tongue caressing the underside of my shaft. She takes it just fine until I start driving my cock into her throat like I'm doing pushups, the bed squeaking. Every little gag makes me want to cum in her mouth and make her swallow every drop, but I'm cumming in her pussy tonight.

I slide out of her, cock dripping with her saliva. She gasps and coughs until my tongue is between her legs again. I stroke up and down slowly, over and over, bringing her back to the brink but never allowing her to go over the edge.

"Please," she begs. I want to hear her beg for me every night.

"Please what, princess?"

"Please make me come."

I slide two fingers inside her and curl them, hitting that sweet spot inside her hard.

"Agh!" she moans.

I suck her clit into my mouth and then she's shuddering again, thighs clamping over my ears as she cries out. Her body twists and turns, but she can't go anywhere. Can't escape me or the pleasure I drive through every cell of her body.

"Good, baby. Only two more to go."

"What?" Behind her blindfold, I'm sure her eyes are bugging out of her head. "I can't come again."

"It's not a matter of *can*," I say simply. "You will. You'll come as many times as I say you will. I don't give a fuck how long it takes. You have no idea how patient I can be. And don't bother faking one because I know what you look and feel like when you come. I'll add ten more to the list if you pretend."

She whimpers.

"This one's going to be really fun, princess."

She stiffens when I start moving on the bed, unsure what to anticipate from me next.

I hook my feet over the headboard by her arms. "Open up, princess."

"Please don't make me gag," she begs.

"That's up to you. Suck hard or I'll have to fuck your throat."

She opens her mouth wide for me and I slide my cock in, her tongue rubbing against the top of my shaft this time. I groan, loving the sight of her perfect lips wrapped around my hard length. I thrust in and out slowly, careful not to go too deep. Yet.

I kiss my way down her body until I get back between her legs and pull her clit between my teeth.

My cock in her mouth muffles her cry, sending the reverberations down my shaft all the way to my fingers. I let out a long groan. "You're gonna make me cum down your throat if you're not careful, baby."

She tries to stay quiet while I nip at her clit again before sucking it into my mouth. I suck hard, like she's my ice cream and we're in hell. She's shaking beneath me, gasping around my cock while she tries to suck in air.

This one's taking longer, like I suspected. A harder climb to get up to the crest of pleasure. I don't give a fuck. If she wants to make me go at her all night, I will. I'll sleep when I'm dead.

The suction of her mouth starts to slacken. Her jaw's getting sore. "The longer you take to come, the longer my cock's in your mouth."

She simpers but keeps bobbing her head, the beautiful wet sounds of my cock sliding on her tongue filling my ears.

I press her thighs against my head, working her so hard my jaw aches, and she stiffens. "That's it, princess. Come for me."

I suck at her clit as hard as I can until she cries out around my cock, writhing and fighting her restraints with every last bit of energy she has. I thrust into her mouth, making her sputter through her orgasm. The hottest fucking thing I've ever heard.

One more to go.

CHAPTER THIRTY-SIX
NOELLE

*A*fter the third orgasm, I'm drained. Limbs weak, mouth dry, eyes leaking beneath the blindfold. His cock is out of my mouth, but his tongue still licks between my legs. At this point, the orgasms almost feel like punishment. "Beau," I moan. "No more. Please."

"You ready for me to fuck you, princess?"

"Yes."

"Too bad you're going to come again on my cock."

I stiffen at the promise laced with a threat. I can't come again. My body is too exhausted, my heart on the verge of giving out entirely. I can only hope he fucks me hard and cums fast.

Beau settles between my legs, rubbing his tip against my clit. My legs jerk and I try to clench my thighs together, but I can't escape the restraints. "Please," I beg.

"Please what?"

"Please fuck me."

He nudges at my entrance, and I brace for a hard, fast thrust. Instead, he slides in so achingly slow, I almost sob. He pulls back slowly, back in even slower. When his thumb lands on my clit and rubs, I bite my lip and whimper. "No more," I repeat.

"Aww, princess." His hips pick up speed and so does his

thumb, the pleasure overwhelming, and I groan. "You've gotta come for me. I want to feel your walls clenching on my cock. Or I'll just have to fuck you all night."

He pulls out of me suddenly, making me gasp, and his mouth is between my legs again. *No*. I need him to finish. I need this sweet torment to end.

"Fuck me," I cry. "Please."

He penetrates me with his tongue, even though he knows that's not what I meant. His tongue and thumb work me, the familiar tingling sensation inching up my limbs despite my exhausted heart.

Though it's a slow climb, he brings me closer and closer to the edge. If I wasn't already lying down, another orgasm would make me collapse. I might pass out.

Suddenly, the restraints around my ankles disappear. Then my wrists. But my blindfold stays on.

I'm about to reach up and pull it off when Beau yanks me down the bed. "Come on my cock, princess," he orders, before slamming into me.

I cry out, and he keeps fucking me, hard and fast. My tits bounce wildly, and all I can do is dig my nails into his arms and hold on for dear life as he slides us across the mattress.

Every ram of his cock into me makes my pussy throb, the ache of pleasure impossibly mounting. My limbs are drained, heart exhausted but pounding, and every inch of me is soaked with my own sweat and wetness. His pelvis hits my clit with each thrust, and I wail every time, unable to take the sensation any longer.

He thrusts into me so hard, the top of my body tips off the bed. But he doesn't pull me back up. He leaves me hanging there, pumping in and out of me while his thumb rubs chaotic circles over my clit, making me scream at the overwhelming sensitivity and pleasure.

"I'm not stopping until you fucking come, princess," he shouts.

Stars explode behind the blindfold as my orgasm barrels

through me, draining me of every last dreg of energy. I clench over and over around his cock, head growing light and mind spinning. The scream rips through my throat, so hoarse I don't know when I'll be able to speak again.

Beau lets out a long "*Fuuuck*" over my screams, not caring that I'm halfway off the bed as he fucks me relentlessly.

Until his cock throbs inside me, over and over, longer than it ever has, as he empties himself in me.

When his panting finally slows, he hauls me by the hips back up onto the mattress. I can't move as he puts the restraints on me again. Can't speak the words to protest.

"Why did you leave me, Noelle?" he whispers.

I'm too exhausted to answer. My lips incapable of forming the words. *I didn't leave you. I came back.*

He kisses between my legs, making me cry out one last time before he leaves me spread eagle, naked, and alone.

CHAPTER THIRTY-SEVEN

CASSIE

Theo's up to bat, and the three of us cheer for him from the bleachers. When the ball sails across the diamond straight for him, he smacks it high in the air and into the outfield. A couple of guys scramble for it, but he's already sprinting for first base without bothering to watch where the ball lands. Both of the players miss and Theo manages to make it to second. I jump up and cheer for him along with everyone else, but I'm the loudest.

Once he makes it to home base, Addison stands. "Let's go grab food."

We head for the concession stand and pass Colin, loaded up with two hotdogs in each hand.

Addison narrows her eyes at his back. "What the hell? He's just going to ignore you? Did something happen between you two?"

"What?" Oh, right. I told them I've been hooking up with Colin. The first name that popped into my head when they asked who I've been sleeping with. "Everything's fine. I told you we're keeping things quiet, remember?"

"Theo's not even around." Piper's eyes are wide, pitying. "He should at least say hi to you. You deserve better than that, Cassie."

"Hey, asshole!" Addison shouts, and I want to slap a hand over her mouth.

Colin turns around, and it's official: I want to die. He lifts a brow and glances around. "Who's the asshole?"

"You are! What, she's good enough to fuck but not good enough to talk to? You're scum."

"Addison—"

He laughs. "I don't know what the hell you're talking about."

Addison folds her arms. "Don't play dumb. Tell him, Cassie. He doesn't get to treat you like shit."

Colin turns to me. "We fucked?"

The tension boiling in my veins comes to a head and I burst. "No, okay? We didn't. I lied. Colin's not the guy."

He gives a low whistle and turns on his heel. "Sounds like drama I don't want any part of."

The concern on Piper's face deepens. "Why would you lie about that?"

"Who's the guy then?" Addison asks.

I bite my lip. Theo and his dad want us to keep this quiet, but Addison and Piper are my friends. They won't say anything. I can't keep lying to them anymore. "Theo."

Piper gives a horrified gasp and Addison hisses, "You're not serious."

"It's not as bad as you think," I sputter. "He and Noelle aren't together anymore. They broke up the day she went missing."

"Oh my god." Piper covers her mouth.

Addison's eyes narrow. "The day she went *missing*? And you *fucked* him? You realize how fucking guilty that makes him sound, right? He gets dumped and she conveniently disappears the same day? And he's been keeping the breakup a secret, pretending like he's still her doting boyfriend? I hope you told the police."

"He broke up with her. You're making it sound way worse than it is."

Disgust contorts Addison's mouth. "Right. I'm sure that's exactly what he told you."

I open my mouth to protest, but Piper cuts me off. "You think that's the news she was going to tell us? That Theo broke up with her? Oh my god. And he did something to her before she could tell us!"

I grip Piper's shoulders. "Stop. You guys are jumping to conclusions. We know Theo. We know he wouldn't hurt her."

Addison steps between us. "You *think* you know Theo because you've fucked him. But you're clueless, Cassie. I thought I knew you too—I thought you actually wanted to find the girl you call your best friend. But instead, you're covering for her ex."

"Please don't say anything, okay?" I plead. "You're wrong about him."

Addison shakes her head. "He has you totally brainwashed. I just hope for your sake he doesn't kill you too."

CHAPTER THIRTY-EIGHT
NOELLE

When I wake up, I'm no longer tied down. I'm curled up, Beau's arm draped around me. Holding me. Protecting me.

Through the window behind us, the sun is shining its first rays. I scoot away from him, making him stir.

"Princess," he murmurs sleepily.

"I didn't leave you." Tears blur my vision as my voice cracks. "I came back. I meant it when I said you can trust me. I wasn't going to tell anyone about you. I don't want to lose you." The words I longed to say to him before.

He sits up, wanting to reach out to me, to get closer, but he stays still like I'm a skittish animal and any wrong move could send me running. "You did. I'm so fucking happy you did." When he finally takes my hands in his, he doesn't squeeze or pull. He holds me like a delicate butterfly. "I panicked. I lost it. I thought you turned on me. I thought you were leaving me. I'm . . ." He swallows. ". . . sorry."

I give his hands a gentle squeeze. "I understand why. But you have to trust me. I'm not your mother. I'm not going to leave you or hurt you. I'm your princess."

His eyes fall shut and he shudders. "Yeah. You fucking are."

His gaze is on me again, and he brushes my hair behind my ear. "Forgive me?"

"Trust me?"

He tips his forehead against mine and presses my hand to his heart. "With my fucking life."

"Then I forgive you."

We stay like that, embracing until he finally pulls away to draw the curtains while I crawl under the covers.

"We should buy this house. When it's safe. Make it our own," I tell him.

Beau grins, slipping under the covers with me. "Yeah? What would you change?"

"First, I'd get blackout curtains."

He presses his lips to my bare shoulder. "Mmm." The word hums deliciously along my skin. "Then we'd never have to leave the bed."

"Except to take baths." When he raises an eyebrow, I add, "Together."

He nods like that's better. "And we'd order all our food and have it delivered right to our room."

"And I can paint on the walls."

"Perfect." He catches my jaw and kisses me, tongue prying me wide to claim me. Claim what's his. I moan and melt beneath him.

His mouth moves across every inch of my body, sucking, licking, nibbling. This time feels different. Like a prayer. Worship.

I'm no longer just the princess in the basement he can't resist —I'm the woman he wants. The woman he's scared to lose.

I'm scared to lose him too.

But I push those thoughts aside when his tongue lands between my legs. His strokes are long, luxuriating. This time, he's giving me pleasure, not wringing it from me.

When my thighs start to shake, he grips them hard, his fingers sinking into my flesh. I'm no longer skin and bone. Gone are the stick-straight legs that made Mother happy, that made me beautiful in her eyes.

Now, I have thighs that touch. And the way Beau is massaging them, it's safe to say he loves them too.

For the first time in maybe my whole life, I love my body. I love the way I feel in it. Especially the way Beau makes me feel in it.

When he sucks on my clit, I drop my head back and groan, pulling at his hair that was made for this. He hums his approval, and the vibration makes me hiss. Wetness pools between my legs, and when he slides a finger in, it's his turn to groan.

He keeps licking and sucking, gradually pumping his finger inside me harder and harder as I get closer to the edge. When I finally go over, heart hammering wildly, he doesn't back off. He keeps eating me, not done with me yet.

I'm soaked, the sound of his tongue penetrating me turning obscene. He fucks me with his tongue while his thumb rubs at my clit, and when pleasure barrels through me again, it's so sweet, my eyes water.

By the time he straightens, I'm a limp, whimpering, wet mess beneath him, but it's not like last time. Not making me come over and over so I regret leaving. This time is fully for my pleasure. To show me how much he wants me here, in this bed. With him.

His gray eyes are intense, trained on mine as he leans over me. "I would walk on glass for you. Rip anyone limb from limb for looking at you wrong. Protect you. Worship you. Whatever you want, I'll give it to you. You want a new art studio? I'll build it. You want to come seven times a day? I'll be on my knees before you. I'm yours, princess. Every inch of me. My entire black and tarnished soul is yours."

A tear slips down my cheek. "And mine is yours."

Just before he slips inside me, he breathes, "I love you."

Then he slides in to the hilt.

I gasp, clutching at him. When I got here, he didn't seem like somebody who was capable of falling in love. He was little more than a beast, terrifying and merciless. Unfeeling.

He's nothing like I thought he was.

But sometimes, I do enjoy the beast.

Like now. When he slams inside me, driving pleasure through every inch of my body.

"Did you say you love me?" I gasp.

He rams inside me again, both of us moaning. "Yes."

He loves me. Beau Grayson loves me.

"I love you too."

His lips curve up in a cocky smirk. "I know, princess."

Then he fucks me harder and faster than he ever has, making the pleasure in my limbs build like a song to its crescendo, until I come so hard, my vision goes dark.

CHAPTER THIRTY-NINE

THEO

"Thank you for coming in today, Mr. St. James." Officer Garcia shuffles papers together in a file, opening up her notebook and grabbing her pen like we're in a business meeting, not an interrogation room.

When the police called this time, Dad insisted on sending my lawyer with me. *Mrs. Lockwood is the second-best lawyer in the state of North Carolina after me.*

She looks like she can't be older than thirty-five, but her lips are pursed and one glance is enough to tell you she means business.

Officer Garcia folds her hands together on the table in front of her. "I'm just going to get right to it. We asked you to come down today because we don't believe you've told us everything about your relationship with Miss van Buren."

Mrs. Lockwood crosses her legs and sighs. "Please ask my client whatever direct questions you have. We don't have time to waste, and neither do you. A girl is missing."

Garcia shoots a glance at my lawyer. Obviously wishing it was just the two of us again. "At the time of Miss van Buren's disappearance, were you still in a relationship?"

Shit. I rub my palms against my jeans, suddenly sweaty like I've stepped in a sauna.

There's no point in lying anymore. She wouldn't be asking if she didn't already know the truth. "Uh. No."

Garcia nods once. Lockwood shifts uncomfortably. Dad must not have told her this bombshell was coming. I couldn't have predicted this either.

"Right. So did your affair with Miss Sinclair begin before or after your ex-girlfriend went missing?"

The words drop in the room like a rock, silencing all of us. Both women's eyes are on me. Garcia's accusatory; Lockwood's horrified. She didn't expect to have the rug pulled out from under her today.

Neither did I.

My chest constricts, air struggling to reach my lungs. How did they find out about me and Cass? Did we slip when we thought no one was watching?

"Don't bother trying to deny it," Garcia says simply. "We know about your relationship."

Lockwood holds up a hand. "Hang on. What could Theo's relationship with Miss Sinclair possibly have to do with Miss van Buren?"

Garcia scowls at her. "You know as well as I do that we have to look at everyone close to Miss van Buren and their potential motives."

"Motives for what? My client had nothing to do with his girlfriend's disappearance. He's an honor student, a scholar, a division-one athlete—"

"Yes, we're well aware of your client's many accomplishments," Garcia deadpans. "But that doesn't mean he didn't cheat on Miss van Buren or harm her in some way to be with another woman."

"I didn't cheat on her." Both their eyes flash to me, at the rough edge to my voice. I pull in a deep breath to calm myself.

"Noelle and I broke up the afternoon she went missing. Cass and I didn't get together until weeks after."

Garcia's eyes narrow. "So you mean to tell me that you and Miss van Buren broke up the same day she was reported missing? Even though you've been claiming since her disappearance to be her boyfriend. Is that correct?"

Now I know why my father wanted me to keep quiet. She's already looking at me like I'm guilty.

I glance to Lockwood for guidance, to get me out of this line of questioning, but she stays silent. "Yes."

Officer Garcia leans back, arms folded. "Did your breakup stem from your feelings for Miss Sinclair?"

"Who made these allegations?" Lockwood cuts in.

"Two of her sorority sisters, close friends, came forward with the information."

Addison and Piper. Fuck. I thought they were oblivious to us. We must've screwed up. Slipped when we thought we were being discreet.

Except the only people who know about the breakup are me, Noelle, Dad, and Cass.

Cass.

No. She wouldn't have told them. Not after my father's warning. Not after we agreed to keep it to ourselves until Noelle came home.

"So hearsay." Lockwood rolls her eyes and stands. "Congratulations, Officer. You have nothing. My client and I will be leaving now."

But by the way my lawyer guides me out the door, nails digging into my back, they have something. A whole shitload of it.

CASSIE

After class, I head right for the baseball field to cheer for Theo at practice. He's had to ice his leg today, so we didn't get to meet up for lunch and we haven't gotten to see each other since yesterday.

Addison and Piper grabbed lunch without me. They've been avoiding me since I admitted the truth about me and Theo—they think I'm the shitty friend who's choosing Theo over Noelle. That I've placed my trust in the wrong person. The guilty person.

But I know Theo. He had nothing to do with Noelle's disappearance.

Gray clouds move in fast from the west, carrying with them the threat of rain. The guys will play anyway, even in a torrential downpour. Then Theo and I can peel off our soaked clothes in the back of his Audi and fuck each other warm again.

A few of the baseball players pass me on their way to the field. I search their faces for—

"Cass."

I whirl, a huge grin on my face, ready to throw my arms around him.

Theo's features are grim. Stony. My stomach gives a sickening churn. "We need to talk."

He pulls me back toward the locker rooms, away from the meandering line of his teammates heading for the baseball diamond, and leans against the wall, arms crossed and eyes anywhere but on me.

"What's going on?"

"You told Addison and Piper we're together. And about the breakup."

My mouth goes dry. I try to swallow down the lump in my throat, but I can't. "I'm so sorry. I didn't want to, but I told them Colin is the guy I've been seeing and they confronted him in public, and I didn't have a choice—"

"Why did you have to tell them anything?" He scrubs a hand

down his face. "Dad was right. This makes us look bad. Everyone always suspects the ex, and now they know we're sleeping together." Finally, his gaze lands on me, and I regret ever wishing it would. I've never seen this look in his eyes before. I don't recognize him. "The police questioned me and basically accused me of being involved."

Fuck. So the news has reached the police.

I grab Theo's hand, desperate not to let him pull away from me too. I never meant for Theo to get wrapped up in all of this. He doesn't deserve the suspicion, the interrogations. "No one who actually knows you would ever believe you'd be capable of hurting anybody."

He isn't looking at me anymore. His eyes are on the field, where his coach is shouting instructions. A muscle in his jaw ticks. "That's the problem, though, isn't it? They don't know me. And they're going to waste time looking at me, trying to pull answers out of me I don't have, and Noelle will still be missing."

The gray clouds have completely blotted out the sun now, and a raindrop hits my cheek. "We'll figure this out together." My voice cracks. "I love you, Theo. I'm . . . I'm in love with you."

My heart has never hammered this hard in my life. Any second, it'll burst. Unless I hear those words from Theo's mouth.

When he pulls his hand from my grasp, I know I won't.

The rejection hurts worse than when he asked my best friend to homecoming. When he asked her to be his girlfriend instead of me.

A new, deeper wound to replace that old scar.

He keeps his eyes on his cleats. "I fucking love you too, Cass. A lot." Hearing his admission aloud makes my chest squeeze painfully when I know there's a *but* coming. "I've never felt for anyone what I feel for you. But I trusted you, and you broke that trust. I didn't want anything getting in the way of finding Noelle, and this has turned into a huge mess. I think we need to take a break for a while. Until she's back. She's our friend, and she's one of the best people I know. We need to focus on her right now. That's what we should've been doing all along."

He's breaking up with me. I finally got Theo St. James, in secret, in the shadows, and now I'm losing him before I even got a chance to call him my boyfriend. We didn't get a first date. We didn't get to meet each other's parents during an awkward group dinner or take cute selfies to post on our Instagrams or disgust our friends with how much we love each other.

I barely got him, and I've already lost him.

He turns to leave, and at the sight of his back to me, at the sight of him walking away from me for the last time, I break.

"Noelle isn't one of the best people you know," I call. "She killed Hunter."

CHAPTER FORTY

NOELLE

*B*eau left his phone on the kitchen island. I sent him to the grocery store with a special request for the marshmallows my father would sneak me when Mother had me on yet another diet before a shoot or a pageant.

Of course Beau has a passcode on his phone. I guess his birthday. Nope. Then the usual string of numbers—1-2-3-4, 1-1-1-1, 0-0-0-0. None of them work.

I'm stumped. I can always wait for him to get home and—

Wait.

I type in 1-2-2-8. My birthday.

The screen unlocks.

I smile. Did he change his passcode to my birthday before or after he brought me here? Before or after we fell in love? I don't care. I'm just glad he did.

I go to Instagram first. My mother has been living on social media, posting daily updates about how I'm still missing, they're searching for me, and our family isn't involved in my disappearance. My heart lodges in my throat. I watched her send my friends off with my car and my dog, but maybe it's not what I assumed. Maybe they really are still searching for me. Maybe they do miss me.

The comments are a mix of people who know her and support her and strangers who blame her. Who claim it's suspicious that we had a fight the same night I went missing.

I clutch the phone hard in my hand, the metal digging into my flesh. She hasn't been the perfect mother. I can't say she's even always been a good mother. But she'd never do what they're accusing her of, and I hate that I'm hiding out here with Beau while they're hurling these disgusting accusations at her.

My friends are still posting the occasional selfie with me, but the posts have become increasingly infrequent, interspersed more and more with their everyday lives.

Except for Cassie. She hasn't posted at all in a week, and she's turned off comments. I freeze. Why?

I go to TikTok and find Cassie's profile. Her follower count has jumped up from a few hundred to over two hundred thousand. Holy shit. Before I went missing, she hadn't posted any videos at all. But now she has countless videos, all of them about me.

One of her pinned videos includes her face and a picture of the two of us in the background, the words: *Help me find my best friend* in big letters beneath our feet. This one has five hundred thousand views. Video after video of her asking people to help spread the word.

The comments on her most recent videos are scathing, everyone tearing her apart with the usual slurs. Whore, slut, bitch.

U literally became famous bc of your missing bff and u go and fuck her bf?

So I guess she and Theo are officially together now, and everyone hates them for it. Guilt washes over me. No one would give a shit about them dating if I wasn't a missing person. They shouldn't be publicly bashed for falling in love.

I need to go home. Right everything. Tell everyone the truth. Or at least, some version of the truth so I don't lose Beau in the process.

His phone buzzes in my hand. The text is about a car insurance payment, and I try to swipe it away but accidentally click. I backtrack to his messages and spot an unsaved number at the top.

> You'll get the rest of your money when they find her body.

My heart stops.
I click on the message and scroll up.

> Is it done?
>
> You need to plant the body soon.
>
> Let me know when she's dead.

These were sent two days after Beau took me. There's only one *she* these messages could be referring to.

Whoever this is, they're asking if Beau killed me. If he planted my body.

Someone else knew Beau was bringing me here to kill me.

They paid him to do it.

Heart pounding in my ears, I stare at the string of numbers that almost looks familiar. The same area code as mine and Beau's. They must be from Westbrook.

I search the number on Instagram. In the seconds it takes for the app to load, my stomach churns so violently, I'm afraid I'm going to be sick.

A girl pops up with a bright, smiling face.

Cassie.

CHAPTER FORTY-ONE

CASSIE

I'd been suspicious of the van Burens since Noelle's father claimed Michael took a joyride in their Bentley. I'd been to the van Burens' house enough times to know Michael wasn't the kind of guy who stole his boss's expensive sports car, even for a night. He was an honest, hardworking man who broke his back—almost literally—saving up for an expensive private investigator who could track down his son.

He certainly wasn't the kind of man who'd hit someone with a car and leave them to die on the side of the road.

Noelle pretended to be a good friend, sticking by my side through Hunter's funeral and the weeks of depression that followed. But she could never meet my eyes when I talked about him.

Then the van Burens offered to pay my tuition. They'd never make an offer that generous unless there was something in it for them. They were buying me off, and I knew it had something to do with Hunter.

So I convinced Noelle we needed a girl's night. Just the two of us.

We giggled in our room, watching reruns of our favorite sitcoms on her flatscreen from her bed and taking a shot every time there was a laugh track or a pun or a corny line. Noelle was hammered within the hour, but I'd dumped the vodka out of my bottle and replaced it with water. I was more sober than I'd ever been, struggling to tamper down the white-hot rage boiling inside me.

Noelle was keeping a secret from me. About Hunter.

She knew something about the night he died that she wasn't telling me.

So I didn't feel bad when I fed her shot after shot. Didn't stop her when she lost track of how much she'd drunk and reached for another. I needed to get the truth out of her.

Around one a.m., her eyes were starting to fall shut. I was wide awake. I swiped open the camera on my phone because I needed to get answers from her while I had a chance.

She didn't even notice the phone pointed in her direction. Too busy snorting at the Netflix show.

"Hey, Noelle. Why did your parents offer to pay my tuition?"

She stiffened, but even drunk, she couldn't meet my eyes. She dropped her gaze to her hands in her lap. "Because they feel bad about your brother."

My stomach gave a hard twist, vision already blurring. I knew it. I knew they were involved. I knew her parents were the ones actually behind the wheel that night. And they framed their employee for it.

The van Burens disgusted me.

I swallowed down the hard lump in my throat and blinked fast to keep the tears at bay. I filled in the blank: "Because they're the ones who actually killed him."

I didn't expect what happened next.

Noelle burst into tears, covering her face with her hands. I ground my teeth together as I restrained myself from screaming at her.

She was sobbing over her parents' crime? My brother *died*. They killed him.

And she had the audacity to cry in front of me.

She wailed something into her hands, but I couldn't make out the words, too muffled and drunken.

"What?" I asked.

She dropped her hands from her face. "Because *I* did!"

My blood stopped cold.

My best friend—who had been consoling me and eating ice cream with me and sitting at his graveside with me—had been the one to put my brother in the ground.

No. That couldn't be right. She said something else. She meant something else. Not Noelle. She wouldn't have done this to me. Wouldn't purposely leave my brother to die when she could've saved him.

The next words left her mouth in a wail. "I'm so sorry, Cassie!"

I ran from the room, knees hitting the hard, cold tile in the bathroom, and puked.

When I listened to the recording the next morning, that same chill ran down my spine when she said those three words. *Because I did.*

My best friend killed my brother.

CHAPTER FORTY-TWO

THEO

Cass calls after me when I stomp toward the baseball field, but I don't turn around. She cuts me off with a hand against my chest and it takes everything in me not to shove her hand away.

"Her parents paid off Michael to take the fall for Noelle and say he was the one behind the wheel that night." Her eyes are wild, desperate for me to believe her. "Noelle is the one who hit Hunter. She left him there to die. And she let an innocent man take the fall for her."

I keep my eyes on the field over her head. Coach shouts my name. "Noelle wouldn't do something like that."

"I didn't want to believe it either." Her eyes are glassy, voice wavering. "She's my best friend. I didn't think she'd ever do something like that to me. Even if it was an accident, she'd at least stay by his side and call for help." She swipes at the tears on her cheeks, but they keep falling. "But she admitted it, Theo. She told me the truth herself."

Cass pulls out her phone and plays a video. Noelle lying on her bed, giggling at the TV. Obviously hammered. My heart squeezes. I miss my friend.

In the video, Cass asks Noelle why her parents offered to pay

Cass's tuition and I freeze. I didn't know they did that. I just assumed Cass got a scholarship or loans.

The line of questioning makes Noelle noticeably uncomfortable. Then she starts crying. *Because I did!*

Every inch of me goes ice-cold. Noelle admitted to being the one behind the wheel that night. She confessed to killing Hunter and leaving his body at the scene. Cass has proof.

Shit.

I swipe a shaky hand over my face, trying to figure out what the hell to do with this information. "If you've known this whole time, why didn't you take this video to the police?"

Cass shakes her head, brows pulling together. "You still don't get it. Nothing would've happened to her. The police would've shrugged it off because she was drunk. They would've called it a false confession or something. Or her parents would've paid to have it swept under the rug again."

The date on her phone screen catches my eye. "You took this video a week before she went missing."

Cass keeps her pink-painted mouth locked shut, brown eyes wide. A bat cracks against a ball and I step away from her.

I shouldn't be afraid of Cass. She's five-foot-three to my six-two. She cares about me. She's in love with me, I know she is. She wouldn't hurt me.

But I can't trust that she wouldn't hurt Noelle.

This is too much of a coincidence. She takes a video of Noelle confessing to her brother's murder, and a week later, Noelle disappears. Cass has been playing the role of the worried best friend, posting countless videos asking the public to help find her best friend, claiming she knew Noelle wouldn't run away or kill herself, crying over Noelle possibly being held hostage and tortured somewhere. She let me and Piper and Addison investigate the van Burens, tried to frame them for their own daughter's disappearance so she could get revenge on them too. For shoving their daughter's crime under the rug. For helping her get away with it.

Then she pursued me. Another pawn in her revenge game. To steal away Noelle's boyfriend as one final way to hurt her.

"You know where she is, don't you? You know what happened to her. You think she killed your brother, so now you . . ." I can't bring myself to finish the thought out loud. Bile churns in my stomach.

She reaches for me, but I recoil. "I didn't hurt her," she pleads. "But I . . . I made a mistake. I got someone else involved. If we can just follow him—"

"I wish I could believe you." My throat bobs and I retreat another step. "But I don't know how to believe anything you say anymore. Goodbye, Cassie."

At her full name, her face falls.

CHAPTER FORTY-THREE

BEAU

*T*hree grocery stores later and I finally find fucking marshmallows. But my princess wants marshmallows, she's getting marshmallows.

The front door squeaks when I walk in and Noelle jumps. I chuckle. She still hasn't learned that I'm the only one who will ever come in or out of this house. That as long as I'm around, no one else is going to touch her. I drop the grocery bag on the kitchen island. "Your marshmallows, princess."

But she doesn't move from her spot in the middle of the kitchen. She just stares at me with those big blue eyes. "Cassie hired you to kill me?"

How the hell did she find out? When I spot my phone on the island, I have my answer. "Offered me a lot of moncy to get the job done too," I tell her.

"How much?"

"Three hundred thousand."

She swallows, nodding. "The money my parents gave her for tuition."

More like hush money. She collapses on a stool at the island, white as bone. "How did she find out?"

She asks it more to herself than to me, but I give her an answer anyway. "That little video she recorded."

Noelle's gaze darts to mine. "What video?"

"The one where you're drunk out of your mind and admit to hitting that asshole with your car."

She claps a hand over her mouth. "Oh my god." Her eyes glisten. "She was never supposed to find out. She was already so hurt about Hunter. I knew if she found out the truth, it would crush her."

"He was a predator," I remind her. "He preyed on girls. He preyed on *you*. You did the world a favor."

"I know," she whispers. "But not Cassie. She loved him. She refused to see that side of him. I never wanted to hurt her like this."

"So why'd you leave the scene?" I finally get to ask the question that's intrigued me from the start.

I didn't totally buy the confession when Cassie showed me the video. Noelle was too drunk to be wholly reliable. Maybe still covering for her parents or her jerkoff boyfriend. But now she's sober, and she's not denying any of it.

"I shouldn't have, I know." Her gaze falls to her hands in her lap, like I'm in any position to judge her. She's taken one life—I've taken five. "I panicked. I was terrified about what would happen to me. It was so, so stupid."

A princess whose whole life revolved around being perfect. She couldn't stomach the thought of being the opposite.

"And Michael?" My nostrils flare now. That's the one crime she still hasn't owned up to. Apologized for. "You let an innocent man go to prison for you?"

Noelle slips off the stool, shaking her head. "I told my parents what happened, and they said they would take care of it. A few weeks later, the news got out that Michael confessed. I had no idea they were going to bribe him into taking the fall for me. If I did, I would've just gone straight to the police. I never, ever wanted anyone to take the fall for me, and I didn't ask my parents to cover it up." She takes a deep breath. "The night you kidnapped me, I was going to turn myself in. I was heading to the police station. I was going to confess to the whole thing, get Michael out of prison, come clean to Cassie. I couldn't live with the guilt anymore. I know you probably don't believe me—"

"I believe you."

I knew it. I knew deep down, she wasn't this cold, heartless rich bitch who'd let an innocent man take the rap for her. She doesn't just feel guilty for what she did to the Sinclair kid or her best friend—she feels guilty for what she did to Michael.

I knew there was more to her than meets the eye. I knew she was nothing like my mother. I knew it.

"Can I ask you something?"

I lean my elbows on the island. "You can ask me anything, princess."

"Why were you willing to do Cassie's dirty work? You work for bail bond agents and hunt down sexual predators. I know what I did is awful, trust me. But a hit-and-run seems a little . . . tame for you. To warrant adding me to your souvenir collection." She nods at the tattoos on my knuckles.

I straighten. "Yeah, well, let's just say your little friend can give me a run for my money when it comes to stalking." Noelle tilts her head and waits for me to go on. "She came to me for a reason. Figured I had a stake in her revenge plot when she found out Michael's my father."

Noelle's eyes bulge and she claps a hand over her mouth. "Michael is your father?" Her mind's scrambling, putting all the pieces of this puzzle together. "Oh my god. You finally found your father, and I took him away from you. That's why you wanted to kill me."

"That, and I thought you killed an innocent guy and got away with it. Typical rich bitch ruining everyone else's lives and not suffering consequences for any of it."

Admittedly, I let my emotions get the better of me. She's right —I probably could've overlooked a standard hit-and-run, let local law enforcement deal with it. I had far worse predators to hunt down.

But then Michael agreed to serve a two-year prison sentence for a crime he didn't commit because his employers bribed him with money they knew he didn't have. Money he needed. Money he wanted to get me out of my line of work. So he wouldn't lose his son after he'd finally found me, twenty-five years later.

He was the only person I had in this world, and she got him locked up.

So yeah. I salivated at the thought of killing her.

But once I learned what kind of guy she'd put in the ground, I couldn't bring myself to draw that knife across her throat. Michael didn't want me getting involved, wanted to keep his deal with the van Burens and collect. Didn't want Noelle's future ruined. He was willing to take her punishment. A better man than I've ever been.

"You weren't wrong." Noelle wrings her hands together, and her words come out small. "I deserve to suffer the consequences for what I did. I'm so, so sorry, Beau. I never meant to hurt Michael, or you."

I wrap her in my arms. "I know, princess." I pull back and smirk. "I kidnapped you, tied you to a chair, and threatened to kill you. You haven't exactly gotten off scot-free."

She takes a steadying breath, mind still scrambling. "So what do we do about Cassie?"

"What about her?"

"Do we go to the police?"

I nod. "That's a great idea. Let's tell them all about how your best friend hired me to kill you and I took the money, but I changed my mind about the whole murder part once I got your pussy in my mouth."

She gives my arm a playful smack. "We could leave you out of it."

"If that's really what you want to do, I'll take you there."

Her brows knit together. "You don't think I should do anything? She tried to have me killed."

"And you killed her brother. She could've turned that video over to the police. You could be locked up somewhere else right now. Maybe you should finally tell her the truth to her face. Sober. Tell her what kind of person her brother was."

Noelle shakes her head quickly. "No, I don't want to hurt her more. She loved him so much—I don't want to ruin the memories she has of him. He's already gone; he can't hurt anyone anymore. Nothing good would come from telling her the truth."

"You should still tell her the truth about that night."

"What if she tries to kill me?" Noelle whispers.

I circle my arms around her waist. "Princess, while I'm around, no one will lay a finger on you but me."

CHAPTER FORTY-FOUR

CASSIE

On the bench beside the pond, I'm hiding my tears behind my hair when I spot Beau Grayson strolling along the sidewalk in his security uniform and leather jacket.

I swipe the tears from my eyes, grab my bag, and follow him.

Everything is going to shit. Addison and Piper suspect Theo. The police know about our relationship. And now Theo doesn't trust me.

He shouldn't. I did a terrible, awful thing. But if Noelle is still alive, if she comes back, everything will be okay again. I'll go to prison for hiring a hitman, but at least Noelle will be home.

We would've found her body by now if he'd killed her. The plan was for him to plant her body somewhere she'd be easy to find, stage it to look like a suicide. Then I'd release the video to the police, so everyone would know the guilt over what she'd done drove her to her own demise.

But with every day that's passed since, the guilt over what I did to her has been eating me alive, Theo the only bright spot in the dark world Noelle and I both created.

Now that I don't have him, I'm surrounded by nothing but darkness.

There's still a chance I can make things right. I just need to figure out where Beau Grayson has her.

I keep a safe distance between us as I trail him around campus.

He strolls casually past buildings and students, acting like he's actually here to keep anyone safe. I pretend I'm looking down at my phone while keeping him in my peripheral vision. When he veers around the corner of the library, I follow.

A hand wraps around my arm in an iron grip, shoving me up against the wall, my phone falling to the pavement with a crack.

"Why the fuck are you following me?" he growls.

My hands are already trembling, but I will bravery into my voice. "Did you kill her?"

His steely gray eyes narrow, but he doesn't say anything. Doesn't remove the hand holding me so hard, my bone is on the verge of splintering.

Over Beau's shoulder, I catch a glimpse of a familiar face hurrying down the sidewalk until he comes to an abrupt halt.

Theo.

His gaze darts between me and the back of Beau's head, but he doesn't make a move to get closer. Probably making all of the wrong assumptions about us.

Then he's gone.

Every time he walks away from me, my heart breaks all over again.

"Where do you have her locked away?" I hiss.

Beau stares at me, unblinking, unwavering. Until he drops my arm, shoving me back into the wall. Pain lashes through my skull.

He walks away without a word.

As soon as he's out of sight and I can breathe again, I take off after Theo, certain he's heading for the parking lot now that his coach told him to take a break from baseball until everything quiets down.

So much has been taken away from him, and he's been nothing but good to me and Noelle. He doesn't deserve any of this.

I spot his tall frame heading for his Audi, the lights flashing when he unlocks it.

"Theo!"

He turns, but once he sees me, he climbs into the driver's seat.

I keep running, even as he backs out of the parking spot and heads for the exit.

I jump in front of his car, his bumper nearly clipping me before he slams to a halt.

His door flies open. "What the *fuck*?"

"It's about Noelle!" I rush to his side, trying not to cower under his blazing green eyes. "I know Beau Grayson is holding her captive. I need you to go with me to—"

"I'm not going anywhere with you," he spits. "I don't believe you. I don't trust you. I told you to leave me alone. Whatever shit you have going on, Cassie, deal with it yourself."

He stomps on my chest every time he calls me by my full name. "Please just let me send you the address." I'm already texting it to him, my screen cracked but functional. "If Noelle isn't back by tonight, if you don't hear from me again . . . at least you'll know where to find us."

Theo climbs back behind the wheel before I've hit Send and peels out of the parking lot. Leaving me behind.

Leaving me to bring Noelle back on my own.

CHAPTER FORTY-FIVE
CASSIE

I knew exactly how I wanted to spend the money from the van Burens. Not on tuition—on getting rid of Noelle van Buren.

She deserved to die for what she did to my brother. She hit him with her car and left him there to drown in his own blood on the side of the road.

She knew how much Hunter meant to me. Pretended to be the best friend standing by my side, comforting me, and all along, she was the reason he was gone.

Then she thought she could get away with it.

Rumors had spread that Beau was already prone to violence. A week's worth of digging and following him to the state prison uncovered a few helpful facts about Beau Grayson.

He was a bounty hunter. And Michael was his father.

Just the guy for the job. The only other person in Westbrook who had a reason to want Noelle dead.

She was letting his father rot in prison. For something *she* did. Beau was already a simmering ember—all I needed to do was fuel the flames.

One night while I supported half the weight of a drunken,

stumbling Addison back to Chi Omega, Beau stepped out of the shadows and offered to escort us home.

"Yes, *please*," Addison slurred, leaning at least seventy percent of her body weight on me. "You're *so* hot."

I didn't feel safer with him by my side, but I didn't need to. I needed someone who made everyone around him feel unsafe. I needed someone who could do what no one else could stomach.

Addison pushed off me and stumbled over to Beau, who caught her but grimaced in a way that made it clear he wished he'd let her fall on her face. "I bet you fuck better than Kyle. You wanna f-fuck me?" She hiccuped before her eyes went wide and she clapped a hand over her mouth. She'd drunk more than usual at the frat party, downing cup after cup while Kyle practically dry-humped another girl in the corner. Noelle had Theo and Piper had Neal, so that left me to take Addison home and hold her hair while she puked.

She ran to the bushes, barfing, and when Beau didn't flinch, I knew I'd chosen the right man.

"I need a favor."

"I'm not holding her hair back."

I'd almost forgotten about Addison, on her knees now and whimpering as more alcohol came back up. Even if she heard our conversation, she'd never remember it in the morning.

I shook my head. "I need someone killed."

Stunned silence fell between us for a few seconds before he burst out laughing. "You're a fuckin' psycho chick, huh?"

I stepped closer. "I'm serious."

He shook his head. "You remind me of my mother."

My heart was pounding. Part of me couldn't believe I was really doing this. Letting these words spill out of my mouth, turning my dark, rage-fueled fantasy into a reality. "What if I told you she's the reason your father's in prison?"

Beau's eyes flashed to mine. All the amusement leeched out of them. "How do you—"

I held up my hand. "I know Michael's your father. He spent

years working for the van Burens to afford a private investigator to find you, then you show up out of the blue and start visiting him once he's in prison. It didn't take me long to put two and two together."

We stood in silence for a few moments while he let this information sink in. Until he finally asked, "Who's the mark?"

Holy shit. This was really happening. "Noelle van Buren."

Beau narrowed his eyes. "Isn't she your friend?"

I almost scoffed. He thought I was a stalker for knowing his father's identity, but he'd obviously been following Noelle around campus. Knew her name, her friends, and probably a lot more. "Was. She's the one who killed Hunter in that hit and run, not your father. Hunter was my brother."

Beau's eyes flashed, but he folded his arms. "Michael admitted he was the one who did it."

Panic made my heart thud harder. I needed him to do this. "You don't actually think your father would hit someone with a car and leave him for dead, do you? Or take his boss's two-hundred-thousand-dollar car for a joyride? Noelle was behind the wheel that night. Her parents paid your father off to take the fall for her."

He let the words settle between us, scanning the sidewalk and the lit houses along Greek Row, jaw tight. Like he was deciding whether to believe me or not.

"I have proof. I have her confession on video." A note of desperation in my voice. I played the video for him, but he remained silent. "I don't think your father should have to suffer for someone else's crime. No matter how well it pays."

The rage was boiling in Beau's veins now, simmering just beneath the surface. But he couldn't admit it. Not yet.

"There's enough money in it for you to buy your own Bentley. Maybe run her over with it. See how she likes being left for dead."

"How much?"

"Three hundred thousand."

He lifted a brow. "How'd you manage to get your hands on that?"

"Her parents gave it to me. Their way of buying me off, absolving themselves of the guilt of covering up their daughter's crime."

Beau nodded. "Bring the money tomorrow. Consider it done."

I was a balloon, floating above my body. Amazed this was working, really happening. Terrified that I couldn't undo this now, a twisted plan of my darkest fantasies that I'd put into motion. But more than anything, pushed forward by the white-hot rage that had consumed me ever since I'd learned the truth about my brother and my best friend.

Screw an eye for an eye and a tooth for a tooth. I wanted both her eyes and all her teeth.

CHAPTER FORTY-SIX

NOELLE

"*S*he's here." Beau's rumbling voice breaks through the silence in the dark bedroom, moonlight shimmering through the window.

Cassie has been following Beau around campus. He confronted her today, and the first words out of her mouth were, *Did you kill her?*

She knows he hasn't gotten the job done. And she wants her money's worth.

So she's come to finish the job herself. Maybe frame Beau for it. Get revenge on both of us.

I scurry out of bed to peer past the curtain with him. My Mercedes in the driveway. She drove *my* car to come kill me.

The driver's side door swings open and Cassie steps out, hood pulled over her head. She eases the door shut behind her. Completely unaware of Beau and me tracking her every move.

"What do we do?" I whisper.

His voice comes out so low and deadly, it could crack concrete. "I'll handle her."

~

CASSIE

My legs tremble as I climb out of Noelle's Mercedes and sneak up to a window. Desperation beats out the fear that pulls my feet in the opposite direction. The same desperation I felt the night Hunter died, in the brief time between his missed curfew and the police showing up at our door, when all I wanted was to go search for him. Find him. Bring him home.

I'm the reason Noelle is trapped here. I'm the reason the psychopath bounty hunter decided to keep her locked up to torment her.

Noelle betrayed me by killing my brother. By lying to my face about his death for months. But my decision to hire a hitman was one I made when I was blinded with rage. Sure that she needed to pay for her crime, and if the legal system wouldn't make her, I would.

But despite all she's done, Noelle is still my best friend. She doesn't deserve this. She loves me, even if she hurt me. Maybe that's why she kept this secret from me. So she wouldn't hurt me more.

Bile churns in my stomach at the thought of the nightmares she's had to endure in the last two months, locked up here with Beau Grayson.

By doing this, I'm no better than she is.

If there's a chance she's still alive, I need to get her out of here. Together, we can outsmart him. Then I'll explain everything.

If I can forgive her for her sins, I hope she can forgive me for mine.

I sneak up the edge of the driveway, praying the cover of darkness will keep me invisible until I can figure out a way inside.

When a door creaks open, my heart stops.

"Come in." The low command makes my lungs twist, unable to suck in air.

Without another word, Beau Grayson disappears into the dark house.

I shouldn't follow him in there. He could hurt me. Kill me. All before I ever get a chance to lay eyes on Noelle. To find out whether she's still alive.

But for her sake, I follow him. I sent her here—now I need to bring her back.

In the shadowy house, I fumble along the wall for a light switch. Maybe it's more dangerous if he can see me, but I'm dead if I can't see him.

The door slams shut.

I whirl, but it's too late.

A heavy forearm pins me to the wall by the throat.

I sputter, clawing at him, but Beau doesn't budge. This close, I can make out the sharp, murderous features cloaked in shadow. The scar over his eye making him more intimidating than he already is.

"Where the fuck is she?" I manage to gasp. I dig as hard as I can into his bare arm, but my nails might as well be made of cotton for all he's affected by them.

His forearm presses harder into my throat, cutting off my air supply. The pain makes my feet scramble, desperate to escape him. But there's nowhere to go.

"I'll kill you before you lay one fucking finger on her," he snarls.

My eyes widen. He didn't refuse to give me answers earlier because he thought I might try to rescue Noelle—he thinks I'm here to kill her myself.

I try to speak, tell him he's got it all wrong, but his arm is crushing my windpipe. I kick out, but he dodges my feet.

I'm up against a guy who regularly takes down men twice my size. Tears spring to my eyes.

I've only got one chance. If I miss this time, I'm dead.

My nails slash across his face. He snaps at me. Doesn't budge. But he's distracted.

Doesn't notice the knife in my other hand.

Not until I plunge the blade into him.

CHAPTER FORTY-SEVEN

BEAU

My guttural bellow sends Noelle charging downstairs. *Fuck*. She's supposed to stay upstairs. Safe, out of harm's way. But she's at my side, hand already covered in my blood.

"Get the fuck out of here! She has a knife!"

"What did you do?" she shrieks at Cassie, still frozen with her back against the wall.

Another psychotic woman with a knife. Should've seen that coming.

"He was trying to kill me!"

Noelle's eyes flash to my face, searching for the truth because she knows she can't get it from the psycho bitch in front of her anymore.

"She asked where you were." I grit my teeth, fighting for the words through the pain. "I wasn't about to let her lay a finger on you."

"I'm not trying to hurt her!" Cassie cries, eyes flooding with tears. "I'm trying to save her! From *you*!"

She points the knife at me, still dripping with my blood.

"Cassie." Noelle's voice, strong and steady. My lighthouse in the hurricane. "Put the knife down."

She lowers her shaking hand but keeps the knife gripped between her fingers. "We need to get out of here, Noelle. While we have a chance."

"I'm not going anywhere with you. We're calling the police. He needs medical attention."

"He kidnapped you! He was going to kill you—"

"Because you paid him to!" Noelle snaps. "Get me a towel. *Now.*"

Cassie flashes me a look like the last thing she wants to do is help me. But she follows Noelle's instructions, grabbing a kitchen towel from below the sink.

Noelle presses it against my abdomen. I'm starting to get lightheaded. *Fuck.* If I go out, I won't be conscious to protect Noelle from the knife-wielding psycho in the room.

"Get out of here," I tell her. Desperate for her to get somewhere safe. I can't lose her too. "Don't worry about me. Just get the fuck away from her."

The last words I hear before I go under are Noelle's. In her perfect, musical voice. "Call 911."

CHAPTER FORTY-EIGHT
NOELLE

Shit. Beau is unconscious and Cassie still has a bloody knife in her hand.

"Put the knife down, Cassie." My words come out steady, but my composure is fracturing.

"I can't. What if he wakes up?" The blade wobbles in her hand. If I knock her off her feet, I might be able to get the knife from her. "We need to get away from him."

"He's not the dangerous one here. *You* are."

Her brown eyes go wide. "He's been holding you hostage here for two months!"

"He hasn't. I've been choosing to stay here."

She presses a hand to her mouth. "Oh my god. You think you're in love with him, don't you?" She takes a cautious step toward me. "Noelle, this is Stockholm syndrome. You don't actually love—"

"Shut the fuck up, Cassie. This isn't Stockholm syndrome. I've had the freedom to leave for weeks. You're the one who hired him to *kill* me."

She crouches, face crumpling. "I'm sorry. I . . . I still can't believe I did that. I was just . . . I was so *fucking* angry at you." Her voice breaks, a tear sliding down her cheek.

And somehow, my best friend crying brings tears to my own eyes. Even after everything, all that we've put each other through, I still love her. Even before she was my sorority sister, she was my soul sister.

I bite down on my lip until I draw blood, trying to stop my lip from quivering with the sob building up from my chest. "I know. I did a horrible thing, Cassie. I hate that I hurt you so badly. I'm so, so sorry. If I could take all your pain and put it in me, I would."

She gives a hiccuping sob, unable to speak.

I want to run to her, wrap her in my arms and comfort her, tell her a thousand times how sorry I am. For running after I hit Hunter. For not coming clean and taking responsibility. For causing her so much pain, and pretending all along that my hands were clean.

But I'm too terrified to leave Beau's side. I don't know how deep the wound is or how much longer before he loses too much blood.

"I get why you wanted to hurt me for hurting Hunter." I don't bother swiping at the tears on my cheeks.

She shakes her head. "You dying isn't going to bring him back."

Part of me wishes she'd learned that before she hired someone to kill me. But if she had, I never would've fallen in love with Beau.

Before I came here, I didn't understand the level of damage I'd truly caused. How many lives I'd affected. Even if she regrets it now, Cassie was right to send me here. To sic the beast on me.

I need to face the consequences of what I've done.

After I make sure Beau is okay.

"Cassie . . . can you please call 911?"

She keeps a wary eye on Beau but doesn't make a move for her phone.

"I know you think he manipulated me or fucked with my

head, but I'm asking you, as my best friend, to please trust me." I swallow down the sob. "Him dying isn't going to make me fall out of love with him."

Cassie stands slowly.

And walks toward us with the knife.

CHAPTER FORTY-NINE

THEO

I scramble out of the car and sprint for the house when I spot Noelle's Mercedes in the driveway and the front door wide open. My heart's in my throat, beating a million times a minute.

I'm an idiot for letting Cass come here alone. No matter what she's done, no matter how badly she's pissed me off or fucked up, I can't let her walk into the arms of danger. I should've been by her side.

Now I might be too late.

The second I'm through the doorway, Cass whirls on me, bloody knife in the air. I hold my hands up, and she halts when she realizes it's me. "Theo?"

Noelle and Beau are crumpled together on the floor.

Noelle.

She's alive.

I've spent the past two months thinking she was dead. But she's okay. She's *okay.*

Her hand is slick with blood, and the rag she's holding over Beau's stomach has gone from white to almost entirely crimson.

"What the hell did you do, Cass?" Maybe shouting at the girl with the knife isn't the best move, but the panic bubbling up in me is exploding out.

"I . . . I stabbed him." Her lip trembles, eyes welling with tears. Her hands shake, but she doesn't make a move to come after me or Noelle or lunge at Beau again.

She's scared.

There's still hope. I have to believe that.

"She thought he was going to kill her," Noelle explains. "And that he was holding me captive."

"Isn't he?" Why would she be here if he wasn't?

Noelle shakes her head. "No. And we need to get him to a hospital." She flashes me a pleading look.

The guy's bleeding and passed out. This isn't good. I may not be in med school yet, but I've learned enough to know we don't have much time.

I lower my hands slowly, taking a single step toward Cass. "Everything's all right now. You're safe. So is Noelle. Just put the knife down."

Without a second's hesitation, Cass lets the blade fall to the floor.

My girl's still in there somewhere. She's just gotten lost, and I need to help her find her way back to herself. To me.

"I didn't mean to hurt anybody, Theo." She bites down on her knuckles, tears streaking her face. "I just don't know how to live without him."

I'm halfway to her now, and I swallow the lump in my throat. "I know it's hard. The days after my grandpa died were hell. The whole year, even. I didn't know what to do with myself." Even thinking back on those days now, all these years later, and tears still sting my eyes. He was the most important person in my life then, and I lost him. That's how Cass feels. "I know you think you can't live without him now, but you can. You have to. He would want you to."

Cass loses it then, dropping to her knees and sobbing into her hands. I rush to her, kicking the knife away before I fall to my knees in front of her and wrap her in my arms. Giving her the hug she's been needing for a long time.

CHAPTER FIFTY

CASSIE

I stabbed someone. His blood is on my hand.

Over my own sobs muffled into Theo's chest, Noelle cries on the floor next to Beau, partly from what I did to the man she loves and partly from Theo's words.

She's frantic, terrified. Just like I was that night the police showed up on our doorstep and told us Hunter was dead.

I spent so much time thinking Noelle had the perfect life. That she had it so easy and it was about time she deal with some repercussions. But I never really put myself in her shoes. What it must be like to have a controlling, demanding mother you can never please. To feel so terrified of making a single misstep that you work yourself to the bone to be perfect.

To feel so trapped in your own life, you'd rather live in seclusion with the man who kidnapped you than return home.

Noelle did a stupid, awful thing. She shouldn't have left my brother alone on that road to die. She should've called the police. She might've been able to save his life.

But she was terrified. And she knew if she left, there was a chance she could stay Perfect Noelle van Buren.

If I was in her shoes, if that had been me behind the wheel

and another guy on the side of the road, I don't know if I would've stopped either.

I might've kept driving.

I hand her my phone, and this time, she calls 911.

∼

NOELLE

THE POLICE ARE on their way. As long as first responders get here soon, Beau will be okay. I squeeze his hand, reassuring him that I won't be gone long, even if he can't hear me. I'm not leaving him. I'm never leaving his side.

I rush for Cassie on the floor with Theo, him still holding her as sobs wrack her body. He lets her go, and she falls into my arms, soaking my shoulder with her tears while I do the same to hers.

She hugs me harder than she ever has. An apology and a promise wrapped into one.

For Hunter. For Beau. For everything she's done. For everything I've done. For this mess we've made together. And that's how we'll have to fix this.

Together.

Behind me, a groan makes my heart stop.

"Princess?"

CHAPTER FIFTY-ONE
BEAU

*L*ast time I was in a hospital, it was a different woman who attacked me with a knife.

Noelle doesn't leave my side for a second. She gives her statement to the cops from my bedside.

She's hanging onto my hand and not letting go. Never again.

"Thanks for not letting her stab me twice," I murmur. Noelle squeezes my hand, biting her lip. "I'm supposed to be the one protecting you."

"You do everything for me. It was about time I return the favor."

I sweep away the tear gliding down her cheek with my thumb. "Didn't think you'd get rid of me that easy, did you, princess? Next time you hire someone to kill me, make sure she knows where to aim."

She giggles, tears in her eyes when she hugs me and whispers in my ear, "My entire black and tarnished soul is yours."

I wrap a strand of her hair around my finger and smile at her. "And mine yours, princess."

CHAPTER FIFTY-TWO

CASSIE

Noelle's story to the police is nothing close to the truth, but it's the one she makes all of us swear to stick to.

So we all relay the same details, in our own versions to avoid suspicion: Noelle ran away to live with Beau Grayson, knowing her parents would never approve of him. She had no idea anyone was searching for her, that so many resources were being expended on her behalf. I stabbed Beau, thinking he was holding Noelle in the house against her will. Theo followed me.

In Noelle's story, I come out the heroine, not the villain. She painted me in a whole new light.

She really is an artist.

In the moments before the wailing sirens arrived, after Noelle told us the story we would all recite, I insisted we should tell them the truth about what I did.

I tried to have her killed. I stabbed Beau. I couldn't just get away with everything.

But Noelle shook her head. "You've suffered enough, Cassie. I'm the reason we're in this mess to begin with. You were right—I should face the consequences for what I've done."

Something flickered over Beau's face then. Concern over what confessing might mean for Noelle and the future of their relationship, but also something else.

Pride.

Addison and Piper are waiting for me when I leave the police station. Piper sprints toward me, hitting me like a linebacker and nearly knocking me off my feet. I can't help but laugh. "Oh my god, we're *so* sorry we doubted you!"

Addison perches with a hand on her hip. "You saw how long I put up with Kyle's bullshit. I don't always have the best judgment."

I smile. "Is that finally over?"

Addison nods and opens her mouth just as Piper blurts, "Yeah, he was a tool."

We all laugh until someone calls my name from the parking lot. My mother next to my rusted old Cadillac, waving to me.

At least she doesn't have to bail me out of jail for stabbing a guy.

"I'll see you guys later."

Piper and Addison both give me one last hug before I head for the parking lot.

Mom's wearing faded jeans and a white T-shirt that's actually clean. Her hair is cropped a little shorter, fresh and bouncy. She might even be wearing lipgloss. She's coming back to herself, slowly but surely. I can only hope I'm starting to do the same.

Before we climb in the car, I blurt, "I'm sorry I pulled away from you." I'm shocked by how quickly tears spring to my eyes. At the pain I've buried so deep down, I almost forgot it was there. "Every time I looked at you, I saw him. I couldn't deal with it."

Mom hugs me then. The first time she's touched me since his funeral, and I didn't realize how much I missed it until now. "I'm sorry I pulled away from you too. A mother should never do that to her child," she murmurs into my hair. "But we can't retreat into ourselves like that anymore. We need to support each other. We're in this together."

A few tears spill out onto my mother's shoulder, but she doesn't care. Only hugs me tighter.

Theo was right. I'll keep living, without Hunter, because I have to. Mom and I both do. But this time, we'll do it together.

∽

THEO

I HAVEN'T SEEN Cass since the day we found Noelle. She hasn't texted or called or come to Sigma Chi. She's giving me space. Time to figure out if I can forgive her, trust her again after everything that's happened.

As far as I'm concerned, if Noelle can forgive her, so can I.

I toss a blanket in my passenger's seat and set two tumblers of hot chocolate in the cup holders. She's been spending more time at home lately, visiting her mom on the weekends. I hope they don't feel like they're a galaxy apart anymore.

Her mom's the one to answer the door when I knock. Her eyes light up, decked out in purple pajamas and fuzzy slippers. "Cassie!"

Cass appears at the door in matching pajamas and slippers, hair tied up in a bun and face void of makeup. She's so goddamn adorable, I'd sweep her up in my arms if they weren't already full.

Her smile falls. "Oh no."

My stomach lurches. She's not happy to see me. She doesn't want me here. "Sorry, I can go—"

"No!" She reaches out, grabbing my arm to stop me, the tumbler of hot chocolate swaying dangerously. "Don't go. I just . . . if I'd known you were coming, I wouldn't look like this."

"Why? You look cute." My cheeks flush when I remember her mom's standing right there.

She doesn't seem to care, though. She's still beaming. "You two go on. I'm going to go finish the ice cream."

Cass follows me around back, where we'll have a bit of

privacy. I lay the blanket out on the grass, a night sky full of stars and a full moon above us, and hand her a tumbler. "I brought hot chocolate."

She grins and sits on the blanket with me. She's so fucking adorable. I don't want to go another day without making her smile.

"This is really sweet." She takes a sip before setting the tumbler down in the grass. "I've really missed you."

I grab her hand. "I've missed you too. A hell of a lot."

Her smile slips. "I'm so sorry for everything."

I lean forward, squeezing her hand. "I just want to understand why."

Cass nods slowly, like she knew this conversation was coming. She swallows and takes a deep breath. "When I heard Hunter died in a hit and run, that someone left him there and got away with it, something in my brain just . . . snapped. I couldn't think about anything else, couldn't focus, couldn't feel anything other than this raw . . . *anger*. Like I just wanted to kill whoever hurt him. Make them pay. I thought that was how I'd finally get closure. How I'd finally stop obsessing over what happened to him and find some peace. Then I found out it was Noelle, and . . . I knew I couldn't do it myself. So I hired Beau to . . ." She can't finish the sentence. Can no longer stomach what she tried to do to her best friend. "At first, I was glad I did it. Then the guilt started to creep in. More and more, every day. Bits of it at first, then it started hitting in waves, crashing over me until I was drowning in it. But by then, I thought I was too late. I thought Beau had already killed her and there was nothing I could do. Once I suspected he hadn't, once I thought there might still be hope, I knew I had to save her. Try to undo the horrible thing I'd done."

I let her words sink in, the only sounds the cicadas and a car's tires passing by.

Her eyes fall to her legs, crossed in front of her. "I understand if you don't want anything to do with me anymore."

I stroke my thumb over her cheek before threading my hand in her hair. "You're all I want, Cass."

Her gaze flashes up to mine, shimmering. "You forgive me?"

"I've never needed to forgive you. Only understand."

A small smile pulls at her lips through her tears and she kisses me. Her lips just as soft and wonderful as I remember.

"I want to know all of you." I cradle her face in both hands, delicate and beautiful and mine. "Even the darkest parts. Even the parts you're ashamed of. I want all of you."

CHAPTER FIFTY-THREE
NOELLE

I turned myself in for the hit-and-run. Michael is finally out of prison, and after a quiet hearing, the judge sentenced me to five years probation. Five years of community service and regular monitoring.

Too light a punishment for what I did, especially given the prison sentence Michael was handed. I told my parents not to meddle, but I'm sure my mother had a hand in this, for her own sake. She can't stand the thought of everyone knowing she's the mother of a convict.

They aren't happy when I tell them I'm switching to an art major, even when I insist they don't have to pay for it. Well, Dad's happy for me—Mother isn't.

"We're just glad you're home and have a future ahead of you," Dad says, wrapping me in his arms before clipping the leash on Angel, back home with me for the weekend until we return to the sorority house. She's much happier there with all the girls around to dote on her. That's why my parents sent her with my friends, not because they were trying to get rid of all traces of me.

Mother bites her tongue and manages, "We're glad you're safe."

They don't have any say over my life and future anymore. This is my life, not theirs. I'm living it the way I want.

My parents met Beau in the hospital the day Cassie stabbed him. Not exactly the introduction I imagined, but it went better than I expected. My mother was civil, even as her mouth curdled at the tattoos covering his arms.

He's nothing like the guy she wanted for me. Maybe that's part of what makes him so perfect.

~

CASSIE

AFTER FINALS, Theo shouts my name and runs up to me, heads turning to follow him. It's like a moment I've daydreamed about. Theo St. James running toward me with a huge grin on his face, everyone aware that I'm the girl he can't take his eyes off of.

"Hey, beautiful. You ready for our trip?" he asks.

I'm loading up the Cadillac with our bags. My car has more room than his Audi, and we'll need all the space we can get.

This summer, we're hitting the road and heading west. Who knows where we'll end up, but I can't wait for this new adventure with him. Just the two of us.

I throw my arms around him. "I'm so excited."

He chuckles, tipping my chin up and dipping me in a mind-blowing kiss, tongue sweeping into my mouth and making me weak at the knees. I'll never get enough of Theo St. James.

"Thank you for forgiving me," I murmur. "Even when I went totally nuts for a minute there."

He squeezes my hips. "Thank you for letting me be the man by your side. I'll do my best every day to make sure I deserve it."

I slip my hand around the back of his neck. "I love you so much."

"I love you too, Cass." Theo pulls me toward him by my hips

until I'm flush against him and kisses me. "I can't wait to fall asleep under Cassiopeia every night."

CHAPTER FIFTY-FOUR
NOELLE

*I*n the back of my Mercedes, Beau thrusts into me again, making the car shake. "Fuck yeah, princess," he groans. "Come on my cock."

My shirt is shoved up past my tits, bra yanked down. He didn't even bother taking my panties off—just shoved them aside, in too much of a hurry to bury himself inside me.

When he bites down on my nipple, I cry out and lose myself, falling over the edge and down into hell where he's grinning at me, fucking me through the throes of my orgasm. I'm so glad we found each other here.

Beau collapses on top of me when he finds his own release, and when we get our clothes in place, we pull back onto the road and head home.

He bought the abandoned house. Turns out the couple who owned it are living in Switzerland now, and while they planned on returning for vacations, they never did.

I'm completely out from under my mother's thumb. Maybe now we can actually have a chance at a decent mother-daughter relationship.

In the headlights, I spot a small cross staked into the ground, dead and wilting flowers surrounding the memorial sight.

This is the road. The spot where I hit Hunter.

I'd been sick to my stomach for days, agonizing over the picture he had on his phone, over the threat he made to take what he wanted from me, no matter how I felt about it. The possibility of his dirty fingers between my legs, his beer breath in my mouth, his cock spilling inside me, made me want to vomit.

That crescent moon drawn on the back of my hand, a reminder of him that I couldn't wash off no matter how hard I scrubbed.

Who knows what he was doing on the side of the road that night. Walking home from a drug deal, maybe. Or maybe he'd just blackmailed and fucked another girl on the side of the road before leaving her there. Used and violated.

When he turned and his face was in my headlights, I didn't move over the yellow lines. I didn't hit the brake.

I pressed on the gas.

I turned the wheel. But not away from Hunter.

Toward him.

His eyes popped and he tried to leap out of the way, but he wasn't getting away with it. Not this time.

The thud of his body against the Bentley was sickening, and my first thought was that Mother was going to kill me for the dent in the fender.

But once I noticed Hunter had disappeared, I couldn't bring myself to care.

I jumped out of the car and rushed to the front, calling his name. He gurgled on his blood in answer.

He was awake, eyes still open when I reached him. That small flicker of light in his eyes when he saw someone approaching, thought they might be there to save him.

That light flickered out when he saw that someone was me.

I searched his pockets until I found his phone. I held it up to his face to unlock it and swiped through photo after photo of girls in compromising positions. Girls like me, passed out and clothes askew. Others that were far worse.

I deleted them all before sticking his phone back in his pocket. Those girls didn't need to be humiliated by a bunch of cops finding those photos. I wouldn't let him do that to them too.

To me.

I got back in my parents' car and drove off. Leaving him to bleed out and die the slow death he deserved.

My only regret was the pain I knew his death would inflict on Cassie.

Beau squeezes my hand from the driver's seat. "Glad that fucker's dead."

"Me too," I murmur.

He kisses my knuckles. One now adorned with my own tattoo.

A crescent moon.

ACKNOWLEDGMENTS

First, thank you to my incredible readers. I will never be able to thank you enough for your enthusiasm and support along this journey. Every like, comment, message, and video means the world to me. I'm the luckiest author in the world to have you all as readers. You make me excited to wake up every day and do what I love. Thank you, thank you, *thank you*.

Thank you to my betas, Lauren, Kelsey, and Jessica. This book would not be what it is without your feedback. Thank you for reading so quickly and for all your enthusiasm and encouragement. I cannot thank you enough!

Thank you to Beholden Book Covers for the truly stunning book cover! You always manage to take my vague ideas and make something beautiful. I'm forever in awe of your talent.

Finally, thank you to Alex, for celebrating every publishing milestone with me and helping me through every step of the process. Thank you for giving me the space to create my stories and live in my own fictional worlds for hours without complaint. Beau supports Noelle in pursuing her passion because you support me in pursuing mine. I love you.

ABOUT THE AUTHOR

Harmony West writes dark forbidden romance. She enjoys her love stories with a side of mystery, twists, and spice.

For updates on Harmony West's latest releases, subscribe to her newsletter at www.harmonywestbooks.com/subscribe or follow her on social media @authorharmonywest.

Made in United States
Cleveland, OH
05 February 2025